little family

little family

ishmael beah

RIVERHEAD BOOKS | NEW YORK

2020

RIVERHEAD BOOKS
An imprint of Penguin Random House LLC
penguinrandomhouse.com

Copyright © 2020 by Ishmael Beah
Penguin supports copyright. Copyright fuels creativity, encourages diverse voices,
promotes free speech, and creates a vibrant culture. Thank you for buying an authorized
edition of this book and for complying with copyright laws by not reproducing, scanning,
or distributing any part of it in any form without permission. You are supporting
writers and allowing Penguin to continue to publish books for every reader.

Riverhead and the R colophon are registered
trademarks of Penguin Random House LLC.

Library of Congress Cataloging-in-Publication Data

Names: Beah, Ishmael, 1980– author.
Title: Little family / Ishmael Beah.
Description: New York : Riverhead Books, 2020.
Identifiers: LCCN 2019049160 (print) | LCCN 2019049161 (ebook) |
ISBN 9780735211773 (hardcover) | ISBN 9780735211797 (ebook)
Classification: LCC PS3602.E2417 L58 2020 (print) |
LCC PS3602.E2417 (ebook) | DDC 813/.6—dc23
LC record available at https://lccn.loc.gov/2019049160
LC ebook record available at https://lccn.loc.gov/2019049161

International edition ISBN: 9780593189283

Printed in the United States of America
1 3 5 7 9 10 8 6 4 2

BOOK DESIGN BY LUCIA BERNARD

For my daughters, Kema and Farah, and my son, Kailondo.
Thank you for providing me the opportunity to reevaluate my
masculinity, for the mirror to look into myself deeply through
your innocence. You have expanded my heart in ways that were
unimaginable to me. I love you with every muscle of my being.

And for my remarkable wife, Priscillia, my muse, my everything.
I have lived a thousand lives because of you. My soulmate, دوستت دارم

For those who have no voice, silence remains the unbroken truth. And every so often, that silence is torn by a roaring.

—MENDE PROVERB, SIERRA LEONE

little family

If you are to walk toward a field that lies at the edge of the small town of Foloiya when the sun is awake in the sky, you will hear the breeze whistling through the grasses, parting the dry and green strands as it makes its way to you. Or maybe you will think it is the rustling of someone hiding under the vast shrubs. At the end of the field, your eyes will light upon the face of a boy among the grasses, peering intently at something. You try to see what it is by following the trail of his gaze, but you see nothing.

"Hello," you say. The boy does not respond, only narrows his eyelids against the wind. You stare back at his face, in which youth is steeped in something serious and old, in stories you want to know. You try your luck again.

"Good morning." You do not know what else to say. Caution trumps curiosity: You sense that you should not move closer. He does not respond. In fact, nothing about his demeanor suggests that he is even aware of your presence.

Your eyes search his face one last time. Then you give a sigh and continue on your way. Yet as you go, you glance back, still hopeful of an answer. And then, just as you have given up and turned your full attention to the road ahead, you hear him whistle. Immediately several answering whistles fill the air. You become confused. Should you move on ahead or go back to the boy? You are more aware of your fear now, but at the same time, your belly burns with cautious excitement. You do not know which feeling to pursue.

While you hesitate, the shrubs begin a vigorous dance. But when you look again to where the boy was sitting, he is gone, without your having heard him leave. You set aside your fear and try all the pathways that are visible to you, but none goes any distance. Each time, you find yourself returned to where the boy was sitting, the smaller plants stretching to regain themselves in the wake of his human weight.

1

Kpindi brushed his hands against the low-hanging branches of the tree under which he sat, the morning dew on the leaves moistening his palms. Shivering, he wiped his face, youthful but coarsening, with his wet hands. This attempt to wake eyes that yearned to slumber was not successful. He sat back on his heels and crouch-walked to a shorter tree surrounded by tall grasses, at the junction of the dusty red paths. From this point, he could hear and see from afar anyone who approached, with plenty of time to decide how to react.

Satisfied with his line of sight, he stretched his bony frame, his rib cage drawing away from his long belly, and sat erect, with an unreadable stare calculated to inspire fear, curiosity, and confusion in anyone who happened upon him. Such an encounter had never occurred, and Kpindi liked it that way. He didn't want to be found. Not by those who were searching for something, in pain or confusion or fear. But even less by the kind of people who bore well-meaning smiles, yet whose eyes betrayed a disregard so habitual that they were no longer conscious of it.

Determined to stay alert, Kpindi concentrated on each of his senses in turn, so that every little whiff of smoke from newly kindled fires where breakfast plantains were frying, every fluttering of a bird in the branches, every whisk of a broom sweeping dried leaves from someone's yard, every bucket that clanked in the grasp of those going to fetch water, pulled him from the grip of slumber.

And then there were footsteps—footsteps that Kpindi did not recognize. He quieted his breathing until it fell beneath the passing breeze.

"She brought me right here every morning, even when she could barely walk." As soon as the next gust of wind shook the grasses, Kpindi hastened to a new hiding place. From this position, he could see the elder whose voice had reached him. She was sitting on a large flat stone, a young woman by her side. Her face, elegantly wrinkled, was lit with memory.

Lost as these two were, in either the joys or the bitterness of the past, Kpindi knew they were no threat. Absently, he pulled a kola nut from the front pocket of his trousers and took a bite, to keep himself awake and steady. The smell of the nut, and the familiar ritual of chewing it, brought his grandmother to mind—his grandmother with her constant joking, no matter how unhappy life had been back then. It was sweet to remember her face. He took another bite of the kola nut, keeping his eyes on the two women.

"Ah, never mind how you came into this world," his grandmother used to say. "You were brought here to live. So live!" And that was all he could ever get out of her.

The wind had dropped, and in the quiet, every sound was amplified. It seemed to Kpindi that his ears were vibrating. From his spot under the bushes, he imagined a context for each noise that reached his ears, a favorite pastime. Sometimes he would spend three or four hours on watch this way. Just then he heard a shriek, followed by a burst of laughter. He imagined the sounds as coming from a house nearby, where a father was getting ready for the day. His wife and five children had showered first, using up all the hot water, so that when it was his turn in the bathroom, cold water struck his body, and he shrieked. "Why must I suffer like this every morning?" he cried, as he did every morning. And the whole family, their faces smooth with Vaseline, the children in their school uniforms and their mother stylishly dressed to go run her waterfront store, joked and chatted as they did every morning too.

Was this a family he remembered, or a family he only imagined? Kpindi wasn't sure. He waited for the next sound to reach him, ready to dream up a fresh scenario.

The elderly woman stood up with surprising agility and began walking back toward town. The young woman looked around, but her gaze passed over Kpindi and went to the sky, and then she followed her companion. No need to warn the others, he decided.

Noises from the market were filling the air. The day had begun. As he rose to embrace the morning, the wind slapped a few leaves against Kpindi's face. Just then he heard the secret whistle. *King's property, king's property, everything is correct.*

He answered in turn. *King's property, king's property, everything is correct.*

2

Usually Khoudiemata made her visits to the market between dawn and the first appearance of the sun. There was a pause that came at this hour, a sigh, when the waking had to decide whether to spend their day being useful or being destructive. Raffia bag slung over her shoulder, beanie on her head, this bright-eyed young woman of eighteen with smooth, sharp cheekbones chose to remain suspended between the two, as her circumstances dictated.

Besides, she was drawn to the hidden beauty of this dilapidated place, which painted over whatever bad memories troubled her mind with the simple and intriguing brushstrokes of all that was on display. She glided among the traders, listening and watching as they called out to the passersby, letting them know what they wanted, what was essential for them to purchase. *Madam, I have a special gift for your lovely daughter.* Or *Mister, don't you want to go home with a gift that says what doesn't exist in words? I have just that for you.* The merchants had sweet words for almost everyone, but when Khoudiemata passed before them, they said nothing. It was as if she did not exist.

She was not invisible—people's eyes caught sight of her—but somehow, she was forgotten as soon as she was glimpsed.

Khoudi did not mind. Because of her invisibility, people spoke honestly around her about their fears, hopes, and dreams. Sometimes she picked up important information that way, information that made it possible to continue to live at the edge of the lives of such people. Some mornings, she simply lingered upon their faces, living in the emotions that they wore—some exceptionally happy, some pensive, some unthinkably sad. Imagining their lives helped her to stay suspended between being useful and being destructive, while turning to her advantage everything that happened.

Now she watched as a fruit seller juggled a pinkish-red mango, a yellow pawpaw, and a green guava in the air before setting them on a platter as colorful as her flowered robe. Khoudi took in the glistening red of the palm oil being poured into bottles, the deep green of the cassava and sweet potato leaves that were constantly sprinkled with water so they didn't lose their freshness to the sun, the shiny dark hand that sprinkled the water, the head wraps of the women, so casual yet so elegant, the blue river nearby, the pink sand on its banks. She never tired of the pleasure of letting herself get swept away by such sights, delighted that their delight never grew stale. How could you not find in them some tolerance for whatever life threw at you?

Then the moment of sigh arrived, and this boisterous place seemed to freeze for a moment. The traders stopped mid-sentence, the echo of the last words they had said reverberating in the atmosphere. Their hands paused midway to wiping the sweat from their foreheads, their lips on the verge of bright smiles, their rumpled brows in the act of releasing sorrow. Khoudi created snapshots with her eyes that she could revisit later, when she was in need of something other than her life. Then, before the sigh came to an end, she took whatever food and money her hands could snatch, hid them in her raffia bag, and made her way out of the market.

Normally she would not stop, but today she came upon a strange sight. A man was sitting on the ground wearing khaki shorts, a long-sleeved white shirt, brown boots, and a brimmed khaki hat. He looked like one of those white men in the books she had read back when she was a schoolgirl, when she was living with that family who had let her stay with them awhile. She pushed the memory aside and concentrated instead on the image that came to mind, from one of those long-forgotten books. There were always photos of those white men standing in the bow of a boat, rowed by a man so shiningly dark that he became the only point of intensity in the photo. In each photograph, the boat seemed to be heading up or down a river, to discover what, she did not understand, then or now. Anyway, this man was not white, but he looked just as out of place. He was looking at an old map of Foloiya, which was itself strange, because no one around here was in the habit of looking to some piece of paper to help them understand the very land they stood upon. The map was flapping against the man's hand in the breeze, as if it wanted to fly away, knowing it had no use. How could an old map help you find your way in a place that shifted constantly, like the direction of the wind?

The man paused, waving her near without looking up. She hesitated, but his demeanor held none of the menace she was used to encountering in men toward young women like her.

"Do you know where this house is?" He extended the map to her, pointing at the far end. "I have covered everywhere except this last place." He kept his gaze on the map, his eyes searching it for an answer as it fluttered even more violently in the wind.

"That house is no longer there. It fell with the last rains," Khoudi told him with certainty.

"That explains it." He took a red pen from a chest pocket that was lined with other pens of various colors and crossed out the indicated location of the offending house. Then he began to fold the map with what seemed like excessive care. "Do you know where the people who lived there went?"

A car with tinted windows and fancy tires, too sleek for the landscape, zigzagged its way along the road, trying and failing to avoid the potholes. The confused fellow stood and saluted, which amused Khoudiemata, who had caught the insignia. It was not a government car.

"Why are you saluting? Do you know Rolls-Royce?" she asked, chuckling.

The man didn't answer, but held his salute until the car slowly disappeared down the mangled road. Then he repeated his question. "Do you know where the people who lived there went?"

"Why do you want to know?" Suspicion rose in her even as her instincts told her he was harmless. *But harmless people work for wicked bosses,* she thought.

"Because I am charged with taking the census. I am doing a thorough count of everyone in this town." He sounded annoyed, and with his index finger he gestured toward his chest and shoulders, indicating that his outfit with its various badges and adornments should have conveyed his importance to her.

"Is that so?" Khoudi stifled the impulse to laugh at how seriously he took himself. She was willing to bet he had not found many houses, or many people willing to come to the door at this early hour. In fact, most had already left, to chase the dreams that no longer came at night.

For the first time, the man looked in her direction, and his eyes went straight through her body as though someone else was standing right behind her. Without saying anything more, he went off in the direction of the house she had told him no longer existed.

Khoudi had long stopped worrying about what people saw or didn't see when they looked at her. Perhaps she was a reminder of the fragility of their own lives. "Don't you want to count me in your census, Mister?" she called after him mockingly, but even his shadow had turned its back on her. She was used to people assuming that someone like her didn't know anything, but she did know one thing for certain: The census meant nothing. It was just another ploy that let those in power pretend that something was being done. Young as she was, she had watched history set its wings and fly off in the wrong direction more than once.

At the end of the open field beyond Foloiya, Khoudiemata counted steps, more with the memory of her muscles than of her head. She cast her eyes about her one last time, then turned left into a wall of bushes. She slid her slender frame beneath them and pulled herself up on the other side, coming face-to-face with a high concrete wall topped with coils of barbed wire. She followed it to the right, stopping at a narrow break. She put her head through first, checking, then stepped through. She wet her lips and whistled the secret phrase to announce her arrival. *King's property, king's property, everything is correct.* Immediately she got a matching whistle back, with the repeated phrases they had agreed upon, to guard against impostors. *Everything is correct, everything is correct.*

She recognized Kpindi's distinctive inflection, confirmed when he continued with a melodic question: *Anything for us? Anything for us?* None of the others did that.

Let's meet at the house. Let's meet at the house, Khoudiemata's whistle replied. Her eyes caught the movement of the grasses as Kpindi made his last rounds.

Jumping over some scattered twigs lest she make any noise, Khoudi landed on the small path, barely body-wide, between the walls of shrubs. This was her path, their path. The other one, wide and easy to find, led people turn by promising turn only back to the crossroads or into town. She and the others had deliberately created these detours to deliver any who sought them right back where they had come.

"Namsa," Khoudi called softly, "you have learned to walk so quietly. I could barely hear your footsteps."

"How did you know I was coming your way, then?" answered the girl, her small voice reaching Khoudi over the wind.

"My nose told me," Khoudi replied.

"How?"

"You always wash yourself with the grass that smells like lemon."

And just as Khoudi heard Namsa sniffing, trying to catch the scent of her own body, she came into view at the bend. The two of them lit up at the sight of each other. Then Namsa placed her arm around the waist of the older girl and looked up at her, her pointed little face not yet even at the height of Khoudi's shoulders. They walked the rest of the way like that, Namsa sometimes skipping, their bodies brushing the branches on either side.

The path came to an end in a clearing enclosed by palm and baobab trees. In the middle, the skeleton of a medium-size plane lay on its belly. Vines had wrapped themselves around most of the exterior, giving it a natural camouflage. Nearly all of the windows in the front were intact, and toward the back, where more were missing, they had been covered with cardboard, plastic, and tarpaulin to prevent snakes and other animals from entering. The faded Air Lyoa insignia could be made out against a background of green, white, and blue. In the clearing in front of the plane, a battered old aluminum refrigerator lay on its side. Khoudiemata placed her raffia bag on top of it, and she and Namsa dragged two upended plastic buckets alongside. The two of them sat facing each other, Namsa playing with her fingers, Khoudi's eyes on the path. The wind gusted up under the bushes and grasses and lifted the nearby heaps of rubbish. A sheet of newspaper took flight in front of one wing, and for a moment, it was possible to imagine that one of the propellers was spinning and the old airplane was going to start its missing engine and take off.

Now Ndevui appeared, from another hidden path that led to the beach. He went for a run every morning, with a white towel around his neck and his earphones deep inside his ears, as if he were afraid of hearing the promises that the new day offered for some. He kept the cord of the earphones tucked under his shirt and into his football shorts, so that no one could see what it was connected to. The truth was that it was connected to nothing, but that did not stop him from singing to himself the songs he had heard on the streets and in the music shops. Who needed a device when you had a mind that could record songs and play them back for free?

"How far did you go today?" asked Khoudi, folding the sleeves of the oversize sweatshirt she wore when she went out into the world, to mask the contours of her body and keep herself safe. But Ndevui was singing whatever his memory was playing, and he didn't answer immediately. He wiped the sweat off his broad forehead and cracked his fingers. Then he removed the earphones and turned back toward her.

"Is your music off now?" asked Khoudi, deferring to his ingenuity. "How long was your run?"

"More than two hours today, without stopping." He pointed with his long fingers beyond the trees and wiped his forehead again with the towel around his neck. He was wearing a TP Mazembe jersey and Kaizer Chiefs shorts—African football clubs, not the European ones most kids flaunted, which were easier to come by. When the others teased him about his choice, he said, "I get to choose the kind of fool I want to be." He had a pair of new cleats too, which he sometimes, like today, strung around his neck as well.

"Are you ever going to play in those shoes, or even run in them?" Namsa teased, a daily ritual.

"I will wear them when I get to play in a game that can get me recognized. They will only add to my natural abilities." He picked up a split-open tennis ball with the sides of his bare feet and began to juggle it.

At this very moment, Kpindi shot into the clearing and deftly intercepted the ball. Some days they used a plastic bottle, an inedible orange or mango, or a bundle of rags. No matter what the day's ball was made of, Kpindi always managed to surprise Ndevui by changing direction at the last split second and stealing it from Ndevui's feet.

"Ha, you have to be alert, big brother." Kpindi snapped his fingers. "It isn't all about stamina and strength." He squeezed Ndevui's biceps, measured and compared them to his bony arms. Though Ndevui was a year older and stronger, Kpindi was taller by a head. He ran circles around Ndevui, juggling the pretend ball. "It is also about using your medium-size head." He laughed and gave Ndevui a shove, then Ndevui shoved him back, the two of them like real brothers, always straddling the line between confrontation and joke. When they had exhausted themselves, they dragged two more plastic buckets hard against the earth and took a seat at the makeshift table.

Kpindi rubbed his long belly. "I am always excited when it's big sister who comes back with food, because I know she has the taste of tastes." Whenever he and Ndevui argued about height, which was often, Kpindi said he was taller because he had drunk more cow's milk, while Ndevui ate only rice and cassava.

"Where is Monsieur La Tête?" asked Kpindi. It was their joke name for Elimane, who was always somewhere reading or writing. Elimane read not with the visible discipline of someone who had acquired the skill later in life but with a kind of effortlessness, a second nature that suggested he had come from privilege. But Elimane never spoke about his earlier life, any more than the rest of them did. They knew only that, of the twenty years of his life, he had spent four living in the plane, the first year all alone. Kpindi had arrived next, then Khoudi, then Ndevui, and last of all little Namsa, only six months before.

"His big head is probably inside one of those rusty books." Ndevui whistled loudly in the direction of the plane, but there was no response.

"I will get him." Khoudiemata stood up and went toward the door of the plane, beside which the painted head of a lion was visible, its eyes vibrant among the painted foliage. She climbed the stairs that they could pull up when they needed to, with a strong tug on thick ropes they had attached to the rails.

Inside, almost all the seats had disappeared, save for seven at the front of the craft, near the cockpit. The seats resembled the cots at the boarding school where the little family had once gone to help themselves to sheets and pillows during a holiday when the guards slept through their shifts. Why would a plane carry little beds, they had wondered. Who could have slept in the belly of this iron bird?

There sat Elimane, scribbling something in one of his many notebooks as usual, every inch of the page crammed with words. He always made an attempt to look well dressed, turning up his faded and tattered sleeves, combing his hair, and shining his black shoes every night as he read a propped-open book by flashlight, if he had a battery, or by moonlight when the moon was bright. Never mind that the soles of the shoes were almost completely gone, so that when Elimane put them on, he was almost walking on bare feet. Poverty has a great appetite for eating one's dignity, but Elimane was one of those people who fought to keep his, even when that was the only battle he was winning.

Now he looked up at Khoudi, his big head heavy on his lanky frame.

"Your body isn't going to survive with only those books for food. So come out and eat, Mr. Serious Gentleman." Khoudi took his hand and pulled him away from his book. He laughed his deep laugh, got to his feet, and followed her out.

Outside, the others had already started apportioning the food from Khoudiemata's bag. They always shared equally, even if all they had was a handful of nuts or a piece of fruit. Today she had brought back fried fish and stewed onions with bread and other things that you would not put together if you had the luxury of considering the pleasure of the mouth.

Elimane went to join the others, but Khoudi remained standing. She looked at each of them in turn, these faces so hidden in the canvas of humanity. All too soon it would be time for them to discuss where they would find the next meal, and what they needed to do to guard their safety while they got it.

Ndevui waved her to the table. He was not one for sentiment, which he regarded as a luxury that made him weak, but he treasured moments of simple enjoyment, like these meals they ate together under the open sky, even though they ate less for enjoyment than simply to stay alive. He knew that there were not only kiosks where you argued with the food seller to add more sauce to your rice or more butter to your bread, determined to get your hard-earned money's worth, but also places where you didn't even see the cook, just some people coming out of a room with your food. And he had seen that people at those kinds of places were always smiling and laughing as they ate. But for this little family too, meals were a time when their faces relaxed—when they looked as they might have if they were as fortunate as some other youngsters, whose faces were always smooth. Ndevui valued even the mealtimes without food, when they sat together before they took up fear and caution again and went out to forage. At such moments of unguarded togetherness, he could stop thinking about all that was against him, against them. It almost qualified as happiness.

"Khoudiemata, please come and sit down before my appetite dies with the morning." Ndevui refused to call her Khoudi as the rest did, saying that her full name suited her best.

"She is memorizing the moment. Give her a minute," Elimane interjected softly.

Khoudiemata sat down, and they all began to eat. If you watched her, you would see that she was eating her bread slowly, her eyes secretively checking to see which of the others remained hungry. She wasn't smiling, but something pleasant and soft had slipped into her face. She had taken off her beanie and let her beautiful dark curls fall free, and now she rested her head on her hand. In this position, even though her eyes were on the others, it seemed her mind had slipped away to somewhere they couldn't follow. But wherever she was, she looked for a moment almost like one of those schoolgirls they sometimes saw chattering like birds during breaks from their classrooms.

Ndevui finished eating quickly, but he pretended to be chewing on something, so that Khoudiemata wouldn't give him the remainder of her food. He was hoping she would hand it to Namsa, the "little one," as he called her. She was licking her fingers like they were sticks of honey. The little one was the only person Ndevui knew who actively smiled while eating. She had told him that she did so to make sure that the food was happy in her belly and would not give her a stomachache. As he had hoped, Khoudiemata gave the last two bites of her bread to the little one, who laughed with pleasure as she brought the food to her mouth.

The wind returned, whispering, and laughter wafted among them too, because Kpindi, their jokester, was smacking his mouth with each bite as though this was the best meal he had ever tasted. Then he began to hum "Dem Belly Full," as he always did. When they had nothing to eat, he sang the lyrics out loud and danced, the words themselves seeming to give him stamina: *Dem belly full but we hungry, a hungry man is an angry man.* But today they had food, and so he hummed, and they laughed and ate and littered the ground with bones that the stray dogs would come for later.

And a strong breeze carried their voices out to the airfield and left them floating in the vast open space.

3

D o not let me fall too far behind," Namsa whispered, looking up
at the sky as she followed the others. She believed that whoever
was responsible for the fate of human beings lived somewhere up
there, even after Khoudi had challenged her to think more deeply
about it. Why up in the sky? Why not in the river, in the forest,
among them, within them? Namsa liked to be in harmony with
Khoudi, whom she secretly thought of as her big sister. But she could
not let go of this belief in a presence-in-the-sky.

They had found Namsa, shivering and alone, in an open field not
far from their home. They tried saying "Hello, please don't be afraid"
in the fifteen languages and three dialects that they collectively
knew, but it was weeks before she did more than nod or shake her
head in response. Even when she began to speak, she seemed unable
to tell them anything about where she had come from, though she
did, as it turned out, understand seven of the languages, including a
lingua franca and some English. In any case, they had an unspoken
understanding not to press one another about the past and its pain,

but to keep trying to live in the present, offering silent understanding and respect.

They had guessed that Namsa was about ten or eleven, though as her playful spirit began to reassert itself, she came to seem perhaps younger. Initially this had been an argument in favor of keeping her—there were times when having such an innocent-looking accomplice could be useful in allowing them to elude notice or suspicion. But as they began to teach her the way of their little world, they had become attached to her for her own sake, and she had completed the sense of them as a family. When Elimane discovered she could not read, he began to give her lessons, in the mornings or in the evenings. Unlike Khoudi, he was always serious with her, even strict, but he spoke to her gently, in a way that she imagined a real brother would. He began to teach Kpindi and Ndevui as well, writing in the dirt with a twig, then erasing the letters with his feet when they had answered to his satisfaction. "Now the words are in there forever, if you choose to keep them," he'd say, pointing to their heads and hearts. He made them feel that the lessons were not for each of them alone, but would make them more useful to the others, and so they paid attention and worked hard.

This morning there would be no lessons, however. After they ate, they debated where to go look for food next. They tried to vary their rounds each day, so as not to create a predictable pattern that might get them caught.

"Not to the airport," Ndevui said. "We were there yesterday." On his run he had noted that things were not so lively at the bars along the beach either, so he thought the ferry landing at the wharf, just past the market, might be a better choice. They had not been there for more than a week, and today was a big day for the arrival of new goods. They could get work carrying loads to various shops or could steal some things and sell them. One of the two was bound to happen—or both. Circumstances would decide, and they would take advantage in the ways they knew.

Reluctantly, they raised themselves to their feet and retraced the hidden path to rejoin the outer world. When they arrived at the wall, Ndevui stopped to listen, to ascertain that no one was on the other side. Then he gave the go-ahead, and one after the other they passed through the opening. Ndevui stepped through last, stopping to camouflage the break with branches so that the opening disappeared behind them.

Disappeared as well was the relaxed mood of mealtime. In the outside world, they walked and spoke with quiet urgency. Gone were the smiles and laughter. They spoke less gently to Namsa as well. *Keep up*, they commanded her. Unspoken were the other commands: *Do not betray emotions. Do not show weakness. Be attentive.*

Namsa still found the transition jarring, and with her shorter legs, she was once again struggling to keep up. She had created a little game that helped. She pretended that whoever was at the front of the group was calling her name, wanting to speak with her, and that she must hurry to catch up with them. Although she never got all the way to the head of the line, she also never got left behind. She preferred it when Khoudi led the group, like yesterday, because even though Khoudi never turned around, she somehow knew when Namsa was beginning to tire, and contrived to slow the group down.

Today, Elimane was in the lead. By tacit agreement, the leader determined where they went and what they did, and no one questioned those decisions unless things were really not going well. Elimane never slowed down, so Namsa said to herself, *Elimane is calling me.* She whispered back, *I am coming, Elimane*, and gave her legs a burst of speed.

The group paused at the edge of the bushes. From here they could see the rutted dirt road with patches of tar here and there. Elimane sighed. "Almost everything in this country is on its way to losing itself." He said something about the road every morning, whether he was leading or not. Namsa didn't always understand what he meant, or why he cared. The road was used mostly by walkers like them, who, like them, took it to town solely to search for something to eat for the day. Most people Namsa had known in her small lifetime seemed to be doing only that each and every day, looking for something to eat.

The five of them didn't all go out onto the road at the same time. They never did anything all at the same time in view of others, in order to avoid notice or suspicion. Elimane looked at Namsa, the newcomer, to be sure she remembered. Namsa returned his stern gaze, nodding slightly to let him know she did indeed remember. Only then did he turn his attention back to the road and, having made sure no one was watching, step onto the road, hitching up his trousers as if he had stopped only to urinate in the bushes before proceeding on his way. One by one, the others followed suit, waiting to step onto the road until he gave the signal, which was to turn around and walk backward a few paces, but without looking at them. Each of them went to a different part of the road, away from the others but within view and earshot. Namsa skipped ahead of all of them but Elimane, as she had been instructed, so that the others could keep an eye on her. She kept her eyes on Elimane's shadow, so it wasn't obvious that she was following him. And just like that, they became part of the road.

It was a brisk fifteen-minute walk to the ferry landing. They passed few other people, mostly men and boys. The air was hot, and the quiet was disrupted only when a van or truck passed, filled with tired faces. These were the faces of people with jobs, but the kinds of jobs that reminded them that their lives would remain a struggle. After a few minutes, a brand-new luxury car came along, weaving from side to side as the driver struggled to find safe passage for his delicate vehicle on the dilapidated road. He could not prevent the tires from landing from time to time in potholes filled with muddy water, which sometimes made the belly of the car drag briefly along the red soil of the road. Just behind the painful passage of this car came a caravan of yellow dump trucks filled with red rocks. This was bauxite from a nearby mining site, the little family knew, en route to the docks, where it would be loaded onto barges.

As soon as the sound of the engines began to fade in the distance, Elimane let out a whistle, without looking in anyone's direction, then broke into a sprint. Namsa was at a loss about what he was reacting to, but she understood that he was running toward something, not fleeing, not alarmed. She almost broke into a run herself but remembered just in time that they must not make it obvious they were together. She stole a glance behind her and saw that Khoudi was walking at a much faster pace but not running, as were Kpindi and Ndevui. Namsa did the same, watching as Elimane's frame disappeared down the hill ahead of them. What had he heard or seen?

Soon enough, a smaller car came into view, stuck in the ditch at the side of the road. Sharp zigzag ruts told the story: The driver had evidently been in a hurry to overtake other vehicles and, swerving to avoid a pothole, had gone off the road. The driver stood by the car, immaculately dressed in jeans and a sweater over a collared white shirt, twisting a pair of gold-framed sunglasses as he scanned the faces of the passersby. He was clearly in need of help to push the vehicle back onto the road but also just as obviously nervous. It wasn't the safest road, and he shook his head at one offer of assistance after another, seeming suspicious. Not all of his would-be helpers gave up so easily. Five thin boys, not taking no for an answer, were attempting to push the car out of the ditch.

Namsa spotted Elimane. He had stopped running and was ambling along, his eyes on a small book he had taken from his pocket, seemingly oblivious of the driver and his predicament. The driver watched Elimane for a few moments, then called out to him.

"Excuse me, young man."

Elimane continued walking, his eyes glued to his book.

The boys had stopped trying to budge the car and were arguing about who was boss and should, therefore, be in charge of apportioning the money they had not yet been guaranteed. They eyed the windows of the car hungrily.

"No. I said no. I don't need your help," the man insisted, waving them off. He turned to address Elimane again, more loudly, his voice a bit thin and strained with the effort. "Excuse me, young man! Sorry to disturb your reading!"

At just that moment, the driver's scent reached Namsa. Had he had showered that morning with a bucket of perfume? she wondered.

Elimane raised his head. "Good morning, sir. What seems to be the matter?" He held the book open with his fingers to emphasize that he had been interrupted in a worthwhile pursuit.

The man opened his palms to Elimane in supplication. "I need to catch the ferry back to the city in time to deliver these provisions. Could you help me push the car out of the mud?"

"Sir, there are so many others on this road who can help you," Elimane replied, nodding toward the youngsters who were hovering around the car. "Besides, I do not think the two of us can get it done."

He closed the book but kept a finger in it, marking the page he had been reading. Namsa was certain he was not pretending about that much, at least.

The man glanced at Elimane's book and then up at his face. "I don't trust any of these people. They have the unpleasant smell of desperation." He lifted his frame off the body of the car and came fully to his feet.

"Well, then, let's get to it." Elimane folded down the corner of the page where his fingers had been, returned the book to his pocket, and turned up the sleeves of his shirt. He made no mention of recompense. His posture bespoke a familiarity with vehicles like this one, and perhaps that is what the man sensed. Khoudi, Ndevui, and Kpindi had only been in passenger vehicles like the ones that had passed them earlier, so crowded that walking seemed preferable and so old that the stones on the road threatened to smack your bottom all the way to wherever you were going or before you got there—unless the heat of the tar on the road melted you first. As for Namsa, she had never so much as been near a steering wheel—at least, not that she could remember. She slowed her pace as she approached and kept to the other side of the road, knowing that if she stood next to a car like that, she would not be able to resist peeking inside.

"It has been a while since I saw such genuine enthusiasm to help another. It used to be common around here," said the man. He got in the car and turned on the engine. With one foot on the accelerator and his other foot on the ground, he began pushing with Elimane. But hard as they pushed, the car remained stuck.

The driver got out of the car, leaving the engine running, and stood next to Elimane. "What do you think, my good man?"

"I think we should offload some things to make it lighter."

Elimane looked down the road, frowning. "But then again, the people passing by may steal it." There were more women walking along the road now, but they remained fewer in number than men and boys.

"Yes, you are right on both points," said the man. "I have to get moving soon so that I do not miss the ferry, or I will arrive very late at night."

"How about we offload some boxes, and then I pick two more fellows to help push with you?" said Elimane. "Then I will watch your things while you get the car back on the road." The man hesitated; his thoughts could be read on his face. He couldn't give his car keys to a stranger, even one he seemed inclined to trust, but he could give him the task of watching some of his goods. It wouldn't be easy for Elimane to run off with the big boxes, and even if he did, it would be less of a loss than the car. The little family watched as the man's eyes darted from one variable to another, making calculations.

"Okay, let's offload that box and that one." The man opened the back door of the car and handed the boxes to Elimane, who set them in the grass, not on the road, where people might rush at them, tear them apart, and run away with the contents. The man closed the rear door of the car and turned back to the road, scanning to see whom he could enlist to help push.

Namsa spotted something that could spoil Elimane's plan, their plan. A woman, not as young as Khoudi and not as old as a grandmother, mumbled as she made her way along the other side of the road. "Eh, eh! This boy is more cunning than Bra Spider's grandfather. Ha! I could get a ride into town if I show him for what he is to that man." She was heading straight for the car, on a mission. Namsa knew the sort—she was one of those who did not want others to succeed at anything, even if they themselves got nothing out of it.

Even if she didn't succeed in convincing the man that Elimane was up to no good, she would plant doubt in his mind, and that would change everything.

Namsa ran across the road to her. "Auntie, auntie, help me!" she cried, reaching for the woman's hand and trembling, as if with fear.

"I am not your auntie, little girl!" The woman snatched her hand away, but Namsa caught it again and held on tighter, this time with both hands.

"I know, auntie, but they will hurt me if they know I am alone. Please just be my auntie for some minutes," Namsa insisted. She fell to the ground in front of the woman, holding her feet the way a child begs for forgiveness, and impeding the woman's progress. When she looked up, she saw that the woman was furious to the point that even her cheeks were trembling. There was no ounce of kindness anywhere on her hard face. But the time Namsa had bought was enough.

Ndevui and Kpindi were approaching slowly, apparently engrossed in a conversation about their final exams, the way they had often heard other kids talk.

"Hey, schoolboys, come make some lunch money." The man waved them over.

"We don't have time, sir. We need to go to our study session." Ndevui looked at Kpindi for confirmation.

The man stepped in front of them. "It won't take long, I promise, and this will be a lesson too."

The boys eyed each other with some reluctance and then agreed. The man began to explain what they were to do, his attention no longer on the boxes.

The woman had lost the opportunity to make a case against Elimane, and now the newcomers had been enlisted. Moreover, while speaking with Kpindi and Ndevui, the man had glanced briefly in the direction of Namsa and the woman, and shaken his head in disapproval at how unsympathetic she was to a child in need. Whatever she said now would have no merit.

"You, if you don't get off my feet this minute, I am going to crush you into the ground. Ah, you think the day is only rough for you!" The woman gave Namsa a knock on the head and stared down at her menacingly for another moment before she continued on her way, grumbling into the day. Despite the pain, Namsa felt proud of her quick thinking and action, and a smile started to rise to her face until she remembered that she must not show such emotions and she quickly hid it away.

Namsa dusted off her clothes and got to her feet, stealing a glance at Ndevui and Kpindi, who were concentrating on helping the man push the vehicle back onto the road, not once showing that they knew Elimane. Now Khoudi and Namsa began to work together, in silent harmony. Namsa went around to the front of the car, apparently transfixed by the sight of its predicament, and so provided additional distraction as Khoudi ransacked the boxes, squatting so that the body of the car hid her from the driver's view. Swiftly she removed a pack of powdered milk, four cans of Nescafé, and a few packets of what looked to Namsa like long yellow broom straws, and placed them in her raffia bag, rearranging the boxes so they didn't look tampered with. Then she duck-walked away from the car before she stood up to walk off.

As soon as Namsa judged it was safe, she herself moved on. She knew that Elimane would make sure that Ndevui and Kpindi helped him put the boxes back in the car, so the man wouldn't have a chance to notice any difference in weight. Khoudi's restraint would also help allay any suspicion. Namsa realized she was learning about good faith and its uses, and the way greed could put it at risk. Playfully kicking pebbles on the ground as she walked, she followed Khoudi to the junction above the ferry landing. Namsa perched herself on a stack of concrete blocks where what looked to be the beginnings of a house no longer appeared to have the possibility of getting finished, as evidenced by the weeds that now grew up and around them. Khoudi had a seat a short distance away, and they stayed like that, not speaking, as they awaited the others.

From where Namsa sat, she saw the ferry approaching. It looked like a dilapidated two-story house floating on water. The rusty hull was stained with salt water, and along it hung old tires. The deck was stacked to the brim with people, cars, and goods, making a festive display of color against the cloudless sky. The sound of the engine became deafening as the boat neared, though for all the noise, the boat moved very slowly. Two concrete pillars, eroded so that their skeletons of iron rods showed through in places, waited to stop the boat's movement before it hit the shallow waters. Beyond them, on the jetty and the shore, an anxious crowd waited, hoping to find their day's livelihood with the arrival of the ferry. Already skirmishes were breaking out, as people hustled for the best spots on the landing from which to offer their services. Ten port guards in green pants and yellow shirts tried unsuccessfully to hold back the crowd by banging their batons against the iron posts of the jetty and dragging them against the concrete as they opened the wire-mesh gates. "Please clear the landing area for arriving passengers and vehicles!" a man shouted from a megaphone when the ferry's laboring engine halted. No one heeded his command. As the ferry neared the pier, he retrieved a hose and sprayed the crowd with it. This time, they moved back just beyond the demarcated area, but just barely, waiting for the moment when they could return, some beginning to claw their way along the wire mesh of the opened gates.

Beyond the crowd, along the side of the road to town, was a long line of vehicles waiting to board whenever the ferry was ready. Namsa saw the man with the car whom Elimane had helped. He was alone now. She guessed that he had trusted Elimane only so far, not enough to offer him a ride.

The man spoke to the guard in charge of the queue, and the guard motioned for him to drive his car past the others to the front of the jetty, where there was a RESERVED FOR OFFICIAL USE sign. The other drivers were disgruntled at the special treatment, and one of them called out, "We can grease your palm too, to become 'official,'" but the guard paid them no mind. And while they stood outside their cars in the heat, their engines off to save fuel, the man stayed inside his vehicle with the engine running and the windows rolled up, talking on his phone, and, evidently, taking advantage of the air-conditioning.

At last Ndevui, Kpindi, and Elimane arrived, one after the other, the hems of their trousers wet. They must have gone to the sea to wash the mud off their feet. They did not greet the girls but moved past them some paces down toward the ferry, surveying the scene as they considered the best approach. By now the place was in turmoil. The vehicles in the first batch coming off the ferry refused to give way to one another, creating a logjam. The arriving passengers squeezed out between the stuck vehicles while the drivers shouted at one another and tried to maneuver out of the chaos. As soon as the tiniest bit of space opened up, one of them accelerated into it, honking, and people sprang out of the way, cursing. But Namsa could tell that the others were more relaxed now, because they had already gotten something for their efforts from the man with the car—Mr. Scent, as Namsa now thought of him, the memory of his heavy cologne still assaulting her nose.

A small stone fell next to Namsa, interrupting her thoughts.

Instinctively she turned in the direction of Khoudi's shadow, which signaled for her to stay where she was by taking a pace forward and then another back. Namsa stayed put as Khoudi's shadow departed toward the entrance to the market. Then she lifted her head to see where Khoudi had gone. The market was less busy at this hour, because most people were at the ferry landing, and she could follow Khoudi with her gaze as she spoke to this person and that. She watched as Khoudi pushed someone out of her way, and then as she shook hands with a barefoot woman wearing a dress with a herringbone pattern in yellow, green, and pink. Khoudi reached into the raffia bag and handed the woman the powdered milk, the cans of Nescafé, and the packets of what looked like broom straws. The entire right arm of the woman disappeared into the pocket of her dress and returned with some bills that she thrust into Khoudi's hands. Reflexively, Khoudi stashed the money inside her bag.

"Who told you to sit here?"

Namsa looked up to see two boys she guessed to be about Ndevui's age. One of them, in tattered clothes that barely covered his body, was pointing at her.

She shooed him away. "Does this place belong to you? Get out of my sight." She had encountered this type before. She had also learned from observing Khoudiemata that she must speak firmly, so as not to leave room to be taken advantage of.

The tattered boy came closer, his face portending no good. "Where is your respect for your elders?"

"How about you give my nose some respect, because you smell," Namsa said, as loudly as she could, giving the boy a shove. Ndevui and Kpindi and Elimane didn't turn around, but she saw that their spines straightened, and the boy noticed it too. His friend was pulling him toward the market, and he let himself be led away, his face telling Namsa that he would find her some other time, when there wouldn't be people around to protect her.

Namsa resumed her position on the column of concrete blocks, this time mindful to stay more aware of her surroundings. Soon Elimane's whistle reached her. *Not as constant as the Northern Star, Not as constant as the Northern Star.* That one was Elimane's own invention. He had said that it came from Shakespeare's *Julius Caesar*, reciting in his deep voice, *"But I am constant as the Northern Star, of whose true fixed and resting quality there is no fellow in the firmament."* So if they whistled, *Not as constant as the Northern Star,* that meant they were moving. Only Khoudi seemed to follow and enjoy this convoluted explanation, but they all knew what the signal meant: *Let's continue.* Namsa rose, dusted herself off, and followed the others on down toward the ferry.

The private cars had finished disembarking, and a procession of trucks and long carts loaded with goods were waiting to go next. But before they could move, three green Land Rovers drove off onto solid ground, and a phalanx of men in khaki uniforms jumped from the vehicles and positioned themselves on either side of the gate. The guards themselves now advanced on the bystanders, waving their batons.

Most of those crowding the landing were young men and boys, but there were older men and some women as well. "Yes, sir, yes madame. Yes, madame," they called. "My boss! You remember me from last time? It's still me, and my price is lower today." Everyone shouted and pushed, calling out their offerings even as their bodies were carried from place to place in the fray. "Only fifty thousand to get all your loads to land!" "I can do it for less and quicker!" "Picking me is the best decision you'll make today!" Vying to offload goods to the vehicles parked nearby, men and boys showed off their muscles, cracking their knuckles and necks, and some even tore open their shirts in a display of strength and readiness. "Sixty thousand for here, thirty thousand for there. What space do you want? What is your last price? I can work with you, my son. You look like my son and brother." The women called out how much they'd charge to stow a load until transportation could be arranged, in spaces that were covered with bamboo and raffia mats and guarded by little girls.

A horn blared from the ferry and the goods were rolled out, while the owners walked beside the carts and trucks. As they advanced, they pointed to those whom they wanted to hire. The chosen were allowed through the gates by the men in khaki uniforms. Sometimes someone jumped in front of the person who'd been selected, and a fight broke out until another choice was made. The workers hoisted the goods off the vehicles and dollies as directed and followed their temporary employers toward the exit, where guards waited to collect their fees, ten thousand per small box or bag, twenty thousand for bigger. One of the guards collected the money as soon as it was paid and handed it to their boss, who reclined on a chair in the middle of the hubbub, a pistol on his lap. He pocketed the cash and gave a slip of paper in return, streaked with a red marker. That was the only semblance of order to the operation, which otherwise had the air of the market just before a holiday.

It was even more chaotic outside. Those carrying the loads had to make sure they weren't pulled in the wrong direction by the crowd and forced to set down the merchandise at the wrong spot. They struggled to stay close to the owners while they dodged reaching hands and pushed their way through the throng.

So transfixed was Namsa by the melee that she nearly missed Elimane's approach until he was directly in her line of vision. Startled, she looked up. This wasn't the way they did things in public. They never addressed one another directly or even acknowledged that they were acquainted. Uncertain about what to do, she simply stood there, her feet seemingly planted on the riverbank.

"Hello, little girl. Can I send you to get me some water over there?" Elimane called out loudly. He reached into his pocket and, lowering himself so that his face was in front of Namsa's, deposited a few coins in her hand as he whispered hurriedly, "When you return with the water, I will give you our cash, and you stay right here with it. Understand?" Although Namsa was staring right into his mouth, she could barely see him move his lips.

She ran to get the water, marveling at this latest magic. How did he do it? She knew to go for the water tied in plastic bags, not the bottled kind. Weaving between people's legs as their eyes stayed locked on the ferry and the possibilities it brought, she ran left and then right to avoid the movement of the crowd that registered from the multitude of their dusty feet and tattered shoes. At times, unable to find a way through, she had to double back, moving a bit farther from the sea to reach the periphery of the market.

She surveyed the sellers, with their coolers and buckets, and decided to go to a girl a bit older than herself, wearing a large red shirt and yellow skirt that she kept pulling up and twisting to make it stay on. She was carrying plastic bags of water on a tray on her head and calling out, "Cold water, cold water here." Impressed with her balancing skills, Namsa approached and handed over the money. The girl lowered herself without touching the tray so that Namsa could pick one of the packets, then stood up and tied the money into the waist of her skirt.

When Namsa returned with the water, Elimane took it, and in the same swift motion deftly slipped her a slender packet wrapped in paper. He bit off the edge of the plastic bag so that he could gulp down most of the water, then held out the remainder to Namsa, muttering, "Your pay," with the same ventriloquism as before, and walked away. Namsa watched as he got closer and closer to the crowd, then, turning sideways, squeezed his shoulders into the writhing, shouting mass, and was swallowed up. Try as she might, Namsa could no longer make him out.

She sat down on the ground and anxiously glanced around. Ndevui and Kpindi were a bit farther down the slope, attentively expecting something from the chaos, and off to the side she once again sensed Khoudi's shadow; she had returned from the market. Namsa searched for a better place to sit, feeling their attention on her even as they fixed their eyes elsewhere. She found a heap of sand piled against an unfinished wall and sat down on it, so that she could see who was coming toward her. She savored the cold water, taking slow sips, as she watched the crowd grow more numerous and more restless. She sensed that something untoward was imminent. She could feel the disappointment and anger rising on the faces before her, while the day continued to deny them everything.

Elimane did not want to drag himself into the gathering madness at the ferry landing, but he knew that he had to become part of it to show a little of his desperation. The traders standing nearby, or really most anyone doing just well enough to pay for the services of people like him, needed to be reassured that those they were considering hiring were in a state of sufficient wretchedness that they could be paid as little as possible for their labor, and never succeed enough to pull themselves up from that state. Thus, the boss men reassured themselves of their own importance. *Pull-down-and-keep-down syndrome* was how Elimane thought of it.

This was something he knew not only by observation but from experience. Once he had lived on the other side of the unnatural human divide. He knew what it was to have a driver, a cleaner, a cook—so many people to do everything for him that the only non-negotiable burden he carried was emerging from and returning to sleep. Oh, to be so beautifully idle once again! But all that had gone up in flames one night, quite literally, and he had been lucky to escape with his life—luckier than the rest of his family. Since then, he had learned how to pretend to be vulnerable, in order to attract those who wanted to take advantage of him, so that in turn he might live. From his reading, he knew that this was the way of the world, all over the world, even where the syndrome was cleverly disguised. Here at the ferry, it existed in its rawest form. In that, at least, there was a semblance of honesty.

He circled the perimeter of the crowd, looking for an advantageous entry point. In most human endeavors, he had learned, there was one. Today, it opened to him thanks to the movement of a beautiful young woman. Nearby, a young fellow with muscles built strong by daily labor was distracted by her, the rest of his body following his eyes and temporarily abandoning the resoluteness required for the chaos at hand. Elimane easily pushed by, taking up a more advantageous position. When the young fellow regained himself, his determination to reclaim his position carried Elimane much farther to the front of the crowd than he would have been able to travel on his own.

Deep in the belly of the mass, Elimane was awash in the stench of other bodies that, like his, must sweat profusely every day to find a living. He was used to his own odor but not to that of such a multitude, whose clothing had soaked and dried on their very backs, under a scorching sun. But he knew that he had the ability to acclimate himself to such circumstances, and he bid his nose to accustom itself to such a smell. It was one of Elimane's strengths, this ability to habituate himself to new circumstances, and he took pride in cultivating it.

It was Kpindi who had taught him not to rely on his strength when inside such a crowd, but rather to sail through it, positioning himself to ride its currents where he wanted to go. "Put yourself here if you want to be pushed there"—Kpindi had used his hands to illustrate the calculated trajectory. Arriving so at the front of the crowd, Elimane knew it was time now for a calculated display of vulnerability. Kpindi was the master at this as well, but it was Elimane's turn to lead today, and they each tried to practice what they learned from the others.

All around him in the melee, people were shouting as they tried to draw attention to themselves. *Pick me, sir! Madame, I am your help, so reliable! I swear I am! I won't let you down!* Elimane could not bring himself to do the same, but he knew he had to play the part somehow. So he opened his mouth wide to give himself the appearance of joining in the shouting, and waved his hands frenziedly.

Most of the people around him continued to focus on the offloading of goods from the ferry. Elimane scanned the fringes of the crowd for other possibilities. His eyes caught a man in a suit and tie—one of the traders, he assumed. He wore the suit completely buttoned up, not the way Elimane remembered it ought to be worn. He didn't like remembering such things, but by now he was used to the way life was punctuated by such moments, which sent hooks into parts of the past one might prefer to forget. Elimane glanced away, as if to clear his mind, then turned back to the man with fresh eyes.

In his buttoned-up suit, the trader was sweating heavily, he could see. He repeatedly wiped his forehead and dabbed his neck with his handkerchief, which soon became so wet that he threw it away and pulled another from his pocket. How many were there in those pockets? He was wearing a cloth sombrero as well. Elimane wondered whether he had just returned from a meeting or other occasion where such attire was required or had retained it because it made him look important. Why else would anyone allow himself to be so punished by his clothes? William Handkerchief, he silently dubbed the man. Elimane and the others were in the habit of giving people nicknames when it benefited them to allow those individuals to take up residence in their minds and be observed properly. Elimane suspected that William Handkerchief would prove worthy of becoming such a person.

Now the trader was pacing up and down and rubbing his fingers, his gaze nervously pointed toward the ferry. He must have goods of his own waiting to be offloaded. What else would a man of this sort be doing around here? In his right hand he clutched a leather bag so tightly that his veins were becoming visible through his skin. He stopped pacing and tiptoed to see what was going on beyond the crowd. He answered a call on his mobile phone with his free hand. The wind came for his hat, and it danced off his head, landing on the surface of the water. Following its path with his eyes as he held the phone to his ear, William Handkerchief was unwittingly moving closer and closer to the edge of the water. Elimane knew that the shoreline was dangerously hollow there, the earth eaten out from underneath by the water that constantly slammed against it, and also by the erosion from the recent rains. Something was bound to happen.

Elimane began to extricate himself from the madness, fighting against the tide. He searched for openings and forced his body through them, swaying to keep a body off balance where he needed to move next. Moving from opening to opening this way, he made his way out. He glanced up, found Kpindi, and pretended to wipe the sweat off his forehead twice. That was a signal to Kpindi to replace him in the crowd, which Kpindi acknowledged by rubbing his right eye. The others also noticed the response, and reshuffled their positions so that they could continue to look at and after one another.

The day sighed with another strong gust that upended a tray from a little girl's head, sending roasted peanuts into the dusty red soil. She held the empty tray with both hands and began to cry, perhaps in anticipation of the punishment she knew was waiting for her.

Free of the crowd, Elimane made his way to William Handkerchief, slowing as he approached so as not to alarm the man or make him think Elimane was coming for his bag. On the very edge of the water, the trader raised himself on tiptoe again, craning for a look at his cargo, and just as his left foot departed the ground, his right foot lost its purchase, and he tumbled into the water along with clods of dislodged earth. No one was looking in his direction except Elimane. *That is one way of cooling off!* he thought, smiling to himself as he rushed forward to help.

In the water, William Handkerchief was fighting to keep himself afloat. Elimane was amazed to see that the man had managed to prevent his bag from getting soaked, holding it on top of his head with one hand while he thrashed at the water with the other. There must be money in that bag, and lots of it, Elimane thought. William Handkerchief was losing the struggle, however. His waterlogged suit was pulling him down, and the waves the ferry had created as it approached the high shoreline continued sending water into his face. Elimane lay flat on the ground and offered his hands, but William Handkerchief's expression said he was not going to give up his bag so easily. Elimane knew that to insist would only feed the man's suspicion. He hastily stripped down to his undershorts, laying his shirt and trousers on top of his shoes, and dove into the water.

Elimane was a strong swimmer, and he reached William Hand-kerchief with a few strokes. Signaling with his eyes, Elimane placed his arm around the man's chest and, without dislodging his grip on the bag, began to tow him to shore, careful to keep his mouth and nose above water. When the water was shallow enough that the trader could find his feet, Elimane set him down, so that the man could walk to land by himself. He hurried out of the ocean, careful to keep his distance.

In Elimane's days as an apprentice learning to navigate the blows of life, he would have been long gone by now, with William Handker-chief's bag in his grip. But he had come to learn that he must always plan for the days on which his wits, cunning, and strength would be no match. For the days when nothing you did worked.

Back on solid ground, a sodden William Handkerchief angrily kicked at the water. He sat down on a nearby rock, his hand still clutching his bag to his head. Slowly he brought it down, but he did not relinquish his grip. He kicked off his shoes, and with his free hand managed to remove his jacket, and struggled to unbutton his vest. He left on his long-sleeved shirt and his tie.

Without a word, Elimane approached again. Requesting permis-sion with his eyes, he took the jacket and vest and squeezed the water out of them. These actions seemed to win William Handkerchief's trust. He removed his tie, shirt, and pants and threw them in Eli-mane's direction. Elimane wrung them out too, then laid the cloth-ing on the grass to dry. He noticed that the man was clutching his bag a little less tightly than before.

Now, finally, Elimane spoke. "It will take them a long time to dry." He nodded toward the clothes. "Your body heat might speed it up. Besides," he added, smiling, "they'll be your own personal air-conditioning in this heat."

His head in his hands, William Handkerchief did not respond. Then, just as the silence was becoming uncomfortable, he dropped his hands to his sides and spoke, the words coming out of him like the last puff of smoke from a dying fire. "I could have died, and no one would have noticed." He nodded at Elimane, perhaps as an expression of gratitude, although his face plainly didn't have the habit.

"Well, every time we wake from sleep that is a possibility," said Elimane. "But you are alive." Then, to push things along and not miss any opportunity, he added, "I am assuming you have things on the ferry. You better get back there, before they belong to someone else." Without betraying any urgency of his own, he made his way back to his clothes. He wanted to retrieve them before they were stolen, but more important, before William Handkerchief could notice the holes in his shoes. If that happened, Elimane knew, he would lose what little edge he had over the man. Here was an occasion when it was important *not* to show desperation. If William Handkerchief realized that Elimane needed him just to survive the day, he would use him only for the day, if at all. And Elimane sensed that there was more to be had here.

He found his clothes and dressed, then sauntered back along the shoreline, as if on his way home.

"Where are you rushing off to?" William Handkerchief sounded less defeated already. "Perhaps I must not ask too much of someone who just pulled me out of the mouth of death. But since you did, you are now responsible for me. At least," he added, "until I sleep and wake again and the possibility of death begins anew. So, a few more tasks before you abandon me, okay?"

At last he laid the leather bag on the ground, unzipped it, eyed what was within, and closed it again. Elimane glimpsed papers, but nothing more.

"So, are you now my boss, or are you asking me for help without drawing that line just yet?" As soon as he had uttered the words, Elimane regretted them, but William Handkerchief only laughed. This fellow was proving more complicated to figure out than some others. He seemed to have different personalities dancing within him, none staying put long enough to be deciphered.

As if he had read and mirrored Elimane's thoughts, William Handkerchief said, "You are an interesting young man. There is some conflict about you. I am not sure what it is, but I like mysterious people. It shows that they know how to guard their secrets well and, therefore, that they will guard other things if they choose to."

He paused for a moment. Then he went to his shoes, drying in the grass, and put his hand inside one of them, rooting around for something. "Can you please go buy me a mobile phone and some dry clothes? I need to make some calls. The fish must be calling their cousins with my other phone by now, so I should hurry before a smart one calls my customers and puts me out of business." From inside the shoe he pulled an inner sole, along with a small plastic bag. He untied it and removed a stack of bills untouched by the water.

"Always wear shoes with laces," he muttered to himself. But he looked at Elimane in puzzlement, evidently surprised that he did not seem more impressed by the money.

The truth was, Elimane was noticing that William Handkerchief kept his money in his shoes, not his bag. It was a good thing indeed that he had not pried the bag from the man's drowning hands and run away with it. What did it contain, then, that was so important that he had almost drowned, holding the bag above the water? At the same time, Elimane was wondering how anyone could walk properly on a wad like that. Then he realized that it must not be as bad as walking in his own ruined shoes. If he, in his poverty, could pretend to be comfortable, he was sure William Handkerchief, with his little riches, could manage the same without any bother. At any rate, he did not want William Handkerchief dwelling too long on whatever was *mysterious* about him. Give no one complete access to your way of being, especially strangers, he had learned, and you may just taste freedom from time to time.

"You make a good point," Elimane said cheerfully. "The least I can do is get you some clothes and especially another phone so that you can talk on it and fall in the water again."

"Don't you worry, young fellow. I have learned my lesson. Thanks for the reminder, though." William Handkerchief handed him some bills. "Here, buy me the cheapest phone you can find, with a SIM card, some calling credit, and one of those clear tough plastic bags. You know the kind I mean?" Elimane turned to go, but the man called, "Wait! Don't you have a phone that I can use in the meantime?" When Elimane made no motion to retrieve one, he said, "Aren't you from this century?"

A strange feeling overcame Elimane, but he responded lightly. "Even if I do have a phone, why should I give it to you?"

"Ah, where am I going to go with it? I just gave you some money without asking any questions." William Handkerchief opened his palms and raised them to the sky, in surrender to the battle to win Elimane's trust.

"That was your choice," Elimane said. "You don't expect me to reciprocate, do you? I have my own measurement of trust. Have a smile now. You are alive! Even if I don't return with your money, it isn't nearly enough for pulling you out of the water." He smiled himself, to show that he was making a joke. Then he jogged away, to make haste in case this whole episode turned out not to be worth his time.

Elimane hurried past the ferry landing, which was still in a state of commotion. It crossed his mind to swipe a phone from someone, but William Handkerchief would surely notice that the phone wasn't brand-new, and Elimane would risk jeopardizing the possibility of future dealings with him. If he bought the cheapest phone, on the other hand, cheaper than William Handkerchief expected, it was possible that the man would give it to Elimane eventually, if he kept him on, in order to be able to reach him. William Handkerchief seemed like the type who would have other phones at home and wouldn't want to carry around a cheap product that might tarnish his image. Elimane decided to avoid overthinking things, lest the iron grow cold and he could no longer bend it to his liking.

At the far end of the market, past the last row of food stalls that had dry ingredients such as salt and pepper, beans, rice, and oil, a set of polished wooden kiosks displayed all manner of electronic devices and appliances on tables and shelves—phones, microwaves, irons, walkie-talkies, computers—along with scattered spare parts for such devices. Some of the traders sat inside the stalls repairing broken items, and others stood by, smoking cigarettes or drinking tea and bantering with one another as they attended to their customers. Elimane's gaze alighted on the shop that appeared least busy, attended to by a scraggly fellow who looked as lost in his thoughts as his body was in his oversize clothes.

Just as Elimane headed for the shop, he noticed Namsa approaching him. She seemed to be absorbed in her own world, jumping and hopping in an invisible game of hopscotch. He was in the midst of debating with himself whether to tell her to focus or to ignore her—sooner or later she would have to figure out how to use her wits on her own, after all—when Namsa gave a big leap and landed right in his path, knocking into him and clumsily falling to the ground. She looked up at him, startled. "Sorry!" she exclaimed, then gathered herself and picked up a small pouch that had fallen from her pocket to the ground. But instead of putting it back in her own pocket, she offered it to Elimane. "Sorry, sir," she said again. Elimane took it, picking up on the cue, though he wasn't sure what Namsa was up to. "Play your games at home," he said sternly, then pocketed the pouch and moved past her, intent on his business.

In a corner of the market, he opened the pouch. It contained a new phone in its box, very much the sort Elimane had been thinking of buying. How had Namsa known what Elimane was going to buy? And when and where had she been able to get her hands on something like this?

Now all he needed was a SIM card and a charged battery. Some stalls would charge your battery for you, for a small fee, but you had to be sure they didn't swindle you by trying to fob off an old battery on you upon your return, or a cheap Chinese-made version that would break if you spoke into your phone at high volume—and high volume was almost always necessary, as the phone network was so patchy and unreliable.

Elimane used the permanent marker he carried in his pocket to write *King's Property* on the battery, in his most elaborately distinctive script. That would make it hard for them to deceive him.

"Hello, a SIM card and a charged Nokia battery, please." He handed over the battery and the exact amount needed to a young boy at a neighboring stall. Elimane had taught the little family to make a point of memorizing the current prices of all sort of commonly needed goods and services; asking the price was essentially announcing your lack of street smarts and pleading to be overcharged.

The boy pointed to Elimane's writing. "This is a used battery, so when you come back, don't expect a new one." Elimane noticed that the boy had a face at odds with his body—a face with the demeanor of an adult. It occurred to him that this was because the boy looked all day into the faces of people who were older than him, and his own face retained the impression of what he gazed on.

Elimane held his ground. "It is a new one. I wrote on it to make sure that you do not give me back an old one." The boss man, who had been hovering in the background, frowned at Elimane but nodded to the boy, indicating that he should bring the conversation to an end and get on with the transaction, before other customers got the same idea. Elimane laughed to himself at having evaded their clutches, for today at least. They would have to content themselves with an honest fee.

Elimane waited for the battery alongside a long line of others who had no electricity to charge their phones for whatever their daily hustle was. He reflected on the undeniable benefits of these devices—the incredible speed with which they transmitted information—but also on their drawbacks. Conversation among the poor was neither free nor as pleasurable as it once was. When someone called you, they spoke fast and so did you, preoccupied as you were with the life of your battery and the unreliability and cost of service. People no longer stopped to ask, "How are you and your family? Are the children well?" or, if they did, waited to attend to the responses.

The boy called to him and handed him the newly charged battery. Elimane inserted it in the phone and waited for it to come alive. The screen lit up and the phone chimed, announcing its enormous importance these days.

Hurrying back toward the ferry landing, Elimane was interrupted by the sudden arrival of a group of a dozen or so men wearing green trench coats and polished boots. Their appearance brought an immediate and unnatural silence to the clamor of people touting their services. The riotous motion of arms and hands ceased as well, and they hung loosely at people's sides. The sea of bodies had parted to make way for the group and remained parted in its wake. Who were these men, so few in number compared with the crowd, yet somehow able to put its very existence on hold?

The men began to unbutton their coats with a deliberate and synchronized slowness, displaying just enough of the metal sticks of death hanging at their sides to give a hint of what havoc they were capable of wreaking. Swamped by the coats, their shadows had no heads or feet. They removed their red berets from their pockets and set them on their heads. The leader of the contingent walked straight to the khaki-clad policemen who were monitoring the unloading.

"You. Stand up."

The officer rose, peanut shells falling from his khaki pants. He hurried to retrieve the boots that were standing nearby, their laces loosened to allow the warmth of the sun to penetrate them. But before he could lay hands on them, one of the red caps kicked the boots into the water. A few in the crowd laughed, but others hushed them, fearful of drawing the red caps' attention. Silence returned, as the crowd, captive spectators to this show of power, waited to see what would happen next.

"You don't need them. Jump in the water and wash that laziness off," the commander ordered the officer. "Now!" The officer hesitated, trying to empty his pockets of crumpled bills and an assortment of cell phones. But before he could finish, he was shoved into the ocean and, right behind him, so was another officer, who had made a move for the abandoned cash and electronics. The crowd murmured in surprise, and some stood on their toes to see if they could spot the policemen in the water.

The commander adjusted his beret so that the wind could not snatch it away, then sat down at the edge of the jetty and laughed at the two men struggling in the water.

"Help us, sir! We'll work hard!" The two men cried out in unison, as though they had rehearsed the words.

"Ah, I get it," said the commander. "The prospect of death brings you together." He laughed with exaggerated loudness. "Look, your boots can swim better than you. You should have kept them on. You are no longer useful." He turned away from the sight of them, and the crowd reluctantly shuffled away from the landing and the gaze of the men with the red caps.

The commander pulled out his mobile phone and dialed, then put the phone to his ear and shouted: "Hello, sir. Yes, I get you loud and clear, sir."

He listened.

"I have control of the situation, sir, and will continue with the search. Thank you, sir." He closed the phone and stood with his legs wide, and his men drew close so that they could receive their directives without anyone hearing. A murmur rose from the crowd as they looked on. At their various points along its fringes, Namsa, Kpindi, Ndevui, and Khoudi sensed that this incident had put an end to the possibility of their making anything of the day here. Such men always invented excuses to disturb the lives of people like them, the ones society had no use for. Today was just another exercise in dehumanization.

Now the red caps scanned the crowd for whoever might be eyeing them displeasingly. And yet if you turned away, this might also be interpreted as a sign of disrespect. It was hard to know how, or where, to look. No one with eyes, in other words, was safe.

When this scrutiny had had the desired intimidating effect, the commander spoke again in his coarse voice, demanding that the crowd line up to be searched. Why was it that those who were about to shatter your lives always demanded order from you, when such directives were invariably a prelude to chaos?

"Why don't you tell us what you are looking for?" came a lone brave voice from the crowd. "Or maybe your bosses didn't tell you? Maybe we can help the government the way it helps us." There was a burst of laughter from the crowd before the red caps pounced in the area from which the comment had come. They dragged one unlucky fellow to the front. The crowd gasped at the bone-cracking kicks and blows that descended on him from the red caps. Who knew if it was really he who had spoken, or if he had even been one of those who had laughed? All the red caps had really wanted was someone to make an example of.

Khoudi sensed that this was the moment to depart, while the red caps were busy and before she was swept up in the chaos that would inevitably follow. She knew that the boys could handle themselves; like her, they had survived such situations countless times. But Namsa was another matter.

Khoudi found her standing next to a wall, near where she had seen her last. She brushed hard against the girl to draw her attention, then began to run, relieved to hear the girl's flip-flops smacking close behind her. Soon enough followed the crackle of gunfire, as she'd expected, and the screaming and thudding as heavy blows met flesh, and the smell of tear gas, and the sound of many others running too. The chaos of violence had begun.

Around a bend, Khoudi jumped over a low wall and sat against it with her nose turned away from the wind. Namsa fell over her as she came over the wall, and Khoudi immediately positioned her face the same way. They rested for a minute, giggling a little at their expertise in knowing what to do in such situations, but then the smell of tear gas grew stronger, so they again ran away from it, toward a section of the beach where Khoudi often went alone.

Elimane had not waited long to leave the landing. As soon as the crowd grew quiet, he had worked his way behind it until he reached the edge of the landing. Then he slid his body down to the water's edge and crouched along the shoreline until he was far enough away not to be seen. He climbed onto the main pathway and returned to where he had left William Handkerchief.

He found the man dressed in his soaked clothes, pacing up and down under a small tree, his bag slung around his neck, muttering to himself. Before Elimane had finished removing the phone from his pocket, William Handkerchief plucked it from his hand without so much as a word. Hastily, he dialed some numbers and put the phone to his ear. He didn't say hello, just, "At the egress." Then he hung up, peeled the sticker printed with the mobile number from the side of the device, and threw the phone back to Elimane.

"Now I can reach the fellow who saved me on my phone that is now his."

"I couldn't find the plastic you asked for, because the red caps are at the landing making the day hell," Elimane said, returning the phone to his pocket.

"What are they up to?" William Handkerchief asked.

Elimane repeated what the commander had said. "The same

excuse they always use," he added, noting that it was no coincidence that the red caps always came to terrorize people when the ferry brought goods.

Suddenly William Handkerchief stopped pacing and stared into the distance. Then, without saying a word, he sprinted into the nearby bushes. Elimane could hear the twigs breaking as he forced his way through. He too started running, in another direction, back to the main road. From Elimane's experience, he knew you don't ask questions when someone near you suddenly runs away: You just run as well. As he sprinted, some of the men in the red caps passed him, and he wondered if they were going after William Handkerchief. When he looked toward the ferry landing, he saw that everyone there had scattered, except for some unlucky captives who were shouting their innocence as they were dragged into the back of military vehicles. No doubt the red caps would exact whatever ransom they could from these unfortunates and their families before they set them free.

The little family had a meeting place for when such things happened. Elimane planned to make his way there once he was certain no one was following him. And the way to be sure of that was to pretend that he was part of a group the red caps wouldn't want to follow. He had noticed that those in charge of order had a strong allergic reaction to proselytizers. Perhaps they suspected that if such a place as heaven existed, they had already been denied entry. Soon Elimane spotted a dozen such people standing by the side of the road, with pamphlets showing pictures of sun rays descending on places where flowers grew and animals roamed among people, unafraid. There was no one in this rendition of heaven who resembled those passing out the pamphlets, he noted.

Without saying a word, Elimane picked up a few of the pamphlets and started handing them to whoever was passing by. When the red caps came by, he held some out to them, but they avoided him with the urgency he'd predicted.

"God bless you, go with God," he called, which sent them running from him. He waited just long enough to be sure they were gone before he took his leave; he didn't want the proselytizers to believe he was truly one of them.

There was a spot on the beach, crowded with restaurants and bars, that was Khoudi's favorite place to be alone. She loved to go there and watch people, imagining what her life as a young woman could be like. She would envision herself as a university student, painting, writing short stories and poems, going to readings and museums, and afterward stopping at these bars to have a drink, read, and meet up with friends. A life in which nothing constrained her from doing and being what she wanted.

But Namsa was with her now, coughing and spitting to get the last of the tear gas out of her lungs, and tugging at Khoudi. "We have to go to Encounter One," she was saying. "The others will be waiting." Encounter One was their rendezvous point for times when chaos or violence separated them before the day was over. There was also Encounter Two, which was to be used as a staging ground to fight back if their home was ever taken over by others. They had not needed it yet.

But now that they were away from the melee, Khoudi was in no hurry. She reassured Namsa that the others knew how to handle themselves and would be fine. They had likely stopped somewhere along the way themselves. She steered them toward the ocean so that they could wash the toxic smoke from their feet, faces, and arms. Salt water was good for that.

When they had cleaned themselves, Khoudi told Namsa, "Come. Let's go sit there at my spot." She pointed to a log. Namsa took a seat next to her, somewhat reluctantly, but she said no more about the others. Khoudi pointed to a boat in the distance and, with her protruding finger, pretended to draw it against the sky. Relaxing, Namsa followed suit, giving the boat an engine and a sail. Then they lapsed into silence, looking around to observe what they were not.

A group of girls Khoudiemata's age strolled by. They had glossy lips and so much confidence in their bodies. There was an ease to their speech and laughter, and they seemed in no rush to get the waiter's attention. Some carried books, and others magazines. They sat together, some chatting about things that didn't chase the joy from their faces, others reading, their eyes drifting from time to time to the sea and then along the hills of Freedom Town, where colorful buildings contrasted with the red soil, as if in an oil painting.

Khoudi imagined herself among them. She was wearing a yellow dress with a simple floral pattern and flat, open-toed shoes with elegant black straps. Her toenails were painted with red polish that matched her fingernails. She was carrying a gold clutch, a newspaper, and perhaps a portable easel to paint on, and her hair was long, neatly braided in two plaits, between which her face shone brightly. She walked majestically, with a natural elegance, a memory of her mother's gait . . .

Namsa nudged her. "Are you there?"

"Yes, barely," Khoudi mumbled, her gaze on the girls, with the image of herself among them. She closed her eyes and lifted her head toward the rays of the sun, now lowering in the sky. She willed Namsa to be quiet until she had finished her imaginings. But to her annoyance, she could feel the girl's eyes burning into her face, and she had to remind herself how young Namsa was, and that she had no idea yet of the things Khoudi was thinking about. Reluctantly she took leave of her fantasy, and the feelings for which she did not yet have words; she could only feel them blossoming inside her. She opened her eyes.

"Look!" exclaimed Namsa. "It is Shadrach the Messiah!"

She was pointing at a man who wore a long robe made of patches of every bright color that could be imagined. He had a wooden staff tucked under his arm, and he held a stack of leaflets that he pressed into the hands of everyone who walked by.

"Yes, where was I?" he called out, to no one in particular. "Oh, I just arrived on that ship out there." He pointed to one of the container ships anchored at a distance.

"But how did I get here? Maybe I walked. But my feet and my clothes are dry! Strange, how strange." He tapped the bottoms of his feet with his staff, then put it back under his arm while he continued his discussion with himself.

"Would you go tomorrow to celebrate a day of independence assigned to you by others?" he asked. "No, I the Messiah wouldn't. You should take your shadows somewhere else tomorrow. Somewhere they can be useful."

Namsa left her spot on the log and ran to him.

He looked down at her in surprise. "Did they send you?" He peered at her more closely, and a look of recognition came over his face. "Oh, you are my shipmate! Forgive me. Sometimes I am not myself."

He took up his path along the beach, carrying on with his discussion.

"Don't let the world ruin you, young child. You do not need a day of independence. You are free every day. Where are my shipmates?" he called, and then he began to sing. *"Don't, don't, row your boat, life's no longer a dream . . ."* He skipped ahead as he sang, tossing the papers into the air and then running to gather them with urgency.

Namsa picked up one of the leaflets and brought it back to Khoudi, who read it aloud.

COME UN-COLONIZE YOUR EARS TOMORROW

SHADRACH THE MESSIAH'S NON-INDEPENDENCE DAY

REFLECTIONS AT BEACH KIOSK

Time: midday-night

Cost: free, as freedom should be

"Can we come tomorrow?" Namsa asked, as soon as Khoudi finished reading.

"Maybe for a bit," Khoudi said. "I have something to do tomorrow." She took off her hat and let her hair free.

Namsa looked at her closely. "This is where you come when you go away by yourself, isn't it?" She found Khoudi's gaze. "I won't tell anyone."

Khoudi smiled. "Thank you for keeping my secret." It wasn't exactly that she was hiding from her family when she came here, she told herself. Besides, she had other places that she hadn't told Namsa about yet. At times she just had this urge that came from somewhere deep inside her, to be alone, to *understand* herself alone, to see how others reacted to her, people who didn't know her. But Namsa was too young to understand.

Khoudi's attention wandered back to the group of girls. Now they were sitting at a nearby café, at a table filled with food and drinks, laughing and talking. Namsa had started playing with her hair, and the distraction of her presence kept Khoudi from fully imagining herself among the group. But it gave her an idea: She would go get her hair done the following day. And for the moment, to occupy Namsa, she instructed her to arrange her hair into two big braids that she could fit properly under her beanie. Delighted, Namsa proceeded to make a beautiful mess of her hair, and Khoudi took pleasure in being fussed over.

They walked on the beach for as long as they could. Then they sat on the pavement, shook the sand from their feet, and put their shoes back on—flip-flops for Namsa, old sneakers for Khoudi, the soles held together by rope and burnt rubber. The image of herself among the smiling, chattering young women made the coarseness of the canvas bearable to her. The two girls made their way along the line of dilapidated Toyotas puffing dark smoke from their dying engines. The cars themselves were another instance of the patchwork that was Freedom Town, Khoudi thought, a patchwork made up partly of reminders of just where you were in society and partly of flashes of what you could not attain but nevertheless longed for, and couldn't help dreaming of.

King's property, king's property, everything is correct.

Namsa tried whistling, but it wasn't loud enough, so Khoudi redid it. Three whistling answers came in on the wind, and the girls jumped over the fallen palm tree and through the low guava trees that hadn't yet borne fruit that season. Encounter One was the ruins of an abandoned chalet. It was completely devoured by vines on every side, so that you might pass without noticing it.

The boys were already there.

Elimane was sitting on the stoop, rolling the tip of his pen against the concrete part of the wall and massaging it between his palms to wake the sleeping ink that refused to come out and write.

Kpindi and Ndevui looked up briefly to acknowledge the girls' arrival, then continued with the game of marbles they were playing on the floor. They had made up the game themselves, using the cracks and holes in the concrete. You got points for rolling a marble into a designated hole in the floor, and if your opponent's marble was blocking your path, you knocked it as far as you could with your own. As usual, Kpindi was irritating Ndevui by flicking the marbles in a way that Ndevui said was against the rules. "That is *fallahand*," he kept saying, explaining to Kpindi that it was cheating to let his hand hang over the line while throwing his marble.

"They are not going to ask how we escaped and where we have been?" Namsa whispered to Khoudi.

"Why are you whispering?" Khoudi asked.

"They seem not to want to be disturbed," Namsa whispered.

"We do not talk about things that happen so frequently," Khoudi answered, in a normal voice. "It is pointless. It is similar to breathing. You do not walk around and say, 'Oh, I am breathing now, and I am breathing again.' You know you are breathing, and that is that, and if you were not, you would know."

She took Namsa by the hand and found a place among the shiny old wooden columns for them to sit.

"I've got four and you've got two," Kpindi called out. "So we are doing best of ten, and when I win, you give me your ganja." He pointed to the rolled blunt behind Ndevui's ear.

"You know we don't gamble for ganja," Ndevui answered. "That we share."

"Okay, okay," Kpindi answered. He threw his marble, and it knocked Ndevui's out of the way.

Elimane had attempted to return to his reading and note-taking, but his pen was still balky. He threw it on the ground, his eyes on where it landed.

The wind brought reminders of the ongoing commotion from beyond—the sounds of people fleeing, or chasing. The sounds drowned out the usual sounds of evening—the chirping of birds, the waves hitting the shores, something being pounded in a mortar, sirens, and a call for prayer. The ears of nature seemed to be listening, waiting for something to snap. Gradually the footfalls of survival and calamity passed, and faded into the distance. The day was drawing to an end.

"I have an idea for a new sign language we might use," said Elimane. "It is from this book. The context is that—"

"Close your bloody mouth that goes on when not needed, man!" snapped Ndevui. "Sometimes I just need to stop hearing you." It was rare for him to go off like that, but Elimane had distracted him just as he was about to make what he was sure would be a winning throw.

A silence fell on them. Then Elimane spoke. "Young brother, there is no need for the unnecessary anger. Smoke your ganja and cool down."

Ndevui offered his hand to Elimane, who took it, breaking the tension. They all had such moments, and knew how to let them pass, and they sat for a while in peace as darkness fell.

They had just started back to the plane together when a phone rang, startling them. They stood there for a moment; then Elimane tapped his pockets, searching. "That's coming from me. I completely forgot." He took out the phone and answered it. "Hello, hello, hello." He moved to different spots in the ruins, searching for a stronger signal.

He listened carefully. "I worry that the red caps are still chasing people around there. They will catch anyone they come across." He listened. "You think they are gone now, and the ferry area is clear? How do you know that?"

When he hung up, he told the others all that had transpired with William Handkerchief. When he got to the part about the phone, he looked up at Namsa and smiled. "That was excellent today." He explained to the others what she had done, and they all praised her.

"How did you get the phone?" Kpindi asked.

"I have my ways." Namsa kept it a mystery, and they didn't press her, as they could guess.

"Don't get comfortable, though," Elimane admonished her. "Challenge yourself to get better and better at it."

Now, he explained, William Handkerchief was calling with an assignment, as Elimane had hoped. The man who usually offloaded his goods for him had been among those arrested, and William Handkerchief needed his "commodities," as he called them, and fast. If Elimane could deliver them in the next few hours, he'd offer one hundred thousand, the equivalent of ten US dollars, per bag. That was quite a sum of money! It could provide not only regular food for a while, but clothes and books and more. And who knew what other assignments might come?

"Does he know about us?" Namsa asked hesitantly.

"No," said Elimane. "He said it is something one person can do, but I think that with all that is going on, it is better to go together."

"We should be out there anyway, trying to get what we can from this madness." Ndevui waited for Elimane to lead them on.

"How did you come up with 'William Handkerchief'?" Kpindi asked, just before they reached the road and resumed their custom of spreading out and comporting themselves as if they were not traveling together.

Elimane explained about the handkerchiefs. "And William? That's after Shakespeare, who you know is a favorite of mine."

This made the others giggle, in one last expression of family feeling before they took the road again.

The road was not as crowded as it had been in the morning, and here and there it was strewn with shoes and clothing that had evidently been dropped by people fleeing. Like the little family's own belongings, these scattered items, worn beyond use, weren't the kinds of things you wanted to pick up. In the distance, a faint voice from a megaphone announced, *If you see anything, please bring it to the nearest checkpoint or police station. You will be doing your nation a great service, and you will be rewarded.* That made the five of them giggle again, to themselves.

As they approached the ferry landing, things grew even quieter. Even the lit interiors of the mostly single-story concrete houses seemed without motion as the group passed the last verandas of Foloiya and covered the short distance to the wharf. The landing now had a ghastly loneliness.

They huddled together behind one of the market stalls. There was no one to see them, so at least they did not have to pretend not to know one another, which was a relief.

"Namsa, you go ahead," Elimane whispered. The reason was obvious to all of them: Should anyone be lurking, her presence would be the least threatening. If someone emerged, she would pretend to be scared and run away, and they could create a commotion to distract her pursuers and protect her. It was just one more in a series of risks and defenses, hundreds of which they calculated every day.

Newly confident and happy to prove herself, Namsa went skipping down the road to the jetty. "Is anyone there?" she called out. "My uncle sent me to see when the ferry would be leaving tomorrow." No one answered. She threw stones at the iron body of the boat, which was shaking with the incoming tide. She whistled, *King's property, king's property, everything is correct. King's property, king's property, everything is correct.*

Elimane, Khoudi, and Ndevui covered the distance from the market stalls to the ferry as quickly as possible, leaving Kpindi as a lookout for anyone coming from inland. They ran past Namsa, who remained where she was as a secondary lookout, and to distract anyone else who might approach the ferry.

Inside, Elimane diligently followed William Handkerchief's instructions. Under the life rings and vests that the crew had long ceased passing out to passengers, as they never wore them, he located the bags he'd been told to look for. They were of waterproof material and so big that an adult could fit inside, sitting down, but were not as heavy as they looked, partly because they weren't full. What could be inside them? Elimane pressed them, wondering, but stopped when Khoudi and Ndevui gave him a cautioning look.

They cinched the bags with the ropes they'd found in the side pockets, as William Handkerchief had mentioned, compressing them to about half their original size. Elimane went to the side of the ferry to make sure all was clear. Then he, Ndevui, and Khoudi each picked up a bag and jumped onto the landing with it. They ran past Namsa, to the market stalls. As soon as they reached Kpindi, Namsa ran to join them. Huddling together, they whispered about how they were going to walk to the delivery point, a bakery just at the entrance to town. Carrying the bags together on the open road seemed too risky. They came up with as much of a plan as they could muster.

Namsa would walk ahead, followed by Elimane, wearing one of the bags like a backpack, his arms through the straps. Behind Elimane, at some distance, would come Kpindi, not carrying anything, then Khoudi with the second bag, and finally, at another distance, Ndevui with the last bag. Once Namsa reached the point of delivery, she was to turn around and walk back to position herself between Khoudi and Ndevui. The hope was that the gaps between them, and the interspersing of those with bags and those without, would avoid rousing suspicion or even memory, should they pass anyone.

Before they could set out, they heard a car approaching. They ran behind the more remote stalls, pressing their backs against some empty oil drums. The vehicle slowed down, and they heard a radio check and then military-sounding footsteps. They heard someone make the rounds of the area and then return to the vehicle, which departed into the silence of the evening.

When the rear lights of the vehicle had disappeared, they began to walk. Namsa went briskly through the lightless, uneven street. After about five minutes, she spotted a man up on a veranda. He was wearing a white gown, and she imagined that he had come out to get some of the cool breeze that had started pushing the humid evening air away. Moving into the shadows, she whistled, *Lazarus, Lazarus.* She knew the others would take shelter, with feathered steps. She remembered that Elimane had chosen this signal because of something about the rising of Lazarus from the dead. She couldn't remember the story exactly, but she knew that they were supposed to use it whenever they encountered someone up and about unexpectedly. The man startled at the whistle and glanced about. Then, unable to see where it was coming from and looking uneasy, he went back inside. Namsa waited until everything seemed to be quiet within, then signaled the all clear, and the little caravan carried on.

After about thirty minutes, which felt much longer in the eeriness of the quiet road, imaginary threats behind every tree, they made it to the bakery. The others waited some distance away, lurking in the dark, while Elimane carried the bags the last stretch.

The baker was waiting in the darkened doorway of the shop. As soon as he saw Elimane and the bags, he took him inside. A kerosene lamp hung in the corner, covered so that it cast its brightness on only a small space. He indicated that Elimane should leave. Elimane insisted on calling William Handkerchief, who didn't pick up, but rang back shortly after Elimane hung up. He told Elimane that he could leave the bags with the baker and said that the baker had his pay. He asked to speak to the baker, and when they hung up, Elimane collected the money, and the baker told him that William Handkerchief was impressed and was going to call him for another job soon enough. In the meantime, William Handkerchief wanted to meet with Elimane in person again within the next few days.

Elimane didn't say much, but he nodded his agreement. Then he left the baker and returned to the others. He showed them the money before putting it in his pocket.

The search for what the day held for them was over. Out of habit, however, they walked home without acknowledging one another, passing here and there others who hoped that the day would yet yield up some generosity before it departed.

A few people were coming outside again, now that danger had once again passed. They sat on their verandas and listened to their radios or checked the dull screens of their badly charged phones.

Elimane was the first to hear the report, which came from a portable radio that hung by its antenna from the branch of a guava tree, blasting music to whoever happened to pass by.

Breaking news. The military police conducted raids today in several locations, looking to retrieve sensitive documents that were earlier reported to be stolen from the government treasury. Anonymous sources indicate that the missing documents relate to government funds. Updates as we have them. Tune in tomorrow at our regular time for a discussion about digitalizing our banking and information systems.

The radio returned to music. Elimane broke formation. "Did you hear that? They have gone far this time!" The others hadn't registered it. But soon they passed other radios that were also blaring out the news.

Khoudi burst out laughing. "Oh, wow, they really think we are all stupid!" she exclaimed, and slowly the rest of them began to laugh too.

"Well, you never know," said Kpindi. "Elimane here knows everything, so it might make sense to him. At any rate, if we ever come across such a stash, he will know what to do." That generated more laughter. Those who searched the day for something to eat were not interested in documents, sensitive or not.

It wasn't yet the season of the harmattan, when the Sahara coughed the cold dry mist of sand that covered the skin like a ghostly garment, but an unusually cold wind came up as they neared home. One after another, shivering, they entered through the break in the foliage, Khoudiemata in the lead.

"Wait. Something is off."

Khoudi stopped abruptly. Before them, in the red mud, were fresh footprints, of people who wore better shoes than they did, and the broken grasses betrayed that they had been recently trampled.

The boys immediately spread out into the bushes to prepare for any encounter, and Khoudi continued cautiously along the path, followed by Namsa. It was possible that whoever had gotten this far had not reached the clearing, stumped by the barrier of thick bushes.

As they neared the clearing, they heard whispers and laughter. In the gloom, their eyes found one another, preparing for a confrontation. Then Khoudi and Namsa continued into the clearing, to announce their presence and give the others a chance to assess what was going on.

A fire in in the center of the clearing was just beginning to gain appetite. Sitting in a circle around it were three young men and two young women, their shadows jumping and stretching in the light from the growing flames. One of the women was in the process of inhaling smoke from a plastic bottle. As she looked up, her eyes fell on Khoudi and Namsa, and her mouth dropped open like the bottle, both openings leaking the cloudlike smoke.

"Eh! Eh! You are wasting. Pass it here," said a muscular young man with a heavy voice. Then, noticing her silence, his eyes followed the path of her bewildered gaze.

He jumped to his feet, snapping his fingers to get the attention of the others. "Come join us!" he called. "You are safe here from the red caps." He laughed loudly.

"Are you from around here?" Khoudiemata asked him, careful not to betray that they were anywhere near her own home. To judge from where they had decided to stop and build a fire, they had not yet found the airplane. Otherwise they would be seated comfortably around the refrigerator-table or perhaps even camped out inside the plane.

"What does it matter where we are from?" said the young man. "Have a seat and join our celebration." He passed by Khoudiemata and grasped Namsa's hand, but she pulled it from his grip and stepped closer behind Khoudi.

He laughed. "What disrespect! Boys, help me convince our guests to join the party." The other two young men stood up and approached. Khoudiemata stepped back, pressing her raffia bag into

Namsa with one hand. She could feel the girl reaching into the out-side pocket where she kept her knife, and an instant later, Namsa had pressed it into Khoudi's open palm. With her hand behind her back, she waited, drawing strength from the knowledge that Kpindi, Ndevui, and Elimane were watching from the bushes nearby, ready to pounce.

The three young men surrounded Khoudiemata and Namsa, edg-ing them toward the fire pit.

"This one is beautiful if you look beyond how she is dressed," said the first. "And I am interested in doing that." He grabbed Khoudie-mata's left hand and pulled her right up against his body. She yanked herself away and returned to Namsa's side. "Ah, she wants it, but she plays hard to get!" He laughed again.

Khoudiemata raised her left fist to him, which made all three of the men laugh. When the muscular one came at her again, with a quick swipe of her right hand Khoudi nicked his arm. She meant to deliver a stern warning, preferring to stop the escalation of violence before it went further. Stunned, he nevertheless came at her again, this time with menace in his eyes. She double-swiped, leaving slashes on both cheeks. Surprised, he reached for his face, and Khoudiemata stabbed him in the leg. He sank to the ground and then fell back in the dirt, howling.

The other two men, who had been headed for Namsa but had frozen in shock at Khoudi's fast action, sprang into motion. Khoudi was ready for them. She met them with her knife raised and a look of determination on her face. But before they came within range, Kpindi and Ndevui were upon them, striking blows to their heads, necks, and torsos all the way to the edge of the clearing, whereupon the two intruders took to their heels. Seeing how things were going, the young women who had been sitting at the fire roused themselves from their stupor and ran away as well.

Clutching her knife, Khoudiemata knelt next to the man she had stabbed, but his body began to slide away from her. She looked up to see that Elimane was holding the fellow's legs and dragging him hard against the ground. He tried grabbing at the roots and branches and grasses, but Elimane's pull was insistent. At the entrance to the clearing, Elimane straddled him and landed punches to his ribs, his throat, his jaw, and his face. With each blow, the young man gasped for air and rolled from side to side, but there was no escape.

Elimane paused, glowering down at him. When he spoke, it was in a quiet but terrifying voice the others had never heard before. "Stand up and run away, or I'll give you another round of that."

The young man struggled to his feet, wiping his face and leaving a bloody streak there from one of the slashes he had received from Khoudiemata. His body was shaking, whether with pain or with anger it was unclear, but despite his muscles and his superior height, he could muster only a feeble fist. Then he unclenched his fingers and staggered away as fast as he could drag his wounded body, glancing back over his shoulder to make sure Elimane and the others were not pursuing him, and stumbling into bushes as he went.

The little family let out a collective sigh of relief, followed by silence as they all found a place to sit or a tree to lean against. Ndevui kicked dirt into the fire until it went out. He picked up the bottle the intruders had been inhaling from and threw it hard into the bushes as though he hoped the thing itself would go up in smoke. All of the others except Namsa knew why.

When Ndevui came to them, he'd been addicted to such bottles. One morning, he'd woken to find himself floating in the ocean. He wasn't that far out, and he could see people going about their morning business, young people running along the beach and fishermen launching their boats. But when he tried to swim for shore, he discovered that he couldn't move his arms or legs, and when he tried to call for help, his speech was slurred. He remembered thinking that it was only a matter of time before he drifted out to sea or some creature ate him or he drowned like a rock, unable to keep himself afloat. In fact, he began to wonder, how was it that he was floating at all? And for that matter, how had he ended up in the ocean? He remembered that he had been inhaling by the docks the night before, with a group of young people like himself, but that was as far as his memory went.

As to the mystery of his buoyancy, that was more readily unraveled. Beneath him, he realized, were pieces of the foam used to protect fragile goods en route to this part of the world while they were in transit. Once they arrived in the port, they were unboxed, and the cartons, foam, and plastic wrappings were thrown into the ocean. But the ocean doesn't like to be fed such foods, and it spits out what isn't natural to its diet. For once, Ndevui was thankful for human recklessness, which had supplied a life raft to keep him safe while he slept. He didn't know how he'd gotten on it. Had he become intoxicated to the point of unconsciousness and, assumed to be dead or nearly so, pushed out to sea by his fellow addicts, lest they be left to answer uncomfortable questions to the authorities about his condition and their own?

Ndevui had floated for a few more hours, until a fisherman in a passing canoe noticed that his eyes were moving and pulled him out of the water and into his boat. Ndevui could not speak at all by this point, but he could cry, and he wondered if his tears of gratitude could be distinguished from the ocean spray on his face. Regardless, the fisherman brought him to shore and laid his body on the beach, out of reach of the waves. "I don't want you dying in my fishing zone and bringing those useless investigators down here. This is my daily living. If you have to die, you can die on dry land."

Ndevui lay on the beach for the entire day, the sun lashing him, until gradually he regained the power of his limbs, and the will to move them. The chill in his bones had stayed with him for a month, and to this day he hated being cold.

But now, the chill that had descended earlier was lifting, departing as suddenly as the intruders, and nothing seemed to be amiss.

Kpindi chased the silence away. "Well, I don't think they found the plane. Which is a good thing, as I don't want to have to go find a new home."

"You think they will be back?" Namsa asked timidly.

"I doubt it," said Khoudi. "I think they just happened on this spot because they were trying to escape the red caps."

"Those particular ones won't be coming back. That fellow is going to have nightmares about Elimane." Kpindi chuckled.

Khoudi's eyes met Elimane's with newfound admiration. She had seen him fight before, but never with so much visible rage.

"Big brother, I never thought you fully had it in you. Did you get that from one of these books, or is it deep in there?" Ndevui picked up the paperback that had fallen out of Elimane's pocket. "I really must work on my reading, if that's how you learn to fight like that." With a grin, he handed the book back to Elimane, who took it and slapped it against his palms, though it didn't need dusting. He seemed to be avoiding Khoudi's gaze.

"I know where that rage came from, and it surely isn't from the books he reads," teased Kpindi, placing his arm around Elimane's shoulders. "There's a cauldron of passion boiling away in there"—he poked at Elimane's chest—"and it finally gave itself away."

"What are you going on about?" said Khoudi abruptly, searching for her bag, which she had dropped in all the commotion. She dusted it off and put the knife away. And with that, the five of them proceeded to the plane.

To their relief, there were no footprints or other signs of intruders there, and when they had completed their inspection, their bodies fell back into their usual state of relaxation in this private world of theirs.

"Ah, now I will finish my day with this purity. Yes, yes, lion rise within I," proclaimed Ndevui, at last taking the blunt from behind his ear and lighting it with mock seriousness. He always spoke like this when he was about to smoke, which was whenever he managed to steal a bit of ganja.

"Isn't it bad to steal something you consider so sacred?" Kpindi took a seat next to him and made a pinching motion with his fingers to indicate that he too wished to partake of the "holy vegetables," as he called it.

"Ganja should be free, so if I take it from someone who doesn't want to share it or is selling it, that is righteousness, justice." Ndevui took a puff.

"Pass on that righteousness, then," said Kpindi, and soon they were passing the joint around until it was finished. Namsa no longer fell into a fit of coughing when she inhaled, as she had the first few times. Everything felt soothing. Even the warm breeze and the familiar landscape became a paradise where time slowed to their rhythm, laughter, and gestures, punctuated by the music of the crashing waves from afar.

Before long, sleepiness overtook them, and one by one, the younger members went inside the plane to lie down. Finally, only

Elimane and Khoudi were left, sitting across from each other at the makeshift table.

"I apologize if I overstepped my role," said Elimane at length. "I just couldn't tolerate how that fellow had behaved to you. I know you can protect yourself." His head was lowered, and he was avoiding Khoudi's eyes.

"Thank you, big brother," Khoudi answered evenly, trying for the same tone she always used with him. It was too much to contemplate the possibility of any of the others changing the way she had.

"Okay, then, I hope the night is good to you." Elimane spoke with his customary calm, but without adding "sister" as he usually did. Khoudi stood and gave his shoulder a friendly jab, to nudge him back to his easy way with her, but he refused to look at her. It wasn't until he had reached the steps to the plane that he sent a quick glance her way.

"Wise choice, Khoudi. Sitting out here a bit with the company of the cool air. Especially tonight." Then he disappeared into the belly of the plane.

Khoudiemata remained outside, thinking. She thought about the many times she had had to protect herself with violence, the only language most boys and men seemed to understand. She liked knowing that she was able to take care of herself, but it bothered her that she had grown so comfortable with violence. And yet, what other choice was she left with?

These thoughts did not open the doors to sleep. She turned her thoughts to the next day, and her plans for herself, and gradually, with the cool breeze sailing gently against her face, the tension in it dissolved.

Her reverie was suddenly interrupted by bouts of shouting from inside the plane. After a few seconds, she registered the voice as Namsa's. She ran up the steps. Namsa was shaking and sweating and rolling in her sleep, in the grip of some nightmare. The others stood by looking on, afraid to get too close. Khoudi sat next to her and held her tightly until she quieted and slept peacefully again.

. The others were all fully awake now. "I am going to the night market." Ndevui glanced around to see if anyone wished to join him. Kpindi nodded, and Khoudi was tempted. A nightmare had disturbed the atmosphere of their home, a nightmare all of them had dreamed. They preferred the risks of nighttime adventures—even in the wake of the red caps—to what awaited them in their own minds.

And the night market was a real escape. It was the only place outside their home where the little family didn't feel the need to pretend not to be together. Like them, most people came to the market after they had finished searching the day and needed a bit of a break. They came to smell what they couldn't afford to eat, to imagine what seemed impossible for them in the grainy television sets people clustered around at the sides of stalls or mounted at the entrance of bars, and in the mannerisms of those better off than they were. To be sure, the group had to keep their wits about them. They usually arrived early and found a place to sit behind the glow of kerosene lamps and the dull bulbs powered by improbably loud generators. If they had money, they bought a couple of beers to share, and some cheap food: stone-hard bread with boiled peanuts or cubed sugar sprinkled with water. Over the din, bits and pieces of banter reached them.

One night not long before, a young man waiting in line to get bread, butter, and tea had called out, to no one in particular, "Why do we always have to stand in line for everything in this country?"

"Eh, you are only asking because you are at the back of the

line," someone ahead of him replied, and the whole line burst into laughter.

Someone else was playing music from a popular radio station on a phone, with the volume cranked up so others could enjoy it. *If I get money, eh* . . . the song blared, echoing the same music coming out of loudspeakers in the distance. Most people mouthed the lyrics, entertaining the dreams the music suggested.

At the end of the song, the radio host made announcements: *Tomorrow, we will have a discussion about whether our politicians should be called corrupt or thieves. If you steal rice at the market, are you not a thief? Join us in the a.m. and call in to be part of the conversation. And now, more music from our own reggae superstar, with a new song: "Mr. Politicorruption," or "You Are Not Fit to Be Called My Leader."* The host sang along a bit as the song filled the airwaves.

The gatherers laughed, and some began humming along.

"Ah, if you steal, you are a thief. Simple as that," someone called out, sparking a boisterous debate.

"No, correction. If you are poor and you steal, then you are a thief. If you are a politician, then you are corrupt." This joking rebuttal brought about more laughter.

"Look at this watch. I *corrupted* it today, oh." A young fellow stood in the middle of the informal circle brandishing a gold watch.

The crowd murmured and laughed, handing the new term around and making it part of the ever-changing local parlance. And the little family listened and took note, eating and drinking as slowly as they could to prolong the enjoyment, keeping at bay the unwelcome memories that grew more restive at night. When fatigue had conquered every cell in their bodies, they'd groggily make their way home.

But tonight, there was to be no night market for Khoudi. While

Elimane went outside and sat in the clearing, fiddling with a paperback as it had grown too dark to read, she wedged herself against the belly of the plane, with Namsa's head in her lap. From time to time, Khoudi read in Namsa's face the signs that her memory was beginning to stir, pursuing her in her sleep. Then she would place her palm on Namsa's forehead until the girl relaxed.

This went on all night, and every now and then, Khoudi would ask herself, "Why must most of those who give life to earth suffer so much?" It was one of those questions that didn't seek an answer. And even as she waited patiently with Namsa, forgetting herself as women do, effortlessly, she wondered if there was a way not to lose herself while caring for others.

4

The sun rose earlier than usual, and harshly, dragged against the sky. Namsa, feeling its warmth on her face, rubbed her cheeks with an effort that woke her, her eyes startling open but softening when they came in contact with Khoudi's. She swallowed to find her voice.

"Don't you like your own sleeping place?"

"I feel safe with you." Khoudi pulled her leg from under Namsa's head and wiggled her toes to return her foot to full life. She didn't mention what had happened the previous night and knew that the others wouldn't either. It was enough that the nightmares took their toll.

Just as their bodies were welcoming the day with yawns and stretches, Khoudi and Namsa heard an explosion of guttural laughter they recognized as Kpindi's and Ndevui's. Namsa went to greet them, and found Elimane outdoors, asleep at the table, his cheek on his book and his hands drooping. Kpindi and Ndevui staggered into the clearing, each carrying a crate of Star beer, Ndevui's with a burlap sack atop it, Kpindi's with a cloth-covered bowl. They slammed the crates down on the old fridge, waking Elimane, the little paperback rising with him, stuck to his cheek.

Ndevui guffawed. "You spend so much time with them, now they are beginning to kiss you while you sleep." He opened the sack and set its contents—beer, vodka, whiskey, and other spirits—on the table. He grabbed a beer and handed it to Kpindi, who had uncovered the bowl to reveal a feast of beignets, fried fish, and pepper sauce that filled the air with its aroma, mingling with the odors of alcohol, sweat, and perfume the pair had brought home as well.

Elimane pulled the book from his cheek, took a beer for himself, opened it with his teeth, and drank long and hard until the bottle was empty.

"That is how it should be done, big brother." Kpindi slammed his bottle against the table in applause.

"You should have joined us." Ndevui struggled to speak through a fit of hiccups. He took a swig and held his breath, attempting to calm them. "Kpindi was a magnet. Everyone wanted to drink with him or dance with him."

"There was fortune in our night," said Kpindi. "We found money where it shouldn't have been left. We *corrupted* it and used it to enter a bar, where we danced all night with beautiful girls." Elimane's eyes widened, reminding them that Khoudi and Namsa were present, but the two of them went on describing their exploits with a couple of the girls who had mistaken them for young men with money. They all ended up going to the home of one of the girls. After the girls had gone to sleep, hoping to wake up with these fellows with money, Ndevui and Kpindi went through their handbags and gathered whatever other valuables they could find, including the crates of beer.

Somehow in all of that drunkenness, they hadn't forgotten to abscond with a feast as well.

This was their code: They were free to do whatever they wanted with what they got on their own, but they had a general understanding that they shared with one another, and even in a state of inebriation, they rarely forgot it.

"The household was preparing for a wedding, so there was lots of food," said Kpindi. "Let's eat and be merry, merry, and merry!" He burst into a song while the others dug into the food.

Khoudi ate as quickly as she could, then wiped her hands, eager to be on her way.

"Are you going now? Already?" Namsa asked, her mouth filled with food.

Khoudiemata nodded.

"Can I come with you?" Namsa pleaded. "We could stop to see Shadrach the Messiah before you go off by yourself."

Khoudiemata hesitated. "He might not even be there." She could see that the boys had decided to go on a binge today. They would drink, smoke, and go wild until they passed out or the alcohol was finished, whichever came first. Much as they loved Namsa, they wouldn't watch out for her the way Khoudi would. Khoudi herself was tempted to join in, drinking some of her own demons into unconsciousness, but it was her day to be alone with herself, and she didn't want to give it up.

"Okay, come with me," she said to Namsa, "but I leave you by the beach when we find Shadrach."

The wind carried all manner of human sounds to Khoudiemata and Namsa from all directions as they walked into the day: singing, jubilation, howls of protest. Every Independence Day since Khoudi could remember, the protests had grown, as people had woken to the irony of celebrating freedoms that existed only on paper.

Shadrach the Messiah could often be spotted all around town, sometimes standing in the middle of the road and pretending to direct traffic, sometimes drunk outside one of the bars the boys liked to frequent, cautioning departing customers in his hoarse voice to "stay hidden, stay in the shadows." The little family always found that admonition funny, because they knew they were already invisible. But today Shadrach would be out in the open, at the kiosk on the beach, or so the leaflet had proclaimed.

They followed the quiet, sun-drenched dirt road until they reached the entrance to the beach, its sand blindingly white. So many people milled around them here that it was no longer necessary for them to work at looking separate.

Beach Kiosk stood a few paces into the sand, but it was no longer as popular as it once had been. Perhaps it was too close to the harsh realities people went to the beach to escape. These days, it was mostly a spot where drivers found parking or dropped off passengers who wanted to walk deeper into the beach. But today a crowd was gathered here, and Namsa and Khoudi squeezed through to see what was going on.

It wasn't Shadrach the Messiah but another fellow they found there. He was obviously young, but he had sprayed his short dark hair and beard white in an attempt to look older. He stood in the water in a white robe, his gaze and one hand raised toward the morning sky. Behind him, a line of people awaited his attention. He lowered his arm and extended his open palm toward them. "My multitude, please approach your prophet." The first person in line, a young woman, advanced, placing some notes in his hand that he glanced at and put away inside a plastic money belt cinched around his waist.

He pulled her into the water and submerged her, holding her nose and head and shouting incomprehensible phrases. She emerged from the water and walked onto the beach with a contented face, and the next person stepped up. Those in line observed the ritual solemnly, while most of the onlookers around Khoudi and Namsa chuckled.

"Ah, even prophets charge fees these days!" said one. "I wonder how you become a prophet. Do you just wake up and say, 'Yes, from today on I am a prophet. I feel it'? Or is there a prophet school where you go to get a certificate, a degree?" The chuckles turned to laughter, but the people in line in the water remained unfazed, their faces reflecting their belief in what, it occurred to Khoudi, was indeed a miracle of sorts.

"My people, my people, that prophet baptized me a while ago, and all I have is the taste of salt water in my mouth to this day!" cried a piercing voice. Shadrach the Messiah was approaching from down the beach, dressed in his usual motley robe. He pointed his staff, with its carved head of a roaring lion, at the crowd, his white beard and hair and broad face giving him a gravitas that belied the rest of his appearance. Then he went toward the people in the water, cutting to the front of the line. The prophet tried to ignore him, reaching for the next supplicant, but Shadrach grabbed his hand and forced a few banknotes into his palm. The prophet looked at the notes suspiciously, then chucked them into the ocean. Shadrach fished them out, carried them from the water, and held each up for the crowd to inspect before laying them out delicately on the beach, each of them weighted down with a little sand so it wouldn't blow away while it dried. The crowd laughed, seeing that this was old currency no longer in circulation.

"Today is a day of thinking, not one of celebration," Shadrach addressed the crowd on the beach. "Think. Think. And rethink." He paced around the banknotes, his ragged robe dripping and sagging

ISHMAEL BEAH

with water. The crowd watched like spectators at a sports match, their attention split between him and the prophet.

"They say April twenty-seventh, today, is our day of independence, of freedom. Well, I ask you, do you feel free? And why do we need some outsiders to agree to our freedom? They came from across the seas and said they had come to save us, to give us civilization. But they didn't even know we existed until they stumbled upon us. So how could they have known what we needed?"

"Amen!" cried someone from the prophet's line.

Shadrach the Messiah pointed his staff at the crowd, which was now shrieking with laughter, whether because of what he had said or a scene that was unfolding in the water. The prophet was arguing with a woman who insisted he hadn't submerged her long enough, even though she had paid extra, and that she was therefore short on the blessings she ought to receive. Finally the prophet had had enough. He exited the water, pursued by the woman, who was now shouting at him, and all the others in the water who had not yet gotten their turn to be baptized.

Shadrach the Messiah started running after the prophet too, pleading, "Come and listen to me, man!" But shortly he stopped and returned to the crowd.

"Eh, that prophet could surely win a marathon." He shook his head. Then he mumbled something that he evidently found so funny that he turned red with laughter, which made those watching him laugh as well.

"How many of you have names such as William, Lightfoot, Boston, Frederick, Cardew, John?" he asked the assembly. More than a few raised their hands. "And how many of you know the names your great-grandmother would have given you, names such as Kailondo, Bai Bureh, Momoh Jah, Suluku, Mammy Yoko, Sarrounia Mangou,

80

Nzinga Mbandi, Nyarroh?" The crowd fell silent. "Even our names are an indictment of the history we have accepted, the one that didn't set us free but made us disbelieve our own worth."

Some people began to head down the beach. They'd come here to have fun, not to embark on self-inquiry, or so they thought. Yet their faces now carried the very questions they had forgotten to ask themselves until now.

Shadrach the Messiah headed back into the water, talking to himself. "They say we are part of the Commonwealth. The only thing common about it is that some of the countries have all of the wealth. *Hahahaha!*" He looked about him. "Where is my staff? Oh, it is right there." He retrieved it from the beach and went back into the water. "So don't celebrate what is not your truth." He bent down to swallow a mouthful of the salt water. "Pure water must have no taste. That is what I had learned in school. But this water is like a meal." He licked the water with his tongue like a dog, then dived into it headlong, holding his staff.

New passersby had stopped to see what was going on, and the crowd was full again. Shadrach emerged from the ocean, his face shining with sweat and salt, more animated by the minute as he continued his sermon. Khoudi noted how easy it was to find something to take away with you when he spoke—curiosity at a question, a fact that needed rethinking, laughter. Even she, skeptical as she was, was tempted to dally, but she knew she needed to go, or her day would no longer be her own.

She looked around for Namsa and was surprised to find that the girl had vanished. Namsa was fascinated by Shadrach, almost obsessed by him. She sometimes thought she'd heard him say something before, or knew what he was going to say next before he spoke. So where was she now?

Before Khoudi could start to search, she spotted Namsa walking from the parking lot with a bottle of water in her hand. She made her way through the gathering and offered the water to Shadrach. But he only looked down at her, as if neither his face nor his hands knew how to respond. Namsa opened the bottle and drank from it and extended it to him again. This time he took it and poured some of the water over his already wet head. "He is indeed an entertaining fool," someone called, and the crowd laughed. Looking in Namsa's direction, Shadrach set the bottle of water on the sand, next to his bare feet. Namsa stayed where she was, in front of the crowd, watching and listening, and Khoudi decided it was all right to leave her there. For each of them, it was a day to get lost in what they liked. Besides, Khoudi hated goodbyes and all the emotions they brought up.

She whistled a goodbye, and thought she saw an answering smile on Namsa's face, but the girl didn't turn around to watch her go.

At the junction where they had gone down to the beach stood a little shop. On one side of the door was a sign that read ALL SHALL COME TO PASS, and on the other COME AND GO WITH ALLAH'S BLESSINGS. Whenever Khoudi looked in the doorway, she saw a smiling old man counting his prayer beads. His face always looked like it had been waiting to meet hers, and he would nod and wave at her. She had wondered if he greeted everyone who walked by like that.

But today, instead of waving, he gestured her inside. In a hammock behind the counter sat a woman as old as he, but whom age had painted with a magnificent elegance. She stood up and came to the counter, leaned on it for support. From below, she brought out a beaded necklace. She unzipped the neck of Khoudi's hoodie, took off her beanie, and placed the beads around her neck. Then she turned

Khoudi around to face a small mirror on the wall, her old hands cupping the girl's cheeks.

"I made this one, and I've had it in mind for you ever since you first walked by," she said. "You remind me of someone I once knew."

Khoudi stared at her image, surprised at how much more slender her neck was than she'd remembered. Then her heart sank as she wondered how to tell the woman she had no money to spare for such adornments.

"It's yours," said the woman. "Just do this one thing for me, when you can: Count the beads, while thinking about what truly makes you happy. And remember, you are always welcome here, especially when you feel your heart is burdened." She led Khoudi to the door. "Go on now, and no need to thank me."

Buoyed by this exchange, Khoudi stepped out onto the road and went on her way, touching the necklace from time to time to reassure herself she had not dreamed the encounter. Where the main road reached a roundabout, she turned onto a small path that zigzagged between trees and dense bushes. She followed the path down through a field of boulders to a hidden inlet with a tiny sandy beach. Here, the salt water met a narrow river that traveled down from the forested mountains. Somehow no one else seemed to know of this place. Perhaps no one explored beyond the boulders. Khoudi herself had stumbled upon it only by accident, during one of her many times running from the police. Since then, it had become the refuge where she took a break from the hardness of the world. An old concrete pillar at the edge of the stones had the inscription 96 DEGREES carved into its base, and that was the secret name with which she'd christened this haven of hers. It made her feel like the title of one of her favorite songs: *untouchable.*

The last time she'd been here was a week earlier, after an

excursion to the Maroon Park market at the center of town, where apparel and cosmetics were sold. Intoxicated with the smell of fabric and perfume, she'd watched for a promising gaggle of mother and daughters to follow into a shop. If she chose a group she sufficiently resembled, and took her hair out of her beanie and removed her hoodie, she could usually pass herself off as a member of the family at least long enough to get in the door, evading the suspicion of the shopkeeper. While her pretend companions shopped, she would lose herself in the smell of the soaps or the feel of the dresses, smiling as though she were in the habit of immersing herself in these luxuries every day of her life. The two young girls and their mother she'd attached herself to that day bought soaps with scents she had never heard of: *bergamot, lavender, verbena* . . . She whispered the names to herself as she rubbed the samples hard on her hand, so that enough residue remained for her to enjoy later on.

That particular family was so carefree and oblivious that she trailed them from one shop to another, managing to slip a bar of body soap and two small bottles of lotion, and, in a coup, two silky dresses into her raffia bag while the girls were trying on outfits and monopolizing the attention of both their mother and the proprietors. While they were distracted, she had quietly slipped away and come to 96 Degrees, where she had hidden her precious soap, lotions, and dresses before returning to the little family.

Now she made her way down through the boulders, then jumped onto the little beach. She went to retrieve her treasures, relieved to find them where she had left them, under a stone in the mangroves. Averting her eyes, she took off her shoes; they were so discouragingly ruined that she no longer allowed herself to view them before slipping them off or on, but accomplished the task by feel. She removed her raffia bag, then her sweatshirt and baggy jeans, placing a stone on them to hide them and prevent water, wind, or creatures from carrying them away. She inhaled the air and closed her eyes, then opened them to see the worn-out underwear, undershirt, and brassiere, whose color and provenance she could no longer determine or remember. Her spare pair of underwear was in the same state, she knew. She would return to the market on a busy day when she might hitch herself to another family out shopping for what she needed.

For a few minutes, Khoudi simply sat by the river with her feet in it. It was warmer than the ocean, and nearly salt free. She looked up at the slopes of the mountain and out at the vast glistening body of the ocean, its blue getting brighter as the sun became livelier. Gently, she touched the necklace the woman had given her, then took it off and put it with her clothes so that it wouldn't get soaked. She found a deeper pool and lowered her body into the water until it reached her neckline. She stayed like this for a while, rubbing her hands against her skin and pouring water over her back, her arms, her face, her belly.

Recently, she had started experiencing a new pleasure while touching her face and body in private like this. Her hand felt wonderful against her own skin, especially along her belly. A tingling rose up inside her body, so intense that she curled her toes and squeezed her legs tight with the pleasure of it. She knew the names for her private parts, but they made her uncomfortable to think about. Instead, she preferred not to think at all, just let her hand pass along the contours of her face and body.

From the plastic bag, she took the soap and lotions she had corrupted at the fabric market. She began washing her body and then her hair with the bar of soap. She tried untangling some of the knots in her lathered hair, but with little success, so she simply gave up and rinsed it with the fresh water.

The next task was to do her laundry. She went back to the stones and collected the things she had been wearing. She wet and soaped them sparingly, then rinsed them, wrung them out, and spread them on the stones to dry. She never felt comfortable getting completely naked, even here where no one was watching. What if someone was spying on her from afar? What if someone showed up by accident? What if she had to run away? The only place she felt less vulnerable was in the water, so she returned to the deep pool, submerged herself, and beneath the water, slipped off her underwear. She washed it the best she could, and then, with her body hunched over, she crouched closer to the edge of the water and laid her undergarments on a nearby stone to dry. Then she returned to the water and waited for the sun to do a little of its magic.

To avoid letting her thoughts wander to places and events she didn't wish to revisit, she started running down a sort of catalogue she kept in her head, of girls she had seen wearing beautiful outfits and enjoying their time together. Would she ever be able to make such friends herself? She had some carefully hoarded money in her raffia bag. Perhaps it was enough to get her hair cut and styled, even a manicure and pedicure. It had been a long time since she'd had any color on her fingers and toes, even painting them herself, and she missed it.

The very thought pulled her from the water, and soon she was back on the sand and putting on her half-dry underwear. She decided to put on the blue dress with yellow flowers that she had corrupted at the shops. She didn't know what size it was, since she had just snatched it when she had the opportunity. She unfolded it, closing her eyes and holding it up to her face to feel its silky softness and inhale the freshness of the fabric, and slipped it on. It came to just below her knees, the way she had imagined, but the armholes were too loose; the dress didn't fit as well as she had hoped. She walked up and down the sand, looking at the shadow of herself in the dress, which exaggerated the loose arms. Then she had an idea. She took off the dress and gathered the excess fabric around the armholes, tying it to form bows on top of each shoulder. She put the dress back on, and now the arms weren't too loose while the neckline was low enough to show a hint of breast. She put on her necklace. Then she poured a bit of each of the lotions into her palm and rubbed them around her neck, wrists, and face. It was delightful to be pleased by the scent on her skin.

But something was missing: her shoes. Reluctantly, she put her feet into her old sneakers. Then she put the other dress back in the plastic bag, along with the soap and lotions, and returned it to its hiding place under the mangroves. She put her jeans and sweatshirt into her raffia bag and slung it on her shoulder and looked at her shadow on the sand, smiling a bit and swaying before she climbed slowly back up to rejoin the world.

About to reenter the road, Khoudi felt suddenly self-conscious. She rearranged her dress, but somehow she could not get it to drape to her satisfaction. Each time she pulled it to one side, she sensed something wrong on the other. Finally, she gave up and set forth, jumping into the road and retracing her steps toward the roundabout. She could not remember the last time she had worn a dress. It felt good, but she felt vulnerable too. Everything felt threatening—even the wind seemed to move her outfit unpredictably.

She took a back way so that she wouldn't have to encounter so many people. Before long, she emerged into a street lined with old one-family colonial wooden homes wrapped with verandas, now lopsided like the history the colonizers had left behind. Most of these buildings were occupied by shops and services. Behind them towered the glass-and-concrete buildings of the government and financial district, with their bright lights.

She stopped across the street from a small building, where there was a salon. Women and girls from all parts of the city came here, she knew. Some of them arrived in big fancy cars, which would wait for them outside, the drivers and bodyguards standing next to them. Others arrived in taxis that looked like their tires would abandon them at any second, though somehow that second never came. Many times, she had watched those women and girls through the window, with halo-like caps over their heads, reading magazines and even drowsing. Oh, to be able to give in to such relaxation!

Today there were no cars outside, which meant that the place wasn't yet crowded. Khoudi crossed the street, her apprehension giving way to excitement. She was so preoccupied with rehearsing what she would say when she entered the shop that she nearly stepped in front of a truck. The driver assaulted the air with his horn, but in her mind Khoudi was already at her destination and did not hear him.

Through the foggy glass window, Khoudi watched the hairdressers and their few customers for a while. Was there a perfect moment to interrupt this coordinated orchestra of hands and heads, and the occasional foot? Mustering her courage, she pushed the door, and it opened abruptly, not with the grace, familiarity, and confidence with which she had seen people open it, the way she had practiced in her mind. The door swung back, shutting out the noise of the street and locking her into a new world of uncertainties. Music, laughter, and the chattering of the women came at her. So did the condescending looks of the hairdressers and the customers, Khoudi thought. She lowered her head a bit, then lifted it again and walked to the desk. As she waited for someone to speak to her, she leaned against the counter, her fingers drumming the rhythm of the background music on its surface.

One of the hairdressers was fiddling with the remote control for the air-conditioning unit, which seemed not to be working properly. It sounded like it was on at full blast, but the place wasn't cool. Exasperated, she set down the remote and approached Khoudi, glancing pointedly at the hand drumming on the counter as if to say, "That is not womanly behavior."

"So, what will it be, miss?" She took Khoudiemata's hand and pulled her until she was standing upright. "That's better." Her eyes spoke again. She took the other hand as well, preventing Khoudi from leaning on the counter again, or departing.

"My name is Kadiatou, and this is my shop," the woman said. "You have money, you are a customer. That is my only rule," she added firmly, deliberately widening her gaze to indicate to Khoudi that she should ignore the other women's condescension. "So, what will it be, miss?" she asked again.

"A deep wash, conditioning, oil, and some big braids, with my own hair, no extensions," Khoudiemata said in one breath, just as she had rehearsed it for so many months.

"Something simple, then? You are sure?" Kadiatou confirmed, once again speaking also with her eyes, which went about the place to show that most of the customers asked to do a little more with their hair.

Khoudiemata shook her head no, not so much because she was sure but because she needed to reclaim at least the appearance of self-command.

"No, just simple, and just my hair." She spoke loudly to make sure the other women heard, betraying no reaction to the looks they cast her way.

"I like your style," Kadiatou said, and Khoudi was uncertain whether she was referring to her choice of hairstyle or her way of standing up for herself. Either possibility was to her liking. She let Kadiatou lead her to a chair and had a seat.

"You have to sit properly so that I can do my work properly." Kadiatou spoke for Khoudiemata's ears alone. When Khoudi looked confused, Kadiatou indicated her posture with her eyes. Khoudi looked around at the other women and noticed that in comparison, she was slouched, with her legs slightly apart and her right arm looped over the back of the chair. This was how she always sat. But now she sat up, straightening her spine, bringing her knees together, and folding her hands in her lap.

"You can return to yourself when I am done treating your hair." Kadiatou noticed how tense Khoudi had become assuming this alien posture. Khoudi watched in the mirror as Kadiatou took a closer look at her hair. First, she parted it with her finger, and then she tried combing it. But Khoudi's hair was so tangled that soon she was on the verge of weeping, her scalp was so sore.

"I'm sorry," said Kadiatou, "but this is going to take much longer than usual. I am going to have to charge you more."

"The prices listed in the window didn't say it costs more if your hair is this or that way." Khoudiemata lifted her head so that her eyes met Kadiatou's in the mirror. "And it's not as if you have so many customers waiting," she went on boldly, indicating the few other bodies in the shop. She sat upright, declaring that she was ready to either get her hair done or leave.

"My, you have gotten sassy all of a sudden!" said Kadiatou. "But you are correct—I should change the sign. But let me see if you have the money to start with." She opened her palms.

"You haven't done anything yet, but you want the money already.

Well, I have it, and that is that. If you don't want to do my hair, just tell me." She hoped her boldness didn't backfire—there really wasn't anywhere else she wanted to go. There were girls on the street who could braid your hair, but they only did things that Khoudi herself could do, if she wanted.

Kadiatou walked away, and for a moment Khoudi worried that she was gone for good. But then Khoudi saw her beckoning from the back of the shop, where there was a sink with a chair next to it.

Khoudiemata lowered herself into the chair, careful to keep her posture ladylike.

Kadiatou applied shampoo and worked up a lather. "When was the last time you did anything to your hair?"

"I honestly can't remember," Khoudi said, then added, "The price in the window is all I have." Abruptly Kadiatou stopped working on her hair, and again Khoudi panicked. "I'll pay the rest in work!"

"I'm just letting the conditioner soak in." Kadiatou smiled. "Usually I get people begging for something for free. You made a good point about the listed price." She began combing through a section of Khoudi's hair, and Khoudi was pleased to feel that it wasn't as difficult to get through it now. She didn't like owing people, but she was starting to enjoy the massage on her scalp and the smell of the oil and whatever else Kadiatou was rubbing on her head. She closed her eyes and enjoyed the sensations, which had the deep comfort of rituals remembered from childhood.

It took Kadiatou quite some time to wash and rewash Khoudiemata's hair, and then to rub in this and that, working and working until the comb no longer struggled to pass through, and her hair could be braided the way she had asked. By the time she was finished, she had to nudge Khoudi out of a half-sleep to give her a mirror.

Khoudiemata hardly recognized the hair on her head, or her face for that matter, to which the new style restored its proper youthfulness, bringing out the supple and untainted beauty that had been hidden. She could not stop returning to the mirror, surprised each time to see herself so pretty. She could not stop smiling either, and she gave up that battle, at least as long as she was inside the salon.

"Now, I want to have my fingers and toes done."

"Good. You are learning to ask like a customer. Don't ever beg if you are the one paying, or you won't be taken seriously. But I thought you said you had only enough to do your hair."

"Since you are agreeing to take me on for labor, I thought why not go for all I really want," Khoudi said playfully, hopefully.

They agreed on a week of work, and Kadiatou brought over the implements. But as soon as she took one of Khoudi's feet in her hands, Khoudi flinched. She was not used to having someone else touch her.

"Just relax and try to enjoy it," Kadiatou said. "No harm is getting done here, young woman." She returned her attention to Khoudi's feet. "So you just want the nails trimmed and cleaned, yes, with clear polish only on the hands? Most people get it done that way." She did not look at Khoudi, and Khoudi did not have the courage to disagree. As Kadiatou worked on in silence, with daydreams of her own, Khoudi's mind drifted to how she would work to pay for the treatment. She hoped that Kadiatou would hold to the week she had agreed upon. She was used to people starting with a pretense of generosity, then exacting some sort of servitude. After all, the little family needed her to search the day for food. Nothing should compromise that.

"Don't exhaust yourself with thinking about every outcome," said Kadiatou, seeming to read her mind. "Learn to accept some beautiful surprises in life."

When she had finished Khoudi's hands as well as her feet, she went to put the tools away, stopping to still Khoudi's left hand, which was just about to touch the nails of her right. "No! Wait until they are dry. I have to watch you to make sure you don't ruin my beautiful work. Good thing I didn't put colored polish on them!" Kadiatou pointed to a bench with a leather top and gestured for Khoudi to sit there.

Khoudi sat and picked up one of the many magazines on the table, flipping it open carefully to avoid damaging her nails, then threw it back down. It was filled with ads for bleaching one's skin. She picked out another, and it was the same. In town, she had noticed that more and more people, men as well as women, and sometimes even children, were bleaching. You could tell by the sickly light pink hue it gave their skin.

Just then, a group of young women about her age noisily flocked in, laughing. She noticed the ease with which they opened the door and entered, as if the place belonged to them. They were moving through a familiar routine. She watched them, intent on learning their mannerisms. They snapped their fingers to get the attention of the hairdressers, and they sat where they wanted, not waiting to be told. And they noticed her—not just as they would any girl, but with their eyes lingering on her, studying the mixed languages of her energy. Under their gaze, Khoudi sat upright again, and brought her legs together and her hands to her lap.

"I want what you did for her with some extensions." The most talkative girl pointed at Khoudi.

"I'm sorry, Mahawa, but we are closing at noon today, for Independence Day," said Kadiatou. "Can you come back tomorrow?" But the young woman was insistent on a quick style for herself and two of her friends, and so Kadiatou and several other hairdressers agreed to pitch in. The three girls took their chairs and their friends hovered nearby, chattering, as the hairdressers descended.

"Can someone put the television on?" Kadiatou called. "Where is that remote?" One of the workers found it in a drawer and turned on the television mounted on the wall. As usual, a Spanish-language soap opera came on, without subtitles. People religiously watched these, Khoudi knew, even though they didn't speak a word of Spanish, memorizing the names of the characters and guessing the plot lines from the action. The hairdressers had their eyes on the screen more than on the girls' hair; their hands went through their tasks by memory.

Meanwhile, the girls continued their conversation as though no one else was in the room, and the women attending to them were mere statues. Khoudi knew what that felt like—it was an experience she had every day of her life. She looked up at the television, which had cut to an ad. A dark-skinned woman was walking down the street, and no one was looking at her. She stopped at the store to buy a "body nourishing cream," as the ad referred to it. She went home and rubbed it on her skin vigorously, with an air of hopeful expectation. The next frame showed her, with lightened skin, walking down the street again. This time, everyone paid attention to her. The ad closed on a message: *Be noticed. Be bright. Be beautiful. Be alive.*

Khoudi stood abruptly. Her nails were long dry, and there was no reason to stay. She went to retrieve her sneakers. From across the room, Kadiatou looked her up and down, her eyes taking in the ratty shoes. With her eyes, she indicated that Khoudi should wait. Then she broke away from the cluster of hairdressers and went behind the counter. She returned with a pair of simple but elegant sandals, and set them down next to Khoudi and indicated that she should put them on. "You don't have to give these back. Someone left them here over a month ago, so clearly they don't need them."

It disconcerted Khoudi that Kadiatou seemed to read her mind so easily, although she appreciated not having to explain herself. A thought crossed her mind: Perhaps Kadiatou used to be like her. She put on the sandals. They were a little too big, but they would do.

The young women were busy admiring their finished hairstyles in the mirrors. "This is why I don't go anywhere else," said Mahawa, rotating her hair to admire the finished effect from every angle. Then, just as noisily and confidently as they had arrived, they made their way out of the shop, restoring its previous quiet. On their way out, Mahawa caught Khoudi's eyes and smiled at her, but Khoudi didn't smile back. As much as she longed to have friends as these girls did, she wanted it to happen without being forced. And she was determined not to show desperation to anyone for anything.

Khoudiemata found a plastic bag in her raffia bag and put her old shoes in it. She needed them for her real life, the one where she owed no one anything and did as she pleased. She gave Kadiatou what money she had, and they arranged that she would come to work off her debt at the shop the day after tomorrow, as the shop would be closed until then. The hairdressers were all preparing to go out themselves to celebrate.

"Come along with us, if you like," said Kadiatou, but Khoudi declined. She knew that if she didn't come back, Kadiatou wouldn't seek her out. She hadn't even asked where she lived or what her name was.

Khoudi walked to a mirror to take one last look. With a shock, she recognized her mother's face staring back at her, with sharp cheekbones and bright eyes. She couldn't tear her eyes away.

Kadiatou roused Khoudi from her reverie. "You are going to look the same, for today at least, even if you stand there for hours. Let the mirror be, young lady." She went to a drawer below the counter and pulled out a belt, which she fastened around Khoudi's waist. "That is what was missing." She regarded Khoudi's image in the mirror with

satisfaction. "It bothered me so much." Then she pulled Khoudi outside, where the other hairdressers were waiting, and closed the door.

The center of town was usually filled with masses of hurrying bodies
and discontented faces. But today, with the holiday, people were
sparse, and what faces there were looked joyful and relaxed. Young
people and old clustered at bars or along the streets or gathered under the eaves of commercial buildings, listening to reggae.

Khoudiemata followed Kadiatou and the others, watching the
shadows of the women that strolled along and beside their bodies,
then glancing at her own to get a sense of how her dress was now
hanging. The best she could tell, it was better than before. She kept
a little distance, so that it would be unclear to those who saw her
whether she was with these boisterous women, who appeared not to
feel the slightest bit vulnerable. But in her new attire and hairdo she
felt conspicuous, and she was glad not to seem entirely alone.

A group of young men were leaning against the side of a four-
story red brick building emblazoned with faded posters of photogra-
phy equipment. All of them wore the same black shoes, black jeans,
and white T-shirts that read

GENTLEMEN OF PURPOSE CLUB (GOP)

PERFECTION EQUALS PROSPERITY

They were indeed outwardly perfect, with neat haircuts, shirts
tucked in, coordinated even in the way they leaned against the wall.
When Kadiatou and her friends came in view, the young men did not
whistle, as men usually did, but blew kisses at them and called to
them. "God, you are the best craftsman!" cried one. Khoudi was so

impressed that she forgot to be self-conscious, until she felt the warmth of their eyes on her and looked up to see them regarding her with a kind of astonishment in their eyes. Was there something wrong with her outfit, she wondered, or with her body?

Then one of the men called out, "Where have you been hiding, O beauty of heaven and earth that has come to bless us?" The speaker had broad shoulders and a face that willingly bent to his smile, a face that hadn't yet been bruised by the world. He rushed in front of Khoudi, and she reflexively folded her fist, ready to punch him in the neck, when she heard Kadiatou and her friends laughing. She looked down and saw that her assailant was offering her a single red rose.

"I apologize for the intrusion," he said. "Please take this as a token of gratitude for allowing us to enjoy your beauty." He indicated his friends, and they all performed a half bow toward Khoudiemata. Then he stepped out of her way, holding the rose before her. Khoudi unclenched her fist and took the rose with a snap of her wrist. The group clapped as she walked away.

She caught up to Kadiatou and her friends, no longer wanting even a little distance between them.

"Give me the flower," said Kadiatou, extending her hand, and Khoudi gladly handed it over, not really having any use for it. Kadiatou broke off most of the stem and planted the rose in Khoudiemata's hair, just above her ear. "You do not know yet what you have, but you will. Now come, we are almost there." She took Khoudi's hand and gave it a squeeze, and something about it reminded Khoudi of how she was with Namsa.

They had arrived at an unfamiliar stretch of the beach, where they were greeted by loud music and shrieks of enjoyment. It was so noisy that in order to speak, they had to shout in one another's ears. The women entered the open veranda of one of the cabanas and sat on plastic chairs at a table facing the ocean, their legs crossed. Khou-diemata sat with her chair turned around so that her chest rested on the back. A waiter brought beer. Khoudi was about to say she had no money when Kadiatou's face told her not to worry. While the hair-dressers belted down their drinks, Khoudi sipped at hers, looking around at the other young women. She wanted to learn how to be like them: the way they laughed and swung their bodies here and there, how they stared at boys and men and captivated them. Ob-serving others was a survival skill, and it was such a relief not to have to turn it toward survival for once. She relished the snatches of con-versation she was catching, about dresses and parties. No one was talking about how and where to get food for the day.

"So, miss, who owes me work for unmasking the beauty of her hair—what is your name? And finish that beer before it gets warm! It is only fun to drink warm beer when you are completely drunk. And you are not there yet." Kadiatou slid another beer across the table, and Khoudi gulped down the bottle she had been sipping.

"Khoudiemata," she said, wiping her lips.

"Khoudiemata. Beautiful name, like you." Kadiatou held her gaze until Khoudi smiled. "There it is, that is the expression of the beau-tiful person dancing inside." She pointed at Khoudiemata's heart. Khoudiemata smiled again, and she could feel her face practicing to accept this expression. She couldn't remember the last time someone had said she was beautiful. She had nearly lost the capacity to believe that she was.

Khoudi went in search of a restroom. She walked along the sand for a bit, through bodies shaking to whatever song came on next, then onto the main tar road and across to a yellow building with a veranda that faced the street. She tried to walk with an easy confi-dence, the way she had watched other young women walking, but she couldn't get used to how strange it felt to be wearing a dress, especially among these chattering people. Apparently they all came here to show that life was good to them. Whether that was actually true, she suspected, didn't matter as much as the ability to pose for their phones, their faces alight with the appearance of joy.

On the way back from the restroom, she was scanning the place when her eyes fell on the group of girls who had been at Kadiatou's shop. She looked away, hoping they wouldn't recognize her, but at the same time found herself half hoping they would.

"Hey!"

Khoudi didn't turn around. Whatever she had heard, it was not for her. "Hello, behind you!" the voice insisted.

Khoudiemata turned around to find Mahawa, the leader of the chatty bunch, waving at her.

"Hey." She waved back, unsure what else to say. Mahawa rushed over to her and gave her kisses on either cheek, then pulled back to get a look at her hair. "With no extensions, that is wonderful! Only at Kadiatou's can they pull off something like this." She looked back at the table on the veranda, where Khoudi could see not only the girls she recognized from Kadiatou's shop but several young men as well. "We are sitting at that big table over there with a bunch of friends. Come join us." Mahawa entwined her arms with Khoudiemata's and led her across the street, forcing the cars to wait for them.

"I came with some people over there," Khoudi felt obliged to say. She was not even certain she wanted to go with Mahawa, but something in her craved just a taste of the company of these youngsters, if only to understand what they were all about.

"I will come with you to ask if they don't mind for you to come sit with us for a bit." She linked her arm through Khoudi's.

The hairdressers greeted Mahawa politely enough, but Khoudi

thought she picked up an undertone of disdain of which Mahawa seemed unaware.

"Can I borrow this lovely creature to visit my table?" she asked, indicating Khoudi.

Khoudi wanted to say that she was not a cup of salt to be borrowed, and that she could speak for herself, but she restrained herself.

"I will take good care of her. We are going to become best friends, I know it!" Mahawa exclaimed. She had a showy way of talking, and it was clear that she liked to be in charge.

"Go and be with those your age," said Kadiatou. "You will have more fun! And in case I don't see you later, Khoudi"—she emphasized the name—"come by the shop anytime." She didn't elaborate, and Khoudi was glad about that. She didn't want Mahawa to know that she owed the hairdresser. She took her beer and her raffia bag and waved to the women, catching a look from Kadiatou that warned, *Have your wits about you and don't lose yourself to newness so easily.* Or perhaps it was only her own thoughts that she was projecting. She caught Mahawa staring at her raffia bag in a way that telegraphed clearly that it didn't go with her outfit, but she ignored the look and pulled the bag close to her body.

Khoudiemata approached the table full of smartly dressed young people apprehensively. There was not an ounce of suffering in their milky eyes or on their relaxed faces. What might they ask her? *Where do you live? What school do you attend? What are you studying? What do your parents do?* These questions had come to replace instinctual intelligence as far as Khoudiemata was concerned. She worried that her mannerisms would betray that this was her first time doing the things they considered normal. She planned to observe every one of their actions before making a move, and to be prepared to counter a question with one of her own.

"Beautiful people. Attention! This is Khoudi, our new friend."

"My name is actually Khoudiemata." She looked at Mahawa, widening her eyes in a way that indicated "Khoudi" was reserved for intimates.

"Ah, forgive me! Khoudiemata, everyone. These are my two best friends, Ophelia and Bendu, whom you remember from the hairdresser," she continued. "And these three pompous fellows"—she pointed to three young men nearby—"are Andrew, James, and Frederick Cardew-Boston. The rest you will get to know as we talk." She pulled out a chair and Khoudiemata took it, her eyes traveling around the table to acknowledge them all and then falling to the ground, where the white sand glistened.

"Khoudiemata. That's a name from the provinces." The one called Frederick Cardew-Boston pointed beyond the mountains, inspiring a few titters.

"We're all originally from the provinces." Khoudiemata raised her head and mimicked Frederick Cardew-Boston's self-important gesture, pointing around them at the colorful assortment of buildings along the hills and the beach. The rest of the group giggled, and the conversation shifted to school dances, and upcoming plans for dinners and beach outings.

These young people seemed to live from one event to the next. Her ears were everywhere, trying to capture as much information about their world as possible, while she guarded her own as closely as possible. Some of the group were couples, she gathered, but it seemed Mahawa and Frederick Cardew-Boston were unattached. His phone rang, and without getting up from the table, he answered. He listened. "Yes, yes," he said, then ended the call. Moments later, he took another call. "Yes." "No." "Let's go ahead with that." He didn't apologize for the interruptions. Evidently the others were used to it.

Mahawa leaned in to Khoudiemata, her voice low. "I knew we were going to be good friends from the moment I spotted you at Kadiatou's. I had hoped to run into you there at another time."

Mahawa's phone chimed. "Hello," she said. "No, I have not forgotten about our dinner. I am driving from the beach area in a few minutes. See you soon, *mwah!*" When Mahawa hung up, her eyes were glittering.

"I have to go for my date, beautiful people! I will see you at dinner." Mahawa stood up hurriedly and put her phone in her bag, then, almost as an afterthought, turned to Khoudiemata. "You should come. I would like to get to know you better. Noire Point, tomorrow at eight. *Ciao-ciao.*" She blew kisses at everyone, then got into a shiny black car waiting nearby and drove off, without waiting for an answer from Khoudiemata.

The gathering had lost its glue, and the various members of the party made motions to leave by paying for what they had drunk. This was when Khoudiemata remembered that she still had her beer. It had lost its refreshing coldness, but no one was speaking to her any longer, so she put a foot up on Mahawa's empty chair and lounged in hers as she finished the beer, then set the empty bottle on the table.

"Wonderful to have met all of you." She stood up and raised her voice slightly to get their attention. And before anyone could ask where she was going and offer her a lift, she made her exit. Once again, she felt eyes on her as she made her way through the crowd.

Her plan was to go to the bathroom and change, certain that those who had mistaken her for having a life like theirs wouldn't recognize her once she had returned to her own reality. Back in her sweatshirt and baggy jeans and tattered sneakers, Khoudi folded her new clothes and put them in her raffia bag. She looked at herself in the mirror and admired her shiny lips and sharp cheekbones. Then she put on her beanie, tucked in her hair, and stepped outside.

The same eyes that had marveled at her were now oblivious of her presence. She was invisible again. Only the displeased looks of the waiters at the bar fell on her, shooing her away. She perched herself on a nearby rock to watch the departure of the beautiful people. Most left in cars that somehow had hardly any dust on them, and a few, Frederick Cardew-Boston among them, had drivers who had been waiting and opened the car door as they approached, as if they had no hands. Ophelia alone hailed a taxi and jumped in.

Khoudi's thoughts turned to the upcoming dinner. She'd need another dress and shoes and money for a taxi. The best place to get those things, she knew, was right where she was—at the beach, where life was laughing through most people and making them forgetful and vulnerable.

A group of young people was carousing nearby. Two of the women seemed to have lots of cash in their handbags—they reached in to pay every time a waiter brought another round of drinks. Then the group went into the water, leaving their clothes—Khoudi counted two black dresses, a short yellow V-neck top with beautifully woven patterns, and new-looking black jeans, plus nice flats and sunglasses—on the sand under the intermittent watch of one of their party, a young fellow who was visibly distracted by every young woman who went by. Khoudiemata moved closer and waited for her moment. The clothes were piled in such a way that she thought she could sweep them up in a few gestures. It was tempting to do it right away, but she had a better idea.

There was a service post close by, where workers, mostly young women around her age, went in and out to change the towels on the beach chairs. They wore apronlike uniforms, some of which were hanging on a post at the back of the service hut. Khoudiemata headed for it confidently, took off her beanie and put on one of the uniforms and grabbed a couple of towels. The young fellow noticed her coming toward him, but at the sight of her uniform he focused instead on the almost naked bodies of two young women giggling past him. Pretending to rearrange the group's towels, Khoudiemata covered the dresses, shoes, sunglasses, and handbags with a damp towel and wrapped the bundle up quickly, so that it looked like nothing more than a load of dirty towels.

She slipped her new possessions into the raffia bag, returned the uniform to the post, and retrieved her beanie. She left the towels behind as well. She'd considered taking them along, to sell at the secondhand market, but she worried that people would recognize the insignia on them and make the connection. Then she hurried back to 96 Degrees to hide her new acquisitions.

She took out the cash and stuffed it into the inner pocket of her raffia bag. She tucked her hair properly under her beanie and, just as carefully, folded away the feelings of the day. She hesitated for a moment, reluctant to return to the reality of her life, wishing there was more strength left in the brightness of the day so that she could stay longer. Had Mahawa really meant what she said about getting to know her better? She'd sounded like she did.

With each step out of 96 Degrees, the tension returned to her face. She no longer swayed and stepped delicately but walked with purpose. The only thing that at first glance distinguished her from the girl who had left that morning was the necklace the old woman had given her. That seemed a fitting token: a gift from hands aged with wisdom.

She stopped by Beach Kiosk to check if Namsa was there, but saw no sign of her, or of Shadrach the Messiah, for that matter. And so she returned home, to the airplane.

King's property, king's property, everything is correct. Khoudiemata whistled twice as she entered the clearing, to announce her arrival.

Everything is correct, everything is correct, Kpindi responded, the whistle followed by his laugh. Ndevui was with him, and they were sitting right where Khoudi had left them that morning. From the laughter and their slurred speech, she knew they were drunk and high even before she came near—but not yet at the stage of intoxication where their inner demons began to dance.

King's property, king's property, everything is correct. Another whistle came through the air, and Khoudi recognized it as Elimane's. Again, Kpindi responded. And then Elimane came into the clearing, and behind him, Namsa, with a beaming face. Khoudiemata sighed with relief.

"Big sister, big sister, we are reciting poems that we are making up on the spot," said Kpindi. "The theme is Freedom. Of course"—he indicated Elimane—"it was his idea. But just when we got started, he had to answer a call from William Handkerchief." Kpindi stood on top of the old refrigerator, waiting to perform. Perhaps they were drunker than she thought, Khoudi reflected, because only in such a state would the boys have agreed to participate in such an exercise.

Kpindi stamped his feet to get their attention.

"O Freedom, O Freedom, free me from Freedom that I do not want." He jumped down and rolled on the ground, laughing. Khoudi didn't see what was so funny, but Elimane and Ndevui were clapping, laughing, and cheering. She removed her raffia bag and set it on the refrigerator, hoping to put an end to its use as a stage. She sat down.

"Why don't you join us with a poem of your own." Kpindi looked at Khoudi. Elimane and Ndevui stopped laughing and horsing around and began to clap, egging her on. Khoudi looked toward Namsa before she spoke.

"I agree with Shadrach the Messiah. Today is not a day to celebrate freedom of any sort. So no poems from me today." She clasped her hands.

"Oh, come on," said Ndevui. "I am sure Shadrach the Messiah, that crazy old fool, would read something if he was here." He stood up, his legs wobbling, and this time all of them laughed.

"So you saw Shadrach the Messiah? Next time we should all go together to listen to him. He makes you think." Elimane opened a bottle of beer and took a swig. He was wearing a necktie, presumably for whatever errand he had been performing for William Handkerchief, and he loosened it now.

"I heard Shadrach the Messiah once tell a story about Bai Bureh. Bai Bureh was a warrior who refused to pay taxes to the British and instead demanded that they pay him for occupying his land. You should have seen how he acted out the story, jumping here and there and drawing images in the sand of a war the British liked to refer to as 'a confrontation.'" Elimane shook his head, and a little silence filled the air. "I would have liked to listen to his stories today," he said solemnly.

"But your boss man summoned you," said Khoudi. "What havoc did you two commit today?"

"He took me to one of those restaurants where all the expats and shady government officials go. We were meeting with a foreign banker. He lent me a suit and had me pretend to be his son, studying at Oxford." William Handkerchief had prepared him with layouts of the campus and names of professors. The banker was an Englishman who hadn't gone to Oxford but was impressed by Elimane and wanted to hear about what he intended to study and how he was going to use his studies to improve his nation.

Ndevui shook his head. "Why do these foreigners always ask how you are going to improve your nation as soon as you do something interesting? And meanwhile they are here in our country, improving themselves."

"I actually enjoyed the conversation," Elimane said. "And when we left, William Handkerchief said, 'You are a natural!' He told me that at one point he really believed I was studying at Oxford. 'In fact,' he said, 'I almost believed you were my son!'" Elimane broke into gales of laughter.

"This boss man of yours is really taking a liking to you!" said Kpindi.

"He says he doesn't like people working for him to have morals, because they become self-righteous as they make more money. Anyway, the food was okay. I liked the jacket more." Elimane undid the necktie and took it off. "You know, I am doing this for us too."

"Yes, big brother. You seem to be enjoying it a lot, though." Kpindi took the necktie from Elimane and hung it loosely around his own neck. Khoudiemata laughed. She sensed that Elimane was enjoying himself during these escapades with William Handkerchief. Not that she begrudged him—the work was yielding them a constant flow of cash for now.

Ndevui stood up and stumbled to where they could all see him.

"Here is my poem: 'Elimane, Elimane, please don't bring the *crooked history* of our land into this space, where we exist as freely as we can.'" Ndevui bowed and got himself another drink. Khoudiemata closed her eyes, remembering the feeling of her scalp being massaged, the smell of the oils on her hair, the chatter of the girls she now knew.

"I am sure Shadrach the Messiah will be there tomorrow," said Kpindi. "He is probably going to be the only one sober then." He sat on the plastic bucket opposite Khoudiemata.

Ndevui extended a bottle of beer and a joint toward Khoudi. "You have to catch up. We have all this beer and smoke. We should celebrate, Independence Day or not."

Elimane had gone to sit by the plane with part of a newspaper he'd picked up somewhere. "This is an interesting column. It asks what people would like to change about their country for Independence Day."

"What do most people want changed?" Khoudiemata came to look at the paper along with him.

"They want to change the names of streets and cities and neighborhoods." Elimane showed her the article.

"I think all the politicians should be changed, because they are the problem," said Ndevui.

"You are right," said Elimane. "I wish you could read it yourself."

"But how will you have time to teach us anymore, now that you are working for William Handkerchief?" Abruptly, Elimane turned the page. He seemed irritated, or perhaps guilty. Khoudi caught an ad for Noire Point. *Come revisit and reawaken the beauty of your tradition*, it read.

Elimane crumpled the newspaper and threw it on the ground and went to get another drink. He opened the bottle and placed it on the makeshift table, tapping the surface contemplatively. Then, with one big swig, he downed the entire bottle of beer, following it with a gulp from a bottle of gin that made him wince. He sat himself down next to Khoudiemata, then turned to her, studying her.

"Khoudi! Something is different about you today. In a good way."

Khoudi had forgotten about her toes, she realized. She wiggled them away from the holes in her sneakers and checked to be sure all her hair was under her beanie. She was glad after all that she had not gotten color on her fingernails. It wasn't so much that she was worried about the little family's knowing how she was taking care of herself as that she wanted to keep that other world as her world, apart. At the same time, she had always loved how Elimane paid attention to the details about her and showed that he understood the way she saw things, and the unspoken language of her thoughts. It occurred to her that he had not asked her how the canvas of her day was, as he usually did.

"Of course, something is different about me every day. I am a woman." She punched Elimane on the arm. She meant it playfully, but she hit him harder than she'd intended. Still, he seemed grateful that she'd fallen back into their old playfulness.

"My masculine brain is incapable of comprehending you fully. But I am aware of my shortcomings." He laughed and rubbed his arm.

"Oh man, don't ruin our enjoyment by talking like a dictionary," Ndevui pleaded. "Live here with us and come out of that head of yours. I ask you, please, man!" They all laughed.

The wind brought them the sound of Afro Trap from town, and it made Khoudi think again about the beautiful people she had met at the beach. What a constant creation life was! Any day, any hour, any minute, something good or bad happened and became part of you for a lifetime.

The sun was beginning its descent from the sky. Khoudi put a spliff between her fingers. "Who has a match or a lighter? Ndevui, Kpindi, you think you can roll enough to keep up?" At such times, she generally encouraged them to smoke more than drink, as alcohol brought out the demons they were otherwise so good at suppressing.

She took another spliff and put both in her mouth. Ndevui threw her a matchbox. She lit up and pulled hard, twice, before passing one to Kpindi on her right, over Namsa, whose head was down on the table with her eyes open. The other she passed left, to Elimane.

"Full circle. I like it," said Ndevui.

"Kpindi, can you sing us a Bob Marley song?" said Khoudi. "'Zimbabwe'?"

"No, no. He can't sing! Just hum the tune," Ndevui said.

"How about if Elimane plays it on the phone William Handkerchief gave him?" Khoudi suggested.

Elimane looked confused. "It's not a smartphone." He pulled it from his front pocket and put it on the table.

"It has 3G, so you can play the song right from the internet, Mr. Bookman," said Ndevui. "It's up to us to make the phones smart these days, until we can afford a smartphone." He took the phone and adjusted the settings. Then he held it up and walked around the clearing until he found the spot with the best reception. In a few minutes the song came through, quiet but distinct in the night air. Ndevui perched the phone in a low bush, and they all sang along.

"*Every woman got a right to decide her own destiny,*" sang Khoudi, certain that Bob Marley wouldn't mind her small edit.

"I wonder what Bob Marley would think about Zimbabwe today?" said Elimane, spliff in hand. "You know—"

"Please don't ruin the song for us, man," Kpindi and Ndevui said at the same time. Khoudi laughed, and Elimane pulled on the ganja and passed it along. When the song ended, Ndevui fiddled with the phone again until he brought in the radio station Lion's Roar, which played only reggae. The music became the background to their laughing and talking, their day of independence. In a sense, they knew, they were freer than most.

"We have to meet this William Handkerchief fellow and thank

him for the phone," said Kpindi. "Look at how we are enjoying ourselves!"

In the afternoon, Elimane told them, William Handkerchief had him go by himself to pick up a white fellow at the airport, take him to the port, and put him on a boat. For this operation, as William Handkerchief referred to it, he was provided with a copy of *Animal Farm*. Elimane was to pretend to be reading the book while waiting for the man; that's how he would be identified. As for the white fellow, William Handkerchief told him, he would look like an older version of Jesus—or at least the way Jesus was portrayed in movies.

As it happened, the man's flight was delayed, and Elimane had to wait for him for hours. Elimane had read the book before, of course, but he ended up reading the entire book again.

"I am sure you would have read it even if the plane hadn't been delayed," said Ndevui, and Khoudiemata and Kpindi smiled in agreement.

"Sounds like you are beginning a whole other life going with this mysterious William Handkerchief," said Khoudi. She wasn't complaining. It was nice not having to do that daily hand-to-mouth out of necessity, like before. Now they did it more out of habit, in preparation for a day that didn't greet them pleasantly, when whatever they had going now came to its end.

Their reverie was broken by the sound of Namsa shuffling her little body to its feet. As she made her way toward the plane, Kpindi and Ndevui began laughing at the way she staggered and stopped to hold on to a bush here and the branch of a tree there, as if her feet had forgotten their natural task. Khoudi and Elimane watched her with concern, though. It wasn't the first time they had seen her intoxicated, but she hadn't had anything to drink or smoke since rejoining them. Khoudi wondered if she'd been running errands for people down at the beach, the way Khoudi herself used to do. You could make a little money buying cigarettes, alcohol, snacks, and the like, and you could take a swig or a bite or a smoke here and there, and no one would notice.

Elimane went to Namsa. She resisted for a moment but then let him help her complete her snail's journey to the edge of the clearing, where he lowered her to the ground. Every time she tried to say something, hiccups convulsed her little body. Kpindi and Ndevui started to laugh again, and this time their laughter was contagious. Even Elimane joined in. While they were laughing, Namsa fell asleep, one side of her face in the dirt.

Khoudi took an empty beer bottle and filled it with water. She walked to Namsa and shook her awake. Namsa grumbled gibberish, and Khoudi handed her the bottle, from which she drank.

Namsa wiped her mouth. "This is terrible beer."

"You should try this one." Elimane gave her another bottle.

Namsa tasted it and made a face. "Horrible. Wait, if you want me to drink water, just say so." She got up and returned to the table, took a bucket, and sat down, continuing to sip water between hiccups. Khoudi knew what to do next. She went behind the plane to harvest some of the aloe that grew all over the clearing. With her knife, she cut the plants into small pieces. Then she squeezed the aloe into a bottle.

"Do we have any ginger beer?" she asked.

"Yes, there's some over there," said Elimane. "What are you doing?"

"Something I learned from one of my aunties who had a drunkard sugar daddy." Khoudi gave the drink to Namsa. "Drink, little by little, and you will be fine in no time."

Namsa drank a mouthful without hesitation. "It is tastier than that water, anyway." They settled back into their usual banter, with Namsa gradually joining them.

112

"You all missed out on what Shadrach the Messiah had to say to-day." Namsa stood up to do her impersonation, reciting what she remembered. "'Look at all of you fools, including me, celebrating an Independence Day we didn't fight for. Some foreigners who didn't own this land decided that today you were free in a land where your ancestors lived before they arrived. This is why we are not free, because we have allowed someone else to decide when and how we should be free. Were we free before they arrived? Hmm? Hmm? Only a colonized mind can even entertain that question. Wake up, wake up, and don't celebrate your imprisonment.'" She sat down. "Some people laughed and others didn't."

"Perhaps the ones who didn't laugh realized something," Khoudi said.

"Many just thought he was a crazy person who goes on and on," Namsa said.

Elimane had heard that Shadrach the Messiah used to be a professor and had held a position in government. It was said that as a professor, he always set aside the textbooks his students were reading and instead took them around the city to show them what was happening. He had tried to organize people too, in the shantytowns. But he grew frustrated at all the corruption, and one day he had just walked away from it, professorship and government post and all.

"Do you know him?" asked Kpindi.

"No, not personally," Elimane said. "He taught my father at university." He followed this admission with a gulp of gin, to wash away any thoughts that might be emerging from the past.

"Please, let's not talk about sophisticated people who lost their minds because of this and that," barked Ndevui. "I hate these sorts of stories! If it can't improve my life now, don't tell it to me!"

Khoudi laughed gently. "If you don't like what you're hearing, just don't listen. Put your earphones on." She knew it was the mention of Elimane's father that was making Ndevui grumpy. No one asked Elimane any further questions, in any case, because they were all afraid of his telling a sad story they didn't want to hear.

Just then, the little phone that had been providing music chimed. Elimane rushed to pick it up, and the others quieted.

"Hello," he said. "Yes."

Then, "However big or small the job, I can find people to do it."

Then, "Yes, yes, reliable people who need the cash and won't have questions." They could hear how hard he was working to sound sober.

Elimane listened some more, then looked up, alarmed. "But why tonight?" He listened again. "Okay, I do not need an explanation. I am aware that poverty has no holiday. I will bring my group. We will be there." He hung up, but just to make sure, he took the battery out and put it back in. Clearly, he had had more than enough to drink and to smoke.

"Ah, this is not good," he moaned.

Kpindi tapped him on the shoulder. "Everything okay, big brother?"

"William Handkerchief wants us to meet him for an errand at the airport as soon as it is dark. So we have to get sober before then. I told you he was unpredictable."

"Don't worry, we know how to hold ourselves up," said Ndevui. "The trick is to drink more and smoke more. We are unpredictable too!" He took several pulls from the ganja, which made him cough. He bit off the edge of a sachet of sassman, the local alcohol that ran to 120 percent proof—it was guaranteed to make you impudent, hence the name—and drank it straight. Then he ran and launched himself into the crotch of a nearby tree in one swing.

"You see that agility? Relax, man! Whatever it is, we can do it in our sleep. This is our life." He returned to the table.

The phone rang again. Elimane took the call and walked around the clearing, hunting for better reception.

"Yes," he said. "I can get them to the airfield without going through the main security entrance." He winked at the rest of the group. It was funny that their boss man didn't know that they lived within walking distance of the place where he wanted them to go.

"I trust every one of them with my life," Elimane was saying. "No, you don't have to worry about secrecy. That is our life. And no one would believe anything we say, anyway. We are useful riffraff, as you told me yourself!"

Another pause. "Yes, right when night sets in, which will be around nine o'clock. Right, twenty-one hundred hours." He rolled his eyes. "Okay, over and out." He hung up the phone.

"This fellow always speaks like he is in the military. 'Over, out, copy, twenty-one hundred hours.'" Elimane surveyed their faces to see if they were all ready for the unknown task at hand. "You heard the time. We aren't to bring any identity cards or anything like that with us." They all laughed. "And he promised to give us five hundred US dollars for tonight." They whistled at the amount, which was equivalent to several million in their own currency.

King's property, everything is indeed going to be correct. They all jokingly competed with one another to say it as fast and as many times as possible, until they fell apart, laughing.

Kpindi took one of Elimane's notebooks, cut out a page, and folded it into a neat rectangle. Then he plucked a pen from Elimane's chest pocket, drew some lines on the paper, and wrote something on the lines.

"My ID card. Now I exist." He laughed.

"Nice photo. It looks so much like you." Khoudi pointed at the smiley stick figure Kpindi had drawn.

"Don't bring it with you, I beg of you. We want that cash," said Ndevui.

Elimane gave a deep sigh they all recognized, and Ndevui raised his hands, surrendering to what had almost become tradition. "Just say it, man, so it is out of the way."

Elimane spoke with reluctance. "You know that we are going to be engaging in the sort of plundering that makes the path of history crooked."

It was an old argument, and Kpindi and Ndevui disagreed with him, as they had expressed many a time. They were already on the crooked path of history, so why walk straight? You either got off or stayed on and lived as circumstances dictated, especially in their position.

If William Handkerchief was willing to give them for one night's work what it took most people six months to earn, they could only imagine how much he was making. They didn't care. Five hundred dollars meant time just to relax if they chose to. For Khoudiemata, it meant more time on her own—or with her new friends. Elimane was thinking about time to read and wander about bookstores and news-stands in town, or to go to the open hearings at the Supreme Court. He could go on his own to some of the places he had glimpsed while working for William Handkerchief. For Ndevui, it was more time to play football or to run as long as he liked. He could even buy his own set of portable equipment, so that he could start a game anytime and anywhere he liked. Namsa and Kpindi just wanted to *be*. Who said that you had to have a purpose? Wasn't the very process of living freely where the purpose lay, where you might find one?

5

It took only a short time for the little family to arrive at the barbed-wire fence from which they could see the entire airfield and the terminal. They knew from previous forays that the fence didn't extend all the way around the field, but enclosed only the parts that were most visible. In the other places, rolls of rusting barbed wire lay scattered about. If the work had once been intended to be completed by a certain date, that time seemed to have passed.

A military vehicle was parked about four hundred yards before them. The two soldiers in it were looking at their phones, the lights from the screens revealing their position in the darkness.

"You see, they have smartphones, but would you say they are smart? And if not, can the phones they carry be smart?" Ndevui whispered to Elimane.

"Good point. But let's discuss later," Elimane whispered back. A breeze ran through the trees, shaking them gently.

"The lights will shut off soon. The generator goes off the same time every day," said Elimane. "I used to come here to steal airplane food, so I learned all the rhythms of this place. I stopped because it was too much work and the food wasn't worth it."

In a couple of minutes, just as he had predicted, the generator coughed, and the lights closed their watchful eyes.

One of the military men broke the sudden silence. "Sergeant, go fill it up and turn it back on."

"Yes, sir." The officer's footsteps echoed as he ran to get gasoline for the generator.

"You'd think they would learn to attend to it before it goes off," whispered Elimane. "Now watch. He is going to turn on the light on top of the jeep and carelessly look around, then turn it off, light his cigarette, and sit facing away from the field."

Just like clockwork, the officer did exactly as Elimane had foretold.

"Well, so much for being a soldier. He doesn't expect anything to happen, and he doesn't care if it does," said Kpindi.

"Let's go," said Elimane, and the five of them ran with feather-light steps behind the soldiers and all the way to the terminal, which they entered through the holes where luggage was thrown onto a conveyor belt. They walked with their backs pressed against the wall, and when it ended, they crouched until they came to the next wall. In this manner, they followed Elimane across the seating area and down a flight of stairs to a dilapidated waiting lounge.

There, pacing up and down and sideways, was William Handkerchief. He was dressed as nattily as when Elimane had first met him, but today's suit was so shiny that it looked like it might catch fire if he rubbed it too hard against another surface.

"He doesn't need a flashlight wearing that outfit, does he?" whispered Kpindi. "We are going to get caught and shot for sure with this guy. Just don't stand next to him."

Elimane cleared his throat, and William Handkerchief gave a start and wheeled around to face them.

"Sam, I was expecting you to come from this way." Sam was a local term of endearment, like "mate" or "pal," but the others guessed that William Handkerchief used it because he didn't care to use Elimane's real name, should he have a sudden need to terminate their relationship. That worked both ways, though. They did not know his real name either, and did not want to. It was better that way.

"Well, I said we would be here, but not how." Elimane approached and extended his hand.

William Handkerchief stared them up and down with intensity, then nodded, indicating that they would do. From under a row of adjoining metal chairs, he pulled out some airport vests and badges and motioned to them to put them on. For Namsa there was a visitor's badge, as she didn't look believably old enough to be working at the airport, or anywhere else.

"You, the little one. You will go and stand behind that." William Handkerchief pointed at a tall mannequin wearing a hat, trousers, and long-sleeved shirt.

"Don't take your eyes off that door over there," he continued. "If it opens, bang on the mirror here twice and we will hear you. If the light comes on in there, bang once only." William Handkerchief again pointed his long fingers at a door that must have been the office of someone high up, because it was not as neglected as the other office doors. "When you hear us banging, come down and wait in the luggage collection hall."

He turned to the others. "The rest of you, do not speak from now on, just listen and follow orders." His voice was strange and stern. He was no longer the fellow who had fallen into the water, as they had heard the story from Elimane. Even Elimane seemed a bit taken aback by the tone of this man he knew so far only as a small-time criminal.

They left Namsa and went out to the runway. Soon, a medium-size plane came through the clouds in the darkening sky. It made little noise, and it bore no markings. It started to land without the usual preparation of fire trucks, movements from the communication tower, or lights illuminating the part of the runway where it would touch down. Nevertheless, the plane seemed to know exactly where to go. It landed and rolled down the empty airfield, parking at the edge facing the takeoff route.

A phone rang. William Handkerchief pulled a bulky device with a protruding antenna from his pocket. "Proceed. All clear." The airplane rolled a bit farther, then came to a stop by two other aircraft.

As the engine died down, William Handkerchief motioned for Khoudiemata, Elimane, Kpindi, and Ndevui to climb into the back of a truck parked nearby. He drove toward the plane and waited.

The main door of the aircraft opened, revealing two men, one in overalls, the other in a leather jacket, and both, disconcertingly, wearing ski masks. Silently they offloaded several heavy-looking black bags and wooden crates directly onto the truck. The four young people organized them so that everything could fit, and then sat on top of the cargo. They could hear William Handkerchief speaking with one of the men in a language none of them knew. The only word they recognized was "okay." They heard the man getting into the truck with William Handkerchief, and then he drove the truck to the baggage area.

As soon as they arrived, William Handkerchief jumped out. The four of them got out of the truck too, though they stayed close to its side, trying to keep a low profile.

"Call our eyes to come down," he said. Khoudi banged on the

large hollow pillar that went up to where Namsa was waiting. William Handkerchief and the other man headed in the direction of the soldiers who'd been guarding the airport. Surely, they must have heard the plane.

Khoudi got back in the truck and tried to peek into the bag she'd been sitting on, but it was too dark to see anything. She put in her hand and felt what seemed to be a block of bills. She had no idea what currency it might be, but she was certain that not even an idiot would waste the paper to print the local currency and then fly it in. The government was already doing that, with the result that every few months there was a new bill that was higher in value than the previous ones. "How did they get money to print money?" Elimane always asked, and of course as soon as the money was printed, there was a shortage and a false need arose for more. The local currency was like a relative who somehow always has a new problem, no matter how many times you help him, and always needs more money, no matter how much you've sent.

William Handkerchief and his companion returned about ten minutes later with a pickup truck. They waved toward the soldiers, who turned off their spotlight. The little family could not help noticing that William Handkerchief and his companion were not hiding anything. The companion motioned with a circling of his fingers, and the army vehicle immediately began to move. It drove around and around the airfield in circles, just as it had been ordered.

Why was William Handkerchief so comfortable with making it clear to them that he had the soldiers in his pocket? Perhaps it was for the usual reasons—that he assumed they would not care, because they were so damaged by their own experiences as to expect nothing from society. Or that no one would listen to them anyway; they didn't exist, as far as society was concerned.

"Time to work. Use the dollies to load these things from there to here," William Handkerchief ordered, pointing at the truck and the pickup and snapping his fingers. They hurriedly fetched the dollies and went to work transferring the bags and crates. Khoudiemata saw the anxiety on the faces of the others and the signs of fear in their movements. It was subtle, but she knew them well. There was something in the manner of William Handkerchief and his companion that suggested they were ready to take any life to accomplish their task.

William Handkerchief sat on his heels to address Namsa, who had materialized from above. "Hey, little one, go to the main gate and keep watch for a green Land Rover. If any other vehicle arrives, press the red button by the gate. It will signal to us." Why hadn't he sent the soldiers, who were driving around the airfield so unnecessarily? The question was almost visible on Namsa's lips, but she pressed them closed and hurried off.

The green Land Rover arrived just as they were about to finish transferring the load. The driver was in military outfit and had on a ski mask too. He stepped out of the vehicle, left the engine running, and went to the back booth, where he lifted the tarpaulin and dragged out someone in handcuffs. The person's head was covered with a brown burlap sack. The driver pushed him to William Handkerchief's companion, and William Handkerchief threw the driver a black bag—much smaller and lighter than the ones that had been offloaded from the plane. The driver squatted, opened the bag, and started counting the money that was inside.

Whether it was excitement at the cash at hand or the fallible nature of human beings, he took off his mask and spoke while holding a wad of bills, as if weighing its worth. "Let me know anytime you want any more prisoners. Happy Independence Day to you—and to him especially." He pointed to the prisoner.

The man from the plane removed a sidearm from his belt and pointed it at the head of the driver. "Simple instructions. No talking unless asked. Do you have anything more to say?"

The driver laughed hoarsely, even though nothing was funny. William Handkerchief snatched the ski mask and the sack of money from him and emptied half of the money into the mask, then handed it back to the driver, who nervously accepted.

"I will hold on to the rest until we know you can follow instructions." He removed his own sidearm now, a twin of his companion's, and pointed it at the driver, who hurried to his vehicle and drove off fast into the night. They kept their guns trained on the Land Rover until it was completely out of sight.

Was this going to be the fate of the little family as well if they made even a small mistake? They didn't want less money, but more important, they wanted to remain alive. Khoudi reminded herself that they had been selected for the job because they didn't ask questions, they followed instructions, and they were expendable and anonymous, which made them a rare commodity. So there was no reason to get rid of them.

While these thoughts were running through her mind, the prisoner with the sack over his head was being loaded onto the airplane. Khoudi could see his legs twitching with fear. William Handkerchief handed his gun to his partner, who got into the plane and pulled the door closed. The plane turned around and headed for the runway, then flew into the arms of the young night. The military vehicle that had been uselessly circling returned to position, and the soldiers turned the spotlight back on, pretending to guard the airport.

Khoudiemata could hear the relief in the breath of the others. They were less afraid now that the strange man was gone, with his aura of evil and his metal sticks of death. They did not think that

William Handkerchief was going to harm them on his own. Even practically, it seemed a lot for him to handle.

"In the back. And hold on tight. We are done here." William Handkerchief indicated the pickup truck. They climbed in and held on as ordered. He swung around to the main gate, where Namsa was waiting. The vehicle slowed down, and Namsa ran to it and flung herself into the back, where the others pulled her in.

It was Khoudi who noticed that something was off about Namsa. She looked a bit fatter, in a funny way. On closer inspection, Khoudi saw that she was wearing some of the outfit from the mannequin under her own clothes. She wanted to shout at Namsa—was she trying to get them killed?—but then she realized that Namsa knew nothing of what had happened with the guns and the strange man from the plane and the prisoner and the money. There was an innocent smile playing beneath Namsa's serious face, as though this had all been a grand adventure. And perhaps it had been. Why spoil it for her? Khoudiemata confined herself to a warning stare to stay silent and not give anything away.

As soon as the truck went through the main gate, which was somehow unguarded and which William Handkerchief somehow had keys to unlock, he turned off the head- and taillights of the car and drove at full speed through the dark night, not once making a mistake, not even going over bumps or into potholes. The night came at them fast, and at each turn or sudden slowdown, Elimane, Khoudi, Ndevui, and Kpindi anticipated a crash and cringed, the bottoms of their bellies bracing for an impact that never came. Then they'd exhale, only to start holding their breath all over again. Namsa alone was calm, opening her arms and lifting her head so that the breeze pulled back her cheeks.

William Handkerchief made a left off the main road and drove to a jetty, where they offloaded the bags and crates onto a speedboat. He reversed the car into the bushes and tossed a wad of cash to Elimane. Elimane caught the money and counted it. Evidently it was all there.

"Do you want me to change it for you to the local currency?" William Handkerchief asked, and Elimane hesitated to respond, unsure whether the sanction against speaking had been lifted. Finally he said, "Please change only twenty of it for us. I am certain I can get a better rate on the street for the rest."

William Handkerchief laughed. "That is why I like you, Sam. You are always thinking about what is best for you. I will call again soon for another errand. Be as safe as you can be." And with that, he jumped into the speedboat and took off.

The five of them knew how to return to the main road and find their way home, but they sat quietly on the sand for a while, letting out all the breath they had been holding in. It was not that they were shocked by the nature of this errand. This was their life; they witnessed daily all the ways life could be threatened, with guns and otherwise. What they were surprised about was how they had been dragged into William Handkerchief's world. Did he have other people for these kinds of jobs who were not available on this particular night? Were they going to be asked to do similar tasks again? Could they refuse without serious consequences?

Elimane sighed. "Well, I am as surprised as all of you. But then again, none of us are saints."

It was their habit not to discuss troubling things in detail. It diluted their ability to stomach what they must. Instead, each of them searched inside for whatever it was that allowed them distance from thoughts and memories that brought pain to their beings. For Khoudi, it was looking for intrigue in what had happened. Who was the man in the handcuffs, and where was he being taken to? Lacking answers allowed her to create distance from the situation.

She recognized that it was up to her to take the first step to put this disturbing night into the past.

"Namsa, let's find a streetlamp that works so that you can show us your new clothes."

Namsa took Khoudi's hand, and they led the way to the main road, where they turned left toward town. Khoudi didn't count on finding a working streetlamp, but the quest kept them going. They passed holes in the ground that were awaiting posts, and poles next to holes waiting to be erected, then a series of posts with no lights, some with broken lamps, and one that had a bulb whose light rose and then fell, rose and fell, and then stopped for about five minutes before resuming its failed attempts again.

"Perhaps we'll wait for the sunlight to see your clothes," said Khoudi at length.

"I will sleep in them so that tomorrow morning I can easily show you everything." Namsa hummed a playful tune and danced a little dance to it as she went.

When they finally reached the airplane, Khoudi, Elimane, Ndevui, and Kpindi went straight back to drinking and smoking.

"So that William Handkerchief is something. I don't want to ruin my night by thinking about it too much," said Ndevui.

"What happened? Did I miss it all while I was upstairs in the lounge?" Namsa looked at them expectantly, but when they did not answer, she went into the plane and succeeded at inviting sleep.

The others smoked until the ganja was finished, and then they drank some more. They were upset about not only what they had taken part in, but what it stirred up for them as well.

Elimane gave voice to the general sentiment. "I have managed to put some things so far back in my mind, and tonight brought it all up for me."

"We have the money, and we're still here," said Ndevui. "We could try to learn how to live alongside society for a while with the cash we have. Anyway, I don't think William Handkerchief would have killed us. And we need errands that give us this kind of money."

"I agree with you. Every day is a dead day for us, and yet here we are." Kpindi smashed his bottle on the ground, as if in demonstration that action would defy the grip of circumstances. Ndevui let out a ghastly laugh into the night air, attempting to make light of their fear.

"Yes," said Elimane, "but William Handkerchief is more than he lets on. So I am not going to underestimate him anymore. As long as we do as he asks, I think we will make cash and stay safe. Mostly I want to live, however, even if it is only to survive. So let's be careful. And I will be more vigilant with him."

"And you, sister?" Ndevui asked Khoudiemata.

"I don't want to choose between surviving and living." But Khoudi was really thinking about tomorrow's escape from their daily harness. Survival had a way of narrowing one's thinking, even about oneself. She longed to be with those who had the luxury of viewing life differently, if naively.

"So when are we changing the money so that I can have my share?" said Ndevui. "I have plans for it."

The night heaved a breath of cool wind that rustled the nearby trees. A few birds chirped monotonously, silencing the hoot of a distant owl. A new day was waiting to be born.

Khoudiemata stayed outside long after the others had gone inside in search of sleep. She was the only one watching as the sun gradually rose into the sky and began to rearrange the clouds.

6

The day following a holiday was also a holiday in this land of theirs. And now they had money to buy food, so there was no need to go searching for it. There was likely no necessity to stand guard either—who would come near their home, today of all days? But as Khoudi was awake and the others were slumbering, she decided to go stand guard. She told herself it was a good habit, but the truth was, she wanted the time alone to practice how she was going to partake in conversations at dinner later on. She headed for the bushes beyond the clearing and found a place to sit against a small tree with her eyes facing the road.

I have lived in the city for a while now. My family has a home in Aberdeen. Khoudiemata sensed that for her, practicing the art of chitchatting demanded responses that weren't too specific, that didn't give away too much or invite curiosity. She was aiming for an aura of reserve rather than mystery, a quiet thoughtfulness. She hoped she would be able to pull it off. Of course, she faced bigger challenges every day, but this was different.

Don't practice too much, think on your feet, she told herself, making a mental note to adhere to big themes that directed discussion away from personal questions. Acting in agreement, the sun found her under the shrubs and brought her back to the reality of her surroundings. Suddenly she was tired, and hungry. The others were probably up by now. It was time to go find something to eat. Later she would go to her secret haven to prepare for her rendezvous. Preparing conversation was not sufficient. There was the question of how she would dress and carry herself, and she couldn't practice that at home. She needed to be able to lose herself in a parallel world. She stood up and headed back to the plane.

Kpindi caught sight of her. "We were coming to get you so that we can go eat. And we need you to comment on Namsa's fashion show. We've told her her clothes look great, but she says that's not enough. And we don't know what that means."

The boys were plainly holding back laughter to spare Namsa's feelings, and they turned to Khoudi with pleading faces that asked her to remedy the situation.

"Ah, you are back," said Namsa when she saw Khoudi. Namsa was standing at the entrance to the plane, wearing black pants and a short red skirt over it, and on top, an undershirt with an unbuttoned man's long-sleeved shirt over it, and a beanie that covered her ears.

"You are beautiful," Khoudi called to her, and Namsa beamed. "You feel good in them?"

"Yes, and they smell new too." Namsa came down the steps proudly, with the aplomb of a model on a fashion runway.

The truth was, Khoudi felt terrible about how badly dressed Namsa was. She wore boys' clothes as Khoudi did, but unlike Khoudi, she had no sense of what colors matched. She looked like a worse version of the Khoudi that Khoudi was just learning to undo.

She will be safe this way, Khoudi told herself. What she really wanted was to take off her own beanie and show Namsa her beautiful new hair, but she didn't, because what she wanted even more was for this fragile new part of her to remain her secret for a while longer.

"So where are we going for food?" Khoudi asked.

Namsa laughed. "Where we always go when we have money. Mama Fofanah's." The rest of them didn't even bother to acknowledge her question.

Khoudi wanted to tell them that with the money they had, they could go eat anywhere if only they dressed differently, so that the money was believably theirs. But their worn-out and ill-fitting clothes, no matter how clean, would raise suspicions. Even Elimane's suit jacket had lost its elegance; its saving grace was the small book inevitably sticking its head from one of the pockets. It was interesting to Khoudi that what you wore had a way of absolving you from suspicion. In this country, many thieves and evil men walked around freely in fancy suits and drove expensive cars, as if those were a measure of their integrity.

They left the arms of the bushes with their usual caution, walking apart out of habit. There were very few people on the road, mostly young girls and boys carrying cooked food to some household or other. It idly crossed Khoudi's mind that they could just hijack one of those succulent-smelling stews and save themselves both the walk and the money.

In town, the usual harried feeling in the streets had given way to a liveliness that smiled through everyone. Speakers blaring different kinds of music competed to conquer the atmosphere, and there were gatherings on every other veranda, in front of shops, under trees, wherever there was shade. People wore their best outfits, their skin so recently coated with Vaseline that anyone who passed them re-flexively checked their own skin for dryness.

Mama Fofanah's cookery bar stood a few footsteps from the beach. Its bamboo roof was held up by four tree trunks rooted in the earth. A low wall of concrete bricks rose to waist level, and benches and tables were arrayed inside in rows, like a classroom. Mama Fofanah stood behind a simple wooden counter, with her eyes on every-thing. There was a fridge that looked like an iron vault, and an open cooking area with big pots, firestones, firewood, and a mortar and pes-tle. It was a place that had never tried to keep up with the times, so going there had the appeal of visiting one's grandparents. And that brought all sorts of people in.

There were about ten customers seated when they arrived, some of the men in suits even shinier than the one William Handkerchief had sported; it must be the new style. A group of scruffy-looking young men—scruffier even than the little family—smelled of the sea. They must be fishermen.

"Good day, Mama Fofanah," called Khoudiemata as she entered. She paused at the stoop to wash her hands in the bowl of soapy water there, then, holding her money in the palm of her hand, took a seat at a table just behind the counter where Mama Fofanah was standing. That was the custom here: You had to show that you could pay be-fore you were served. Kpindi followed, and then Namsa, Ndevui, and Elimane, each of them pausing to wash their hands and greet Mama Fofanah the same way before going to sit at separate tables.

"Good day, child, and welcome." Mama Fofanah greeted each of them in turn. But when she got to Namsa, she cupped the girl's cheeks in her shiny, warm hands and poured love into the child's face. This was Namsa's favorite part of coming here and the reason she always chose Mama Fofanah's when they had money to pay to eat.

"What is available today?" asked Khoudi.

"Chicken stew, jollof rice, okra stew with dried fish and beans." Mama Fofanah pointed in turn to the pots simmering on the coals. One after the other, the five of them came to the counter, made their choices, and paid. Mama Fofanah reached to the money sack at the side of her wrapper for change. Bills she kept in the fridge, for fear of fire, and she kept the fridge locked with a key she wore around her waist.

They sat down and waited for the food, their appetites awakened by the good smells around them. A girl brought a tray of chicken stew and jollof rice and set it on the table before Elimane. She left and then reemerged with another tray, of okra stew and more rice. She went away again and brought a cup filled with spoons that she set on the table next to the trays of food. The little family were puzzled. Usually the food here was served in individual plastic bowls, and the five of them would look at one another's bowls and harass the server to add more of this or that, claiming that one portion was bigger than another.

"It is for all of you." Mama Fofanah circled the group with her finger, starting with Namsa, then circled the trays of food. She knew they were a group, and somehow, today of all days, she wanted them to eat together, like a real family. With Mama Fofanah's eyes cutting the strings of their reluctance, they found themselves quietly taking their seats around the trays of food. It was almost painful to begin, to dip a hand into this delicious food, with its irresistible aromas. To do so was to awaken memory, to risk waking up the past.

"Hello, Mama. Multiparty for me as usual." The voice ordering a some-of-everything plate was startlingly familiar. The five of them eyed one another without looking up, then, on the same impulse, each placed a finger over the food. Namsa was slowest, which meant that it would be her task to confirm their assumption. She left the table and went to the stoop, pretending to wash her hands again. She returned with the answer: a nodding yes. It was William Handkerchief. The group sighed. They didn't want to see him today of all days, and especially not while they were together like this. Yet the place was too small to ignore his presence. At least, they thought, if they listened, they might learn his real name.

"Eh, my son, how are you? My place is never backwards for you even when you climb higher in life," Mama Fofanah joked. The little family gave up the hope of finding out William Handkerchief's name. He was not Mama Fofanah's son, of course. Elders like her didn't call younger people by their names—they were all sons, daughters, or just children, regardless of who they were or what they had done. Your given name came up only when you had done something worthy of serious reproach.

William Handkerchief was wearing a tight white shirt that was struggling to accommodate his belly. He had on white shorts, white socks, white sneakers, and a white headband, and he was carrying a brand-new tennis racket that still had a price tag hanging from it. He must be up to something sinister, the group thought. They were so preoccupied with interpreting his presence that the painful intimacy of eating together in public was forgotten. They ate quietly, enjoying their food but staying alert. It was up to William Handkerchief to make it clear whether they could show that they knew him or not.

He didn't even look their way. He ate with gusto, laughing with Mama Fofanah. In fact, he ate a lot for someone getting ready for a tennis match, or even returning from one. The little family couldn't remember seeing a tennis court nearby. Perhaps there was one on someone's private property, but they had poked around most of the fancy houses in town when the owners were away, and they'd never seen one.

When William Handkerchief had finished eating, a car pulled up outside, and as abruptly as he had arrived, he departed.

Elimane's phone vibrated. He showed the others the text. *Good to see you and your friends. I will be in touch Sam.*

They departed one at a time, trying to shake off the slight pall that William Handkerchief's presence had put on this favorite place. They regrouped outside, but loosely, unable to shake off the habit of pretending that they weren't together. It was early for them to go their separate ways.

As usual, Namsa wanted to go listen to Shadrach the Messiah. Khoudiemata agreed, thinking that it would give her ideas on what to talk about that evening. Ndevui and Kpindi decided to go too. "Elimane, are you coming?" Ndevui asked. "Perhaps you will be able to engage him in conversation. It will be like two dictionaries talking to each other."

Kpindi led the way, laughing, and Elimane followed, a bit reluctantly. He preferred not to fall into conversation with Shadrach the Messiah. He didn't want such an incident to remind him of his family, or to reveal more of his background to the others than he chose to share. However, he was certain that he was going to enjoy listening to this madman of intelligence, as he thought of Shadrach.

They made their way to the beach without haste, befitting the nature of that day. Shadrach was not by the kiosk, however. They continued along the beach until they arrived at the docks where private boats brought those who could afford such conveyances across the water to catch a flight. A crowd had gathered there. The five of them squeezed into the throng of people to see what was going on.

A formation of uniformed and armed men was waiting at the jetty. They seemed to be searching each boat that arrived, for something or someone in particular. They had just finished checking one boat when another came into view. It slowed down as it approached the narrow dock, then all of a sudden veered toward another landing at the sandy beach nearby. A fellow in a well-cut suit and new black dress shoes jumped out, briefcase in hand, and made his way onto the beach with so much agility it almost looked as if he was walking on the water. Before the uniformed men could cut him off, he hopped into a jeep that had just pulled onto the sand and it sped off. The uniformed men jumped into their own vehicles and took off in pursuit.

The crowd began to clap. People had recognized the escapee as the former minister of finance and mayor of the city. Everyone knew he was under investigation for embezzlement, but until now, the authorities had never been able to amass enough evidence to arrest him. The truth was, such corruption was so common that it rarely resulted in arrests. But—as someone in the crowd commented—apparently this man's greed had gone too far, so far that others in power wanted him out of their circle. As the crowd looked on in amazement, the jeep circled back by the beach, and the fellow in question jumped out while it was moving and made a run for the water, seemingly attempting to reboard his boat and get away. But this time the uniformed men caught him and hauled him off.

The crowd, having expected a better show, grumbled with disappointment. But some other type of entertainment was never long in coming along the beach.

Khoudiemata made her way through the onlookers until she was situated just behind Namsa. She whispered, "Follow Ndevui when he leaves for his football match, and tell me if he has improved since the last time we saw him play together." This was not only an instruction; it was also a goodbye. Khoudi knew that Namsa would understand that, and that the others would be aware of her exiting toward the main road even though they did not turn around. Behind her, she heard the crowd roaring with new laughter.

As soon as she reached 96 Degrees, Khoudiemata felt her body relax. She stripped to her underwear, raised her face to the sun, and opened her arms as if she was preparing to be embraced by the sky. She inhaled and exhaled, feeling the warm ocean breeze and the sun against her skin. The soft rhythm of the water against the rocks lulled her for a bit.

She went to retrieve the items she had corrupted after her visit with the beautiful people. They were where she had hidden them, dry and scented with the perfumes of their previous owners. Khoudi held up each item in turn to admire it, these new belongings that she would use to access a world that pretended to be unaware of her existence. She laid them out on the sand and went into the water. It hadn't been that long since she had bathed last, but she was getting used to being cleaner. Besides, she needed to wash off the dirty feeling that the jobs they had done for William Handkerchief had left. That was what really needed washing away.

The sun had warmed the water, and Khoudi lingered in it even after she had washed her body and her underwear and had laid it out to dry. The low sky seemed to glisten with perspiration as it hovered over the calm sea, nearly merging with it. From this distance, the boats looked painted on. Khoudi tried covering each of them in turn with her hand, and then removing it after some minutes to see if the boat had moved. Then she remembered her mission, and checked to see if her underwear had dried enough to be worn.

Climbing out of the water, she glanced at her shadow on the sand. With the sun nearly straight overhead, her figure was etched sharply there, even her cheekbones captured. Watching her shadow, she touched her face, then traced her lips, neck and collarbone, and breasts, along her belly and down to her legs, which were longer and smoother than she had expected. It was a completely new experience, exploring her body instead of constantly struggling in it.

She put her underwear back on, then stood above her clothes spread out on the sand, held open by rocks. She paced, thinking about which outfit to wear. She settled on the yellow V-neck top with woven patterns. It held her figure nicely, and her necklace fell right where the neckline split, and each time she breathed in and out, she saw it rise and fall sensually there. Pleased, she pulled on the black jeans, discovering that they were tighter than any trousers she had ever worn. She was surprised at how closely and comfortably they fit her buttocks, and how aware she was of the shape they made. She tried on the sandals with the straps that buckled. They fit well enough, and she loved how her shiny toenails showed in them, though she realized that walking in them would require getting used to. She practiced on the sand, making random chitchat with herself as she walked.

She took one of the new black handbags, which contained sunglasses, lipsticks, a makeup case, and other items she didn't know what to do with. But they made the bag feel full, so that it sat comfortably on her shoulder. She transferred the money from her raffia bag, along with her knife and a tattered newspaper clipping she always carried with her, a relic of a previous life. She never unfolded it but could not throw it away. She found a small inner pocket for it, a new home. Then she stashed all the rest of her belongings in the raf-fia bag and hid it in the usual place.

Khoudi had observed that many of the girls of the sort she would be joining had glossy lips, so she retrieved the makeup kit from the handbag and riffled through it until she found a little pot of colorless gloss. It felt funny on her lips, and she had to restrain herself from licking them, especially as it smelled like some kind of ripe fruit. There were all sorts of other sticks and tubes in the kit, but she let them be.

It took quite some time for Khoudi to work up the courage to depart 96 Degrees. She paced back and forth, watching her undulat-ing shadow on the sand. She felt beautiful, but she also felt exposed, in a way that was new and uncomfortable. Dressed this way, she knew she would draw attention, and that worried her. She had re-moved the armor of invisibility that allowed her to move through the world as she chose. But the desire to pursue this new direction that responded to the changes occurring in her was more compelling. At last she made her way back up to the road, careful on the stones in her new sandals.

She paused behind some bushes, in view of the road, watching as people passed, going about their day with an aura of persistence in the face of defeat. The contradiction was familiar to her, from that other life she had hidden away at 96 Degrees. Then she stepped out onto the road. Soon enough, cars were honking at her. Men older than her grandfathers would be—if they were alive—called from their cars, offering to take her wherever she was going. She was not surprised, having witnessed this entitlement that boys and men had, to feast their eyes on women and intrude on their existence with calls and stares, but the immediate surge of attention was over-whelming, nevertheless.

A cluster of young women and girls standing nearby were watching her as well, swaying their bodies and pouting. "Useless girl," one of them said, loud enough for her to hear as she passed by. "She doesn't even know what to do. How is she going to get herself a sugar daddy?" Khoudi eyed them up and down, banging her fist in her palm to signal what she would do to them if she did not have something more important to do.

She knew all about sugar daddies, as it happened. A woman she had stayed with at one point had several of them. One of them had locked Khoudi inside his room when the woman sent her to deliver his food. He had said, "I am going to make a woman out of you." She had found his words strange: How could a man make a woman out of a girl, even with violence? What he hadn't expected was the knife Khoudi carried. It had prevented him from doing more than removing her clothes and had done enough damage to send him to the hospital and, she'd hoped, to make it difficult for him to force himself upon another girl or woman again. But the woman, her "auntie," had not believed her, and had accused her of forcing herself on the sugar daddy instead.

It had been a long time since Khoudi had thought about this incident, and how she had been forced to run away to this distant part of the city where she was certain no one would recognize her. That was the last time she had lived with a family. Until she had joined Elimane and the others.

Another car honked at Khoudiemata, and she had the urge to shout at the man inside it, to make him aware of the pain he and all the others like him revived in her. She knew she wasn't the only girl for whom this was true.

She stuck out her hand and hailed the first taxi that came by. It was almost full, and most of the passengers were men, but a spot remained in the backseat. She was about to squeeze in when she caught the look on the face of her would-be seatmate, his eyes tearing into her body with a repugnant longing.

She slammed the door and stood back. "I will wait for another taxi."

The driver shouted at her, "Don't destroy my door, ah!" and Khoudi sent the vehicle off with a departing kick.

This time, she waited until she saw an empty taxi to stick out her hand.

The driver had a youthful face and an inviting smile, a genuine-looking smile. He waited patiently as Khoudi got into the back. She sat quietly for a moment, thinking—there was something familiar about the man that she could not place. He did not hurry her, and when other passengers approached, he waved them off.

"Is everything all right, little sister?" he asked gently. When she saw his face in the rearview mirror, Khoudi decided that he wasn't as young as he had first appeared. He put the car in gear and began driving slowly, even though Khoudi hadn't yet mentioned her destination.

"Don't worry, wherever you are going, you need a fresh breeze on your face before you get there. So I will take the beach road if you don't mind." He glanced back at her in the mirror, trying to catch a response. Then he turned up the music a bit. He drove to the beach, passing other potential passengers along the way, and pulled over next to a bar. He turned off the engine and got out.

"I will be back. I am going to get some water there." He pointed at the bar. It was early to go to Noire Point anyway, and it was good to be back at the beach, Khoudi thought. She leaned her head out the window, allowing the breeze to soothe her face.

Before long, the wind brought her the roar of a crowd. She knew it must be coming from the red gravel field nearby, where Ndevui was playing football. She pictured him dribbling a ball past one, two, three, four, five! players—counted in elation by the crowd as he took the ball to the goal and scored for a fourth time. She imagined him carried around by his teammates, his face shining with a joy that he never allowed to surface otherwise.

"Barefoot Omam-Biyik, *wow!*" she heard someone exclaim, and looked up to see a group of youngsters running by, from the direction of the gravel field. I bet they are talking about my brother, Khoudi thought. She wanted to ask them, but of course, how would they know who her brother was?

The taxi man returned just as Khoudi had decided that he wasn't coming back. He held a bottle of cold water toward her.

"No charge," he said. "These days everyone expects an ambush for the smallest favor." Khoudi believed him but refused the bottle, nevertheless.

"Ah, no worries. Men are horrible, generally speaking, and the rest of us take the blame for the majority. And the majority think the rest of us are weak!" He got back in the car. "So now I'll start your fare. Tell me where you want to go, miss." He turned in his seat to look at her.

"Noire Point."

"She speaks! I was beginning to think you never would. But you have a determined face, one that says, 'I am always going to do what I want.' I have a younger sister with a face like that." He turned back to look at the road. "Okay, I am talking way too much. Let's go to Noire Point."

Gradually, the taxi made its way away from the beach and up into the hills, on a winding road that took Khoudi higher than she had ever been. The houses up here were different from the neighborhoods she knew too. Down there, they were mostly small and crowded close together, and they often looked wounded or deformed, with parts of their roofs missing, their walls collapsing, septic tanks overflowing. Here, the houses were bigger and more elaborate, with more space in between. Everything about them looked manicured— they were freshly painted, and even the gates looked polished, as if no dust existed in this land of theirs. Every so often, the taxi passed a structure made of scraps of zinc or sticks, with a torn tarp for a roof, like a reminder that those who had nothing continued to exist among those who had it all. The city was like that; even the wealthy had to drive on broken roads through reminders of desperation to arrive at their mansions.

"This is how the others live, eh?" said the driver. "Whenever I come around here, it makes me feel bad. It really shows me how far down on the other end of things I am." He fell silent again as the engine labored up a hill, as if a poor man's car was reluctant to enter here.

Until this point, the way had been clear, but now he turned off the winding road, then turned again. Khoudi tried to pay attention to the route, in case she needed her feet to get herself back down later, but she could not resist answering.

"You are right. I wonder, though, how the people who own these houses got this kind of cash. After all, every rich person in a country where the overwhelming majority of people are desperately poor is an automatic suspect. And if they are politicians, they are almost certainly stealing. Even the foreigners who come here do so for money, easy money, and lots of it. Of course, they love to express their love for this 'beautiful country.' It is a way to remain connected to the money, this expression of love. I mean, who loves dysfunctionality?"

The taxi man laughed. "Two kinds of people love dysfunctionality. Those who benefit from it and can go elsewhere from time to time to take a break. And those who have gotten used to it, because they know nothing else." They went over a speed bump, then accelerated again as the road flattened, the tires spinning faster now that they were atop the hill.

"You sure you are just a taxi driver?" Khoudi smiled at him for the first time.

He pulled up before an imposing gate and stopped.

"We are here. Do you want me to go inside, or shall I drop you out here?" the driver asked, his eyes on the high, glossy dark metal gate with its intricate design of a man and a woman dancing. The gate spanned a driveway wide enough to accommodate four vehicles at once. Khoudiemata's eyes ran along the concrete wall next to it, which was a sparkling white; it was obviously painted often. The faint sound of music reached them from scenes beyond their view. The driver whistled in awe, bringing Khoudiemata back to his question.

"Out here is fine." The taxi man rushed around to open the door for her, but she was already out. Khoudi knew she looked the part of someone who was used to being attended to in such a manner, but she felt strange about having that sort of attention. She regretted not having settled on the fare in advance. She had wanted to get off the road so badly that she had forgotten. Now the taxi man had the upper hand.

She offered first, bracing herself for an argument. "I'll give you fifteen thousand."

"Twenty thousand, miss. That is the price for coming up here." The driver looked around, indicating all the wealth.

Khoudi extended a ten thousand note and a five thousand. "So you charge me more because I am coming to a nicer part of town."

He did not take the proffered bills. "No, I am charging you that way because if my car breaks down here, there is no one to help. Also, I am not going to get a return fare out of here. And standing here reminds me how much more money I have yet to make today."

Khoudi relaxed, acknowledging the merit of his argument and the appearance of the situation—for once, she did not look like a woman with no money. She reached into her bag and retrieved another five thousand note. The driver laughed and took the cash.

"I will give you my number in case you need me to come pick you up." He began to recite it to her, but stopped, his face puzzled, when he realized that Khoudi was not pulling out her phone to take note of the number.

"Let me write it down for you." He got back in his car for a moment and returned with a piece of paper on which he had written three different telephone numbers.

"And you say you are poor," Khoudiemata joked, taking the paper from him.

"Thanks to the Chinese, I can afford a phone that holds three SIM cards. This way, wherever there is a network, it is bound to be one of my SIM cards. Even a poor man must have a choice somehow."

Khoudiemata looked at the paper again. *Manga Sewa, your humble and reliable taxi man,* he had written.

"Manga Sewa, the defiant king of the Northern Province!" Khoudiemata exclaimed, with more excitement than she'd intended. But it was not often that someone said something that triggered a good memory from her past. Her mother used to tell her stories of remarkable people—stories that weren't necessarily written about in history books. Manga Sewa was one of those who had fought to have a say in how his land was used by the foreigners who came from across the seas.

"Ah, so you know your history!" said this latter-day Manga Sewa. "Well, that will earn you an excellent discount on your next trip!" And with that he got back into the car and drove off, leaving Khoudiemata with a wave and a smile.

The sun was still high above the horizon, and Khoudi knew she had plenty of time before dinner. Besides, she wasn't quite ready to brave Noire Point yet. But this part of the city was not made for strolling, and she knew that a pedestrian would look suspicious. She needed a destination.

She remembered that not far down the road, the taxi had passed a supermarket. She set out in that direction. The going was awkward, as she was the only one on the road, and the road was narrow. Cars didn't pass frequently, but when they did, they had tinted windows, so even though they were almost close enough to touch, she could not see who was in them. She encountered only two other walkers, an older woman and man who were plainly returning from the market down below, carrying baskets laden with produce, not packaged supermarket goods. Their demeanor was familiar to Khoudi, and she reciprocated their unspoken acknowledgment in this oasis of wealth. She guessed that they worked in one of the huge mansions nearby.

At the supermarket, Khoudi thought about buying a phone, but up here, the cheapest was more than she could afford. Even if she'd had the money, she couldn't bring herself to pay for what she knew she could get at half the price, by bargaining the price down—an exchange that took place in a friendly transaction and a cordial parting, no matter how vociferously the parties haggled. In this quiet, sterilized environment, where you had to speak lower than your natural voice, the price was marked on the phones, and she knew there could be no discussion about that.

To avoid looking more suspicious than she already felt, she decided she had to buy something—another unfamiliar custom. Normally, she went to the market to see what was available and to memorize what things cost, so that when she had money, she knew how to bargain. There was no need to buy until you were ready. Here, she tiptoed along the air-conditioned aisles, lined with many foods that she had never laid eyes on and wouldn't even know what to do with. After a few minutes, she was aware that one of the staff was quietly following her. She looked for the most common foreign foods, a can of Coca-Cola and some chips. They were also the least expensive items, and the ones she was certain her stomach wouldn't disagree with. At the register, the proprietor, an older Lebanese man, examined her money suspiciously, his glances reminding her that she wasn't behaving like the store's normal customer. Why was it necessary that he made her feel out of place?

Outside, she sat on a bench facing the parking lot and ate the chips slowly, her appetite diminished by her treatment inside. She didn't feel welcome out here either. The stares followed her through the window, insinuating that she was up to nothing good. She had planned to dawdle there awhile, but instead she headed back up the hill, sipping her Coca-Cola. She had stolen a look at the proprietor's watch, and she knew she had about an hour to kill before her dinner. She decided she would spend it getting a look inside Noire Point, though she planned to stay far from the dining area so that none of the beautiful people would be aware of her early arrival and think her overeager.

Nervously, she waited at the side gate for someone to notice her and grant her entry. Each time a car pulled up, it honked twice and the big metal gate with the dancing woman carved on it swung inward. But the guards on the other side took no notice of her as they ushered the cars inside and the metal gate returned the carved woman to her dancing partner. While Khoudi waited, she occupied herself by imagining what Kpindi might be up to. She decided that he too had joined a party, on a veranda not far from Mama Fofanah's. His entry ticket was a case of beer he'd corrupted from a few houses away, where a private celebration was unfolding. Like Khoudi on the beach, he had pulled off this feat by pretending to be one of the help. Such is life, Khoudi reflected. It always had sweet words for some, and if you were cunning and kept your wits about you, you could taste some of those sweet words too.

And what might Elimane be up to? Khoudi could not bring as clear a picture of him into focus in her imagination, but she knew it had to do with reading.

She was not wrong. As it happened, Elimane was at that very minute inside an old building in the center of the city. He sat on a rickety wooden chair behind an ancient wooden desk as the sun fell lower in the sky and the light pouring in through the broken rafters diminished. Around him, floor to ceiling, were stacks of newspapers, crumbling with age. They weren't arranged in any particular order, but Elimane liked to come here and randomly pull them out to read. He'd found some that dated as far back as the 1950s. The place was not guarded like the banks or the statehouse. No one expected anyone to steal knowledge, even though knowledge could sometimes cost you your life, as Elimane well knew from his own past. But once you ceased to exist, he also knew, knowledge could give you life.

Right now, he was reading an article headlined "Reversing into the Future." A vein pulsed in his forehead as he read, concentrating so deeply that his ears were deaf to the sounds of the city surrounding him. He used to sit like this with his father, he remembered, the two of them reading together for hours, smiling at each other from time to time. Only afterward would they discuss what they each had learned.

After standing at the gate of Noire Point for some time, as one car after another pulled through the gates, Khoudiemata screwed up her courage and called out to one of the guards on the other side. He did not seem to see her at first, but out of habit, he pressed a button that commenced the opening of the gate. Then he took in her unusual mode of arrival and halted the opening abruptly. The gate swung back into place, and at first Khoudiemata thought he had closed the door in her face. She began to weigh her next move, but then a smaller gate opened within the frame of the larger one, like an inner pocket.

"Welcome, miss." The guard's suspicion showed on his face.

"Thank you." Khoudiemata nodded. She did not want to say anything that would further reveal her to be an outsider to this place, to this way of living, so near-silence and gestures seemed the safest route. Trying not to make it obvious, her eyes searched for the way inside. She saw a cobbled stone pathway lined with flowerpots that led to a heavy wooden door. It looked like an entrance, she thought, and she made her way to it confidently, passing by rows of gleaming, neatly parked cars.

A fellow around Elimane's age opened the door for her and bid her welcome in a respectful tone. Intricate carvings, paintings, and photographs by contemporary African artists lined the short hallway, which opened onto a lounge area strewn with colorful throw pillows and a bar on either side. Walkways near both bars led to a veranda lined with stools and benches. Beyond, to the left, was the dining room, with elegant tables and chairs of polished brown wood. Every touch of the place was a feast for the eyes—and there were many eyes, people of all ages who sat about in their best outfits, drinking, chatting, laughing, looking at the vast early-evening sky. They seemed content, as if they were in on a beautiful, eternal secret. It wasn't crowded at this hour, and the space, though big, felt intimate. A few people milled about, not yet absorbed into the calm of the place. Perhaps those were the newest arrivals. There was soft music, a tune Khoudi remembered from childhood. She found herself humming along with it as she made her way across the room to the veranda, this small familiarity calming her nerves.

From the veranda, the view was stupendous: the mountains and in the distance the ocean, where the sun was setting, its glow painting the sky with spectacular colors. Up here the air was cooler, she noted. She found a place to sit behind a pillar, where she wouldn't be easily noticed by whoever entered the dining area, but where she could easily see them.

Watching the entrance, she noticed something funny and strange. Young men and women would come in, pose at one of the tables or by the bar, or out on the veranda looking at the view, take photos of themselves, and then depart. The entire exercise seemed designed to give the impression that they had spent a glorious time at Noire Point rather than for them to actually have one. A few couples even posed for a series of such photos; the woman would go to the bathroom and change into another outfit and return to take another set of photos at the same locations, pretending to be doing different things, smiling wildly the whole time. This process would repeat itself through several outfit changes before the couples left, and was abetted by the purchase of a small bottle of water so that they would have something to pretend to drink in the photos. There were even people taking selfies of selfie-takers. Khoudi found the self-obsession hilarious, but there was something off-putting about it as well.

"Will you be dining with us this evening?" A polite young fellow presented Khoudi with a menu. She glanced down at the long list of food and drinks, which reminded her that she was a long way from Mama Fofanah's place.

"Yes, I will be dining here tonight with some friends," she said, with as much self-possession as she could muster. "I am early, though, so I will get a Star beer and some cacahuète if you have some." She had memorized that order from listening to people at restaurants by the beach.

"Yes, of course." The waiter took a pen and pad from the side pocket of his green-and-yellow cotton shirt, the same uniform all the staff wore. Khoudi was mystified that he needed to write down such a simple order. Was he worried he would forget it before he got back to the kitchen? He reached to retrieve the menu.

"I will keep it to look at for later," Khoudi said. Her confidence was growing, she noticed with pleasure.

Almost as soon as he had left, he returned. Another difference— in the places she knew, you had to shout at the server to bring you your drink before you grew old and no longer needed the joy you had wanted from it. Another difference—the server didn't ask Khoudi to pay when he set down her drink and snack. She tried to eat the cacahuète, which were nicely roasted, the little nuts whole and well browned, as delicately as possible, and took small sips of the beer instead of gulping it. Then she thought to herself that a real mark of confidence was to do as she wanted, as she had always done. She took a handful of the nuts and a hefty swig of the beer, confident that this time she had enough money to pay for her own drinks, even if they were more expensive here.

She finished the beer and ordered another, then studied the menu for a while, slouching in her chair. What should she eat for the dinner with the beautiful people? She didn't recognize any of the dishes on the menu. She flagged down the waiter again.

"Are there any dishes on this menu that you and I grew up eating?" she asked the waiter. "You know, from here?" She flipped the menu around so that it faced him.

"Ah, those dishes are on the native menu," he said. "You have to ask for it."

Khoudi persisted. "I certainly will later. But why wouldn't they be included here?"

The waiter looked confused by her question, not, as Khoudi was, by the fact that a place called Noire Point had no food that corresponded to its name. Finally, he resorted to the stock phrase by which people accept what they believe will not change and move on. "That is just how it is here, miss."

She wondered what the beautiful people thought of the absence of local foods on the menu, or whether they thought of it at all. Would such a question suffice for chitchat? It was certainly a conversation starter, even a debate starter. She continued reading the menu, just to pass the time, having a good laugh to herself at *Succulent simmering cage-free chicken with a hint of black man's pepper*, for example. She really had to meet the house poet! Big of him to grant the black man some pepper of his own to go with that cage-free chicken . . . If you talked this way about food where she came from, people would come just to listen and laugh, thinking it was a comedy show. Food was either good or wasn't, simple as that.

Thoughts of her little family sprang into her mind, unbidden, as she tried to hold back the laughter building within her. Elimane would have loved entering into this banter about the menu, the public one versus the hidden one. Ndevui and Kpindi would have made jokes about everything in the place, and quite possibly Ndevui would have jumped into the selfies uninvited. Namsa would have gone about the place vocally admiring the setup and asking questions about it of Khoudiemata and Elimane.

Khoudiemata didn't want to be thinking about them right now. She called the waiter over, wanting to engage him in discussing the beverage options, but he didn't stay long enough this time to allow her to distract herself. Instead she turned her attention back to observing what ridiculousness passed as sophistication in this new way of life she was tasting. She was just watching someone take a selfie at the entrance to the bathroom when she sensed someone blocking the remaining rays of the sun on her skin. She looked up to meet the eyes of a forcefully smiling man full of self-importance.

"Come. Join me at the bar," he said, extending his hand. He was the sort who was used to getting what he wanted—it was written on his face and in his every gesture, especially toward those he thought were beneath him.

Khoudiemata pushed his hand back, gently but with emphasis, so he knew not to try again.

"Let me buy you a drink," he insisted.

"Okay," she said. "Please have it sent over here. Thank you. You seem to be a gentleman." She forced a smile that said, *Leave me alone now.*

"Your drink will taste better if you sit with me." He reached for her hand again, and this time she escaped his grasp by removing her hand from the surface of the table. Broken as her life was, she had never been able to tolerate the company of such men, not even for as long as it took to down a free drink.

"Thank you again, but I chose to sit here for a reason," she said, this time without any kindness in her voice. But he seemed not to hear her. He pulled up a chair and sat next to her, forcing her to sit up to attend to him.

"Would you like to be my special friend?" he said, smiling in anticipation of the response he was used to getting.

"No. I am not in need of a special friend." Khoudiemata turned her body away, but not before catching the man's look of surprise and displeasure at her audacity.

"Then what are you doing, sitting here by yourself and enticing men like me?" He raised his voice for all the room to hear. He walked away but turned back to look at her, as if expecting her to change her attitude.

A girl couldn't sit by herself? Khoudiemata was honestly a bit confused and dismayed by this world she was entering. Evidently, the attitude of most men toward women didn't change simply because they were richer or educated. She watched as the man began chatting up another girl at the bar.

By the clock over the bar, it was a few minutes past eight when the beautiful people started to arrive. Khoudi heard a group of three young women she hadn't met before say that they were there for Mahawa's dinner reservation. They were done to the nines, wearing cocktail dresses, heels, and lots of makeup that made them look unnaturally pale. The waiter showed them to a huge table set with glasses and glasses and silverware and silverware. Khoudi couldn't imagine what they could possibly do with so many implements. As soon as the girls sat down, some new selfie-takers came and joined them, taking photos of themselves sitting at the table, with open arms or even holding empty glasses until the waiters came by and told them it was a reserved table.

Ophelia arrived next. To Khoudi's relief, she was dressed much as Khoudi was, casually and smartly, and not overly made up. She nodded hello to the other women, with a smile that to Khoudi's eyes seemed forced, then took a seat at the end of the long table, far enough that the others would have to strain their voices to talk to her. She immediately began fiddling with her phone, making it unmistakably clear that she didn't want to engage with them at all. Was this how the beautiful people were going to treat her? Khoudi wondered. Was it only Mahawa who welcomed her? And was even her interest genuine?

Khoudi's excitement diluted these concerns as she watched more and more of the party arrive: Bendu, James, Andrew, and Frederick Cardew-Boston, and then Mahawa herself. Each time a new person came to the table, everyone stood up and kissed them on the cheeks. I will have to do that too, Khoudiemata thought. She preferred hand-shakes, which allowed you to look in a person's face. The eyes, in her experience, usually gave away a lot more than any other part of the body.

She decided to wait for a few more minutes, watching. They had ordered bottles of wine, red and white, and were holding the glasses in ways Khoudi had seen in movies. She called the waiter over and paid for her beers, then made her way to Mahawa's table, with an air of having only just arrived at Noire Point.

"Khoudiemata, welcome! You know most of us." Mahawa stood

up to hug Khoudi and kiss her on this cheek and that. Khoudi couldn't tell whether her enthusiasm was genuine. The rest of them didn't show much excitement, it seemed to her. She dismissed her worries, telling herself that she had simply grown too suspicious. Her hostess was enthused, she reminded herself, and that should be sufficient for tonight.

"Beautiful outfit," said Mahawa. "Some eyes aren't going to stay off you, my dear. You should show that body more often. Someone has already been asking about you since our time at the beach." She winked in the direction of the young men. Khoudiemata had a sudden rush of fear that Mahawa or one of the others would recognize her bag, or her clothes. It was a small circle of young people to whom life was so good, after all, and their families tended to know one another. It seemed unlikely, but she always tried to stay a step ahead of what might be possible.

She went around the table to kiss everyone, starting with the pale-faced girls who scrupulously avoided letting their cheeks touch skin but made unnecessarily loud smacking sounds with their lips. She let her smile open up as she approached Ophelia, Bendu, James, Andrew, and Frederick Cardew-Boston, who kissed Khoudi's cheeks longer than the others but avoided looking her directly in the eyes when they pulled away. It reminded Khoudi of how Elimane had begun to avoid her gaze lately. What was the matter with these young men?

Mahawa seated Khoudiemata between herself and Frederick Cardew-Boston, and everyone settled in with shuffling of chairs and small talk and laughter. Andrew and James went to the bar and returned with additional drinks in hand and a newspaper. Some story caught their attention and they hunched over the paper, their faces gradually becoming veiled with disbelief. Mahawa, annoyed at having distractions from her party, demanded to know what they were reading, but they were too intent to answer, so she plucked the paper from them and scanned the page herself.

"What? No! I know his children," she said. She left the table abruptly and went to the bar, then took out her phone and paced as she spoke agitatedly to someone.

"What is it?" Khoudiemata asked, turning to Andrew and James.

There were two stories of interest, they explained. The first was about a high-level prisoner the government refused to name, according to the article. The person had been imprisoned for "violations of national law and attempted treason," an unnamed government spokesperson had said. Now the prisoner had escaped, which implied that people on the outside were involved, and investigations into that had started. It was suspected that the prisoner had been flown out of the country on an unauthorized aircraft.

The second story was about the former minister of finance and mayor of the city, who had been arrested upon his return from abroad. Unable to pin down enough evidence to charge him with anything else, he had been taken into custody for the crime of attempting suicide, since he had jumped out of a moving vehicle while being chased.

Khoudiemata tried to match their surprise about the first story and not to laugh regarding the second. "Interesting times" was all she was able to utter. It occurred to her that she was probably the only person in the restaurant who knew the real stories, but she couldn't tell them to anyone—and no one would believe her if she did. It bothered her that her experience of those events, especially the first, was creeping into her evening and threatening to spoil it for her. She envied the beautiful people and their naive connections to these events, which went no deeper than knowing the families of the powerful. She excused herself to go to the bathroom. There she could fight with her memory in private, to make sure it didn't write itself on her face in public.

By the time Khoudiemata got back to the table, Mahawa had returned as well. The worry on her face had receded, and the newspaper was nowhere in sight. Khoudiemata caught the end of a conversation in which Mahawa was giving an update that the finance minister had threatened to name others if he was brought to trial, and so had been released. Then she turned the conversation to other matters, and soon she was making everyone laugh.

She turned her body toward Khoudiemata. "Which do you prefer with dinner, Khoudi, red wine or white? Frederick Cardew-Boston here is making the case for white."

"Yes," he said, his deep voice filled with self-assurance. "It is hot, and something fresh and soft on the palate is required. Besides, I am having fish."

Khoudiemata wondered how she could be simultaneously so annoyed by this boy and drawn to him. "Can I just call you Frederick?" she asked him. "To say your entire name all the time is just too much." She pulled herself upright and tried to cross her legs the way the other girls did, but it was not comfortable for her.

Frederick Cardew-Boston laughed loudly, and it sounded genuine. "My grandmother used to say to my father, 'Why did you give your child this burden that you call a name? People have to eat several cups of rice before they can pronounce it, and when they are done, they will be looking about for him, because his name has no resemblance to him or his spirit.' She refused to use it and just introduced me to others as Grandson."

"Well, I don't think we will be calling you Grandson tonight,"

Khoudi said, bringing laughter to the entire table. She did not think what she had said was that funny, but she recognized how getting a favorable reaction encouraged you to speak more.

Mahawa was holding a bottle each of white wine and red. "Okay, fancy girl, we are waiting for your answer."

"I prefer red," said Khoudi, "because I like to drink what I like, whenever I like, regardless of anyone's rules for what goes with what, or the type of weather we're having. We only ever have hot weather here anyway."

Frederick Cardew-Boston raised his hands in mock surrender, so more laughter.

Mahawa filled Khoudi's glass with red. The truth was, Khoudi was not really sure of her preferences in wine, because she had never had it. She had watched as the others twirled it around in their glasses, looked at it, smelled it, and then sipped before taking a mouthful. Aware of all the eyes on her, she did the same, and Mahawa toasted her. The taste of the wine didn't quite agree with Khoudi, but she gave it another try. Nothing. In time, she told herself.

"Actually," she told the table, "that's not my real reasoning. This place is called Noire Point, right? So if there were black wine, that is what I would have chosen. But since there isn't, I choose red, because the blood that runs through my veins—through all our veins—is red. So I drink to celebrate life." Khoudiemata was astonished at how such things popped out of her mouth in this company. Granted, she had said smarter things, and better, in conversation with Elimane any number of times, and she noticed that a couple of the girls at the other end of the table had rolled their eyes at her nonsense—or perhaps because they wished they had some of her audacious spirit. But Mahawa gave her a kiss on both cheeks and said, "I am falling in love with you, my dear Khoudiemata." And Khoudi felt Frederick Cardew-Boston's eyes on her in a different way. There was something familiar about the look, and with a pang she recognized who it reminded her of: Elimane.

By now, all the wineglasses were full, and the energy of the table dissipated into separate conversations. Khoudiemata turned to Frederick Cardew-Boston, but instead of meeting her gaze, he hid his face in the glass of his wine, smiling. This too reminded her of Elimane, and it irritated her. Why did they all evade you like that, these boys on the verge of a manhood that might never arrive?

"You are not going to ask me why I am smiling?" Frederick Cardew-Boston looked at his glass.

"You should ask your wineglass, since you are looking at it so intensely," said Khoudi. That got him to look at her. To her surprise, she saw that he was nervous, and that he was not good at wiping his emotions from his face. He certainly wouldn't survive in my world, she thought.

"You are different," he said to her, "the way you think and respond to things. There is this mystery and challenge about you. I can't put my finger on it, but I want to." He wiggled his long fingers in the air.

The waiter had arrived to take their orders, and all of the others ordered things from the menu that sounded like gibberish to Khoudi, pronouncing the names of the dishes with a sort of glee. When it was her turn, she asked, "Do you have any food from this country?" She wanted the others to witness what she found so strange.

"I will bring you the native menu." The waiter finished taking the others' orders, then rushed away and returned with a battered-looking sheet. Khoudi glanced at it, and ordered potato leaves with barracuda, rice, and sweet plantain.

Noticing the odd looks from the others, she said, "Don't you find it strange that here we are at a restaurant in our country—a restaurant that is called Noire Point—and when you want a local dish, you are making things difficult? I find it strange!" The table had gone silent, and Khoudiemata thought that perhaps she'd gone too far. Maybe this wasn't the time or place.

But then Frederick Cardew-Boston jumped in. "I agree with you. We should have the choice of other foods on the menu that are not foreign. If anything, the foreign menu should be the hidden menu, and not the other way around."

Khoudiemata was not sure if he really meant it or was just coming to her rescue, but she was grateful regardless.

"So how come you never order the local dishes?" Ophelia challenged him. James and Andrew looked amused.

"None of us do," he said. "I never thought about it. We eat that kind of food at home, but not when we go out."

Andrew broke in. "It is simply about choice. We choose what we want to eat, and that is that."

"Maybe that is part of the reason, but it is also that we think that ordering these foreign foods in public makes us sophisticated," said Bendu, surprising everyone. "That is the truth."

"I had no idea you thought about such things," Mahawa teased her. "But Andrew, if it is about choice, why don't they have all the dishes listed on one menu?"

He scoffed at her without answering, so Mahawa turned to Khoudi. "Well, since Khoudiemata is the catalyst for this vigorous conversation, why don't we let her have the last word before we move on to other things?"

"I think that if we choose not to eat our own food in public because we don't think it is as sophisticated as other foods, it means we believe deep down that our heritage is inferior. If we were truly just choosing what we like, that would be another matter. But most times our choices have been made for us, with a systematic brainwash that starts at birth, on the first day of school." Again, there was silence, mercifully broken by the arrival of the food itself, and the attendant commotion. The conversation turned to where the next parties would be, where people were going for the holidays. Most of the others were going out of the country, almost all of them to Europe— England, France, Germany, Italy.

Khoudiemata noticed that Frederick Cardew-Boston had taken a forkful from her plate without asking, but she stifled the urge to say something about it, feeling that she had already said enough for one night.

"So where will you be going for holiday?" Ophelia asked Khoudi.

"Oh, I am not going anywhere. There is much to do here." Khoudi spoke as lightly as she could.

"I am not going anywhere either," said Ophelia. "My parents won't pay for it, so I will have to probably work if I want to do anything fun this holiday. Perhaps we could find a job together."

Mahawa broke in. "No, no, Ophelia, don't steal my friend. Only when I am not around—otherwise I get to decide what we do together." She was laughing, but it was clear that she was serious. Again, Khoudi restrained herself. She loathed it when others thought they could make decisions on her behalf, but she made herself laugh along with the others.

The drinking continued after the eating, and Khoudi began to worry that even with all the money she had on her, she would not have enough for her share. Others joined them. The heavily made-up young women added more makeup to their faces, right at the table. The music got louder, and so did the conversation.

People got up to dance, boys and girls dancing with each other interchangeably, except Mahawa, who refused to dance with anyone. It became clear why when an impeccably dressed fellow arrived, surprising her with an embrace from behind. Mahawa turned around, glowing, and they went to the dance floor. From their movements, it was clear that their bodies well knew how to follow each other. Then Andrew pulled Ophelia onto the dance floor, and Khoudiemata was left alone.

Frederick Cardew-Boston leaned in close to her and whispered in her ear so that she could feel the warmth of his breath. "I am not going to ask you to dance with me, because I know you are going to respond in a sarcastic way."

"I don't need you to dance," Khoudi said. "I can do very well on my own." She went to the dance floor and he followed her, weaving around her uncertainly as if hesitating to get closer. Khoudi was thankful, because she was not sure she would be comfortable with the way the others were dancing now, their bodies so close.

When the song ended, she headed back to the table, and again he followed her. She sat down, picked up her water glass and drank, while he watched her.

"There are so many things I want to know about you. And so many things I want to say. First, I am sorry for what I said last time about your name. It is a beautiful name, and I should have said that instead."

She said nothing.

"I am waiting for you to jab back at me with some sharp comment," he said.

"I will spare you for the night, but don't push your luck. You are on quicksand."

He laughed. "You know what my mission is for the night?" A vein in his forehead had begun to pulse, and again, Khoudi found herself thinking involuntarily of Elimane.

"Why does it have to be a mission?" she said. "You are going to tell me, whether I want to hear it or not."

"Precisely. I am going to surprise you and make you laugh, and I will tell you why after." He left the table abruptly, and Khoudi's eyes followed him. It was easy to spot him, as the restaurant had now been completely converted to a dance hall, the tables and chairs pushed aside, and he was the only one dressed all in white. She spotted him by the DJ's booth, saying something in the DJ's ears. Then an Afro Trap song came on, and he took to the center of the dance floor. Khoudi had thought to herself that a boy whose father had given him a name like that likely couldn't dance, and their first dance had convinced her she was right, but it turned out she was mistaken. Frederick Cardew-Boston was one with every instrument, a natural. He ended his performance to resounding applause, and then he took off his jacket and threw it at Khoudi. She caught it, laughing so hard that her body heaved, and she had to sit down before she fell to the floor. When she looked up, Frederick Cardew-Boston was standing next to her.

"Now I can go home for the night with the image of that beautiful smile." Immediately her face turned serious.

"Too late," he told her. "I know it is there, and now that is what I will always see, no matter how tough you look at me." He mimicked Khoudi's no-nonsense face.

"Good night," he called, giving a general wave to the room. Then swiftly he turned and planted a kiss on Khoudi's cheek before she could avoid it. From across the room, she saw Mahawa winking at her.

Khoudiemata noticed that as soon as Frederick Cardew-Boston departed, the heavily made-up girls got up and rushed out as well. Were they with him? she wondered. And then, annoyed with herself, pondered why this would be of concern to her anyway.

She decided to take her own leave. She gathered her bag and went to the cashier to pay her share of the meal, but the woman behind the desk told her that the fellow in white had paid for everything. Khoudiemata was relieved but also unsettled, because she didn't like owing people, especially men.

Outside, she spotted Frederick Cardew-Boston vanishing into his car and closing his door. There was no sign of the girls. Khoudi waited behind a pillar. Was it that she didn't want to be offered a ride, with all the complications that would entail, or that she didn't want to discover whether the girls were in the car?

Ophelia emerged at her side, swaying a bit. "I am ready to go home, or rather I should be." She giggled, and continued. "That was fun, and it was great to have you with us. I know why Mahawa adores you. You are fresh, original, real, and mysteriously unusual in a great way." She was grasping Khoudi's arm, both for balance and in intimacy, it seemed. "Would you like to share a taxi?"

Much as the idea appealed to her, Khoudi was nervous. She didn't want Ophelia to get the remotest idea of where she lived, and she had no phone to call a taxi in the first place. She was searching her mind for a way out of this dilemma when a taxi parked in the lot honked and flashed its lights to get their attention. The driver stepped out.

It was Manga Sewa. He acknowledged Khoudi's pleasure at seeing him with a playful smirk.

"My friend Ophelia." Khoudi introduced them. "We will make two stops."

"Ophelia first, and then my old customer after, yes?" he said.

"This way, Ms. Ophelia doesn't feel worried about a new taxi man late at night. After tonight, though, it will be different." That got a laugh from Ophelia, who gave him her address.

During the ride, Khoudi learned more about Ophelia. Her father was the government's logistics manager for imports and exports. He was a strict man who refused to spoil his children, so Ophelia didn't have a car of her own, or a driver. Her father said she must work to get those things if she wanted them.

"Can you believe that I am still paying him back for a school trip to the UK? He is impossible. I don't know what he needs with all that money he has." Ophelia went silent then, and soon Khoudi realized she had fallen asleep. Perhaps it was for the best, because what could Khoudi possibly say? That it was a luxury to be able to complain that way? That she had never met anyone who went to the UK for a school trip? She also found it alarming that Ophelia would simply fall asleep in a taxi, deep in the night with a woman she barely knew and a driver she'd just met. Such naiveté came only from those to whom life has been consistently good.

Manga Sewa had put music on, low, and he was humming along as he wound his way around the curves. Khoudiemata made up her mind that it was too risky to go to 96 Degrees at this hour. This late at night, her presence might draw the attention of a passing driver, and she could not take the chance of being followed. She would have to return to the plane dressed as she was, then leave in the morning before the others woke up. But what if she overslept or one of the boys—or Namsa—woke before her?

She was fretting about all this when the taxi arrived at the entrance of a sprawling property. A gate and a cobblestone driveway made your eyes walk some distance before a hint of the enormous house came into view.

Khoudi woke Ophelia, who looked around herself. "Just here at the gate is fine." She pulled out her phone, the expensive kind you only had to touch lightly, rather than laboriously pressing down on each key. "Take my number, Khoudiemata, and call me tomorrow."

Khoudi pretended to riffle through her bag. "I don't know where my phone is, so let me write it on a piece of paper." Manga Sewa took paper and a pen from the glove compartment and pushed them into her hands. She passed them to Ophelia, who wrote her number, exited the taxi, and wobbled toward the gate. She pressed some buttons, and an armed guard emerged. Ophelia gave Khoudi and Manga Sewa a parting wave before she disappeared.

Manga Sewa had been driving for a minute or so before Khoudiemata remembered that she had not told him where to go. She realized that he was simply going in the direction of where he had picked her up several hours before. "I am thinking that when I get closer, you can direct me," he said.

"What makes you think that I live near where you had picked me up?" Khoudi asked, a bit sharply.

"Because when you hailed me, you were not sweating, and your face seemed to be newly consumed by some annoyance. So I put those facts together with some other knowledge that is part of me, and then I calculated my conclusion." He sounded as if he chose his words to express himself precisely, whether they sounded graceful together or not.

"Do you always calculate your conclusions?" Khoudiemata asked, smiling.

"Yes, with formulas of observation, experience, the unknown, and imagination. Very complex and at the same time simple formulas always variegated with various knowledge that is part of me." Khoudi wanted to ask him what knowledge was part of him, but once again she restrained herself, recognizing that she might be opening a longer conversation that would be best to hold for another time. It occurred to her that Elimane would like this fellow.

She had Manga Sewa let her off at the corner of a field not far from the airplane. There was a rumor about this field—actually, two rumors. It was perfect for football, with beautiful grass, and the story was that it had once sported fancy goal posts, complete with nets. But legend had it that anyone who played on it would soon be beset by some calamity, because spirits played there. The other story was that it was filled with unexploded mines. Either way, people avoided it. So as soon as the taxi's brake lights disappeared around the bend, Khoudi headed for the far edge of the field. But as she drew near, she heard motors approaching, and then saw headlights coming her direction. Immediately, she hid in the bushes at the edge of the field.

There were three 4x4s, and they stopped right nearby. Uniformed men jumped out, talking loudly and argumentatively, and they removed makeshift barriers from the back of the vehicles and placed them haphazardly across the road in a way that would force any passing vehicle to stop. Khoudi knew that soldiers were in the habit of doing this in order to ask for money in the name of security.

Soon enough, a vehicle approached. As it halted, the driver rolled down his window and turned on the lights inside the car; he was used to such interruptions. The soldiers pretended to search the vehicle, but stopped as soon as they spotted two cartons of beer on the floor of the backseat.

"Ah, boss man. This one is for us now," the lead soldier said, as the others flanked the car with false politeness. The driver gave up the beer, undoubtedly knowing it was best not to protest, and the soldiers waved him through. As soon as he was gone, they descended on the beer.

Khoudiemata retreated silently, making her way back to the roundabout where Manga Sewa had dropped her off. It was safer to retreat than to try to pass the checkpoint, alone as she was at this hour.

An idea came to her. She remembered the empty homes the little family had come upon here and there—homes wealthy people built but seldom lived in, as they lived mostly in other parts of the world. The family had been astonished to discover that such homes—and such people—existed. She remembered one in particular that she knew was empty most of the year. They had scouted it during last year's rainy season and discovered that the guard who was supposed to look after the place did so only during the day, so that people could see him at work. As soon as night fell, he turned the lights on around and inside the house and went home.

Khoudiemata and Elimane had been back to the house since, to check its potential as a refuge for their group in case something happened to the plane, and they had figured out how to break in. It was too exposed and risky to be more than an emergency measure, but one night, for one girl, didn't seem like an unreasonable risk. Besides, for once she wanted to sleep in a real house, in a real bed.

She covered the distance briskly, glad to have a way to warm up in the cool night air, ignoring the dogs that barked at every sound and movement at this hour. When she got to the house, the lights were on, inside and out, as expected, but she could discern no noise of movement. She looked around to be certain that no one was out on the verandas of nearby homes and might be watching her. Then she went to the rear of the building, which was surrounded by a concrete wall with a guava tree growing next to it. She threw some stones over the wall to make sure there was no guard dog. Then she climbed the tree and jumped over the wall, landing in the soft dirt of the yard. In sandals, the impact hurt her feet a bit, but she was not really injured. She made her way to a little toolshed next to the back door. Inside, she found a wire and a screwdriver, with which she easily picked the simple lock. She opened the door carefully, raising it on its fragile hinges so that it didn't squeak or grate against the floor, and entered.

Inside, the smell of cleanliness overwhelmed her senses for a moment. She had to shake it off to focus. She tried to recall the layout of the house, thankful for the lights that had been left on. The first room she came to was a bathroom. She ran the hot water tap for a few seconds to wash her hands and then her face. It was a miracle, warm water whenever you wanted it. She longed to take a shower, but it seemed too big a risk. She contented herself with squeezing a little toothpaste on her finger, intending to brush her teeth with that. But as soon as she put her finger in her mouth and looked in the mirror above the sink, she had a powerful flashback, of being held up to a similar mirror as a child, so that she could brush her teeth. She rinsed off her finger and closed the tap abruptly, afraid of letting the memory jolt continue.

Next to the bathroom was a bedroom, and she did not press her luck by venturing much farther. She lay down on top of the bed, fully clothed, her bag and shoes within arm's reach in the event of an emergency departure. She tried to sleep. Her body was exhausted, but her mind began a tug-of-war with it. A house like this brought her at once a sense of familiarity and a sense of strangeness that made it hard to relax.

She thought of Frederick Cardew-Boston and his dance, which had revealed a more interesting person than the pompous young fellow she had first met. She touched her cheeks, where she could still feel his warm breath.

Her thoughts shifted to Namsa. She wondered what the little one was doing and whether she was sleeping well, fending off the torment of her memories without Khoudi's comfort tonight. She thought about the rest of the family in turn, what each had done for the remainder of the day and how it had come to a close. She would find out tomorrow, but she had already decided that she wasn't going to tell them about her own day. She did not want to bring her little family into the fold of her new world just yet, or it into theirs.

The drumming of a heavy downpour announced itself, muffled by the thick walls and tight windows. The rainy season was beginning. It was a harder time to live in the old plane, which leaked a little more each year. That was the reason she and Elimane had first gone looking for another home, and had found this one.

Her eyes caught a framed black-and-white photograph on the wall. It was a family portrait: mother, father, and three children— two girls, who looked to be about ten and five, and a little boy of three or so. The girls wore matching dresses embroidered around the shoulders and necklines, and the boy was in a dark caftan. The children were all smiles, showing teeth and leaning in to their young parents. The picture had been there the last time she was here, though she could have sworn it was hung elsewhere, in a hall rather than in a bedroom. She was staring at it, trying to see beyond the smiles, when at last she fell asleep.

7

"We just have to find the right person, so that no one runs away with our money," Elimane said. He was putting on his old suit jacket, in an effort to look the part of a man in possession of the amount of US currency they were going to change. He was well aware that one ploy for someone to steal it would be to accuse him of having done the same. Even on the occasions when they'd changed smaller amounts, they always had a plan. Elimane would dress presentably, and beforehand they'd research what the street value of the money should be. The others would shadow him, just in case.

Khoudi had gotten back to the plane early in the morning. *King's property, king's property, everything is correct,* she had whistled as she approached, and Namsa had replied, but hadn't run to greet her as she usually did. Nor did Khoudi see her in any of the usual guarding locations when she came into the clearing. She was just starting to worry when she heard Namsa giggling. Khoudi turned and saw a bush shaking. Namsa had so completely adorned herself with leaves that Khoudi had passed her a few times without noticing.

Namsa was delighted by Khoudi's amazement, but her tone turned serious. "You didn't come back last night," she said. "Are you starting to leave us?" And though Khoudi hastened to reassure her and to change the subject, asking about Namsa's adventures since they had last seen each other, her own sense of uneasiness nagged.

Inside the plane she found Ndevui and Kpindi snoring—even in their sleep, the two competed with each other—but Elimane had already gone to get food, and when he returned he greeted her more formally than usual and avoided meeting her eyes. Now everyone was ready to go but Khoudi, which was so unlike her that the others questioned her with their eyes.

"We do not all have to go," she said. She pointed out that people tended to feel more desperate in the aftermath of a holiday, which could put the family's home at greater risk than normal.

"Yes, and it's also a good day to change money—a holiday always pushes the exchange rate higher," said Kpindi. "And with no business happening the last couple of days, we may also be among the few changing, so that will give us the upper hand too."

"Just tell us you don't want to go today," said Ndevui, knowing that Elimane was already annoyed, and Namsa's face registered her disappointment at Khoudi's not going. But Khoudi was tired, and it was weighing on her that she had to return rested to Kadiatou's shop to begin the work of repaying her. She didn't want to leave her debt unattended.

"So, who wants to go?" Elimane asked curtly, and when all of them raised their hands except Khoudi, it was settled. They left carrying the sheets of plastic they used over their heads when it rained, as the skies threatened. Elimane was the last to go, and from the look he gave her, Khoudi could tell that he suspected something was off about her.

"I know you are going to make sure we get a good rate," Khoudi said, attempting to dispel the tension. "Perhaps you will buy yourself that book about the Nile that you had told me about, eh?" Elimane smiled despite himself, pleased that she had remembered this detail of an earlier conversation, and the mood of their parting lightened.

Khoudi waited at the entrance of the plane for the last sights and sounds of the others to disappear before she allowed herself to immerse entirely in reliving the details of the previous night, or to consider how she felt about it all. It was not the dinner or the dancing afterward that was drawing her, she realized, though that other life was indeed enticing. The driving force was more an almost intolerable desire emerging within her these days to embrace what she was becoming, and a growing frustration with the need to swing between two worlds while that was happening.

She closed the door of the plane most of the way, but not completely. She wanted to be safe but also able to help if one of the others returned suddenly in need—the habit of preparing for the worst was second nature to her. Then she sat on her bed and looked around at the other small beds. All of them except Ndevui's were neatly made, with their tattered blankets and sheets. Next to each was a sack of belongings, mostly clothes, except in Elimane's case, where the books outnumbered everything else. How would he run away if he had to? She imagined him struggling with the sack, as it would probably pain him to lose his books more than anything else, and smiled at the thought. Makeshift as their little home was, she was comfortable here, and her body was already entertaining sleep more readily than it had the night before.

She thought about all that had come to pass in this space. There was that time they had decided to celebrate Elimane's birthday inside and nearly set the plane on fire. Another time they returned home to discover that they had not closed the door properly, and found a deer sleeping in Ndevui's bed. The deer had panicked every time they tried to get it out, and it tore their sheets to pieces and broke some windows. Ndevui and Kpindi ended up having to kill it, so they had had meat for days, until they tired of it and buried the remainder of the carcass so that the scent wouldn't attract other animals. And then there was the time the army was searching the area for criminals, and everyone was being asked for identity papers. Those who couldn't provide them were supposed to be followed by officers to their homes to prove that they lived at whatever address they had stated, while those who had the money simply paid off the soldiers. The little family, having neither papers nor money, stayed put in the plane for three days, eating bread and butter and taking turns being read to by Elimane and making up stories and jokes.

So much had happened here that it was difficult for Khoudi to imagine a life elsewhere, and yet there was that nagging feeling that pulled her elsewhere, out into that parallel world. She looked out the windows and imagined the plane as a real plane taking her on a trip around the world. "Well, Miss Khoudiemata, where have we set our sights on this time?" the pilot would ask as they took to the skies, the clouds awaiting her answer. Lulled by this reverie, and then by a patter against the windows as the rain started up again, Khoudi let sleep fully take her body at last.

She was awakened by the roar of an incoming plane. It was so loud that it seemed to make her bed shake. Something was strange, and it took her a moment to realize what it was. Incoming planes normally arrived twice a week, late in the afternoon. There were also unscheduled planes that came and went during the night, without the full waking functionality of the airport. The family was used to irregular flights interrupting their sleep, and after their night working for William Handkerchief, they had a better idea about what such comings and goings meant. But an irregular daytime flight was an unusual occurrence. Khoudiemata sat up and went to the cockpit for the binoculars. She searched the sky, blurred with gray, until she spotted the airplane, its green body pulling away from the clouds. Her gaze followed it as it descended toward the airfield.

She lost sight of the plane in the trees, but her imagination readily supplied what her eyes could not see: The aircraft rolling to a stop. The men emerging and offloading mysterious cargo or bodies or both. The plane taking off again, and everything returning to normal, as if nothing had happened. And sure enough, before long, the green plane shot up into the sky and disappeared into the clouds.

Khoudi's body had lost the desire to seek sleep again. Besides, she wanted to get to the city and back before the others returned. She took her raffia bag and headed for 96 Degrees.

Her things had stayed dry in their plastic bag and hiding place. She changed into one of the black dresses, but it felt strange to be wearing only underwear beneath. She decided to wear the jeans under the dress, and to take the same bag as the night before.

Once again, as soon as she was on the main road she began to attract looks and honks. When she reached the commercial district, she stopped at a kiosk and bought the simplest phone available, and a SIM card to go with it. While the phone was charging, she found the paper where Manga Sewa had written his name, and as soon as the phone had enough power, she called one of his numbers. She did not want to sit next to strange men or boys now that their eyes followed her everywhere. Waiting for him to answer, she admired her reflection in the window of a shop nearby. Who was the striking woman sprouting out of that invisible girl?

"Hello, hello," said a familiar voice. "This is the taxi service of Manga Sewa."

Khoudi felt an urge to giggle, amused at the snappy way he answered his phone. Even his hello telegraphed: *Let's ride quietly, or exchange thoughts, or laugh, or sing, or cry, or be angry but never bitter. Hello.* But it was not the little family's manner to give away so much of their mood to a stranger—or a near-stranger in this case—so she suppressed her laughter.

But he recognized her voice anyway and remembered where he had dropped her off. Was he nearby?

"Yes, I am nearby. Always nearby," he said, and this time she did laugh. He was quite a good businessman, this Manga Sewa!

And he truly must have been nearby, because he arrived within ten minutes. He waited without blowing his horn as she retrieved her phone and explained to the kiosk owner, who had been sitting with his head in his hands, watching her movements, that she wasn't going to pay the extra fee since she hadn't had time to fully charge it. She was braced for a battle, but the man simply smiled and said, trying to catch her eyes, "Come and charge your phone anytime, beautiful woman. You will bring me luck." She had an impulse to shout at him, but a little thrill as well, and while she avoided his gaze, she also held her tongue. She was beginning to understand the power her new way of being in the world gave her, and to take control of it for her own ends. Knowing that he was watching her, she made her way to the taxi and got in. And as soon as she was inside, she relaxed. Manga Sewa greeted her with a smile, but his gaze was simply welcoming, and it put her at ease.

"Welcome, Miss Khoudiemata," he said, and something about the way he pronounced her name told her how genuinely happy he was to see her, and she felt happy too—so happy, in fact, that for a moment she forgot to be surprised that he knew her name, which she had avoided giving him.

"Your friend used it last night," he said, and she was surprised again, at her own inattentiveness. Of course. Ophelia had been tipsy and talkative, and for that matter, probably so had she.

Emboldened, she asked if she could finish charging her phone with the charger on his dashboard. "You are welcome to it, Miss Khoudie-mata," he said, lingering on her name again as he took her phone.

"So where to today?"

She described the location of Kadiatou's shop, and he set off. Today he said nothing, only glanced at her from time to time in the rearview mirror. But as he pulled up in front of the shop, he said, "Have you ever lost something, and after you have given up finding it, the most wonderful thing happens?" He looked back at her, his face full of unreadable emotion.

"No," said Khoudi, a bit overwhelmed by this display, "but I often wish I had." Attempting to lighten the mood, she added, "And I am glad if that has happened to you. This time, take care not to lose it!" She reached for her phone, and he swiftly unplugged it and gave it to her. But this time, when she tried to pay him the fare, he refused.

"Today your advice paid for the trip." He jumped out of the car and came around to open the door for her.

Kadiatou beamed like a proud big sister when Khoudiemata entered the salon. And before Khoudiemata could even utter a greeting, Kadiatou took her by the hand and brought her to one of the empty chairs, where she proceeded to touch up Khoudi's hair.

"You want me to owe you for the rest of my life? Is that it?" Khoudi was smiling, but she was also serious. In fact, it occurred to her that she had enough money from what she had corrupted at the beach simply to pay her debt. But it was work to which they had agreed.

"I honestly don't need extra help," Kadiatou said. "But I did want to see if you were willing to do what it took to get what you wanted. And young as you are, I enjoy your company." Kadiatou spun the chair around to look at Khoudi directly, her face carrying the burden of words that remained on her tongue. Khoudi wondered whether somehow Kadiatou had discovered her address, and her story.

"You have an admirer on whom you have put your feminine magic so badly!" Kadiatou burst out with laughter.

"Badly? What do you mean?" said Khoudi, at a loss.

"You remember when I told you that you were discovering your power? Well, it has been unleashed earlier than I thought," said Kadiatou, but she said no more.

Khoudi decided she didn't want to push her—it was better to wait until Kadiatou spoke of her own accord. Besides, she wanted to get back before the others did. She stood up. "Since you are speaking in tongues and have made it clear that you don't need me to work for you, I am going to go," she said. "But I will come see you again soon. I do want to pay you back somehow."

Khoudi said goodbye to Kadiatou and her friends. A customer who was just arriving held the door for her, and as Khoudi turned to thank her, she noticed how the woman's eyes were following her. Kadiatou, greeting the customer, looked past her to Khoudi with an expression that said, "See, this is what I'm talking about! Even other women feel your power and magic."

Khoudi took out her phone and began to dial Manga Sewa's number, but then she stopped. She would walk instead. She paused to text Mahawa at the number she had been given—why not do as the others did? Then she set out. With each step, she realized, she was becoming more comfortable with how she was carrying herself. Yes, she was drawing attention, but the attention wasn't entirely bad. It was, she recognized, a form of power.

"Khoudiemata!" Someone was calling her name. But who did she know who would shout her name like that in public? Certainly none of her little family. She turned around and saw that Frederick Cardew-Boston was running after her. As he approached, he stopped running and straightened his suit. The closer he came, the more nervous he seemed.

"Is everything okay?" Khoudi said, but it wasn't until she touched his shoulder that she realized she was the one making him nervous. He did not respond, only leaned forward and kissed her on each cheek, attempting nonchalance but arriving at awkwardness. Where had all his confidence and sophistication gone?

"So what are you doing wandering around town without your driver?" Khoudi ribbed him. "Are you sure you are going to be okay? You might break your feet on this rough sidewalk."

"You are funny," he said, regaining a little of his composure. "I go places without my driver—I am an independent man! But I am glad to have run into you."

He averted his face and eyes as he spoke. Khoudi knew he was lying, yet she was enjoying his company, nevertheless.

"Can I buy you lunch?" he asked. "I know a place nearby. That is, if you are not busy and haven't yet eaten. Even if you have, come sit with me and have a drink while I eat." His phone rang, but he ignored it.

"Okay, I will let you buy me lunch," said Khoudi, "if you promise that we will have a great conversation." She tried to catch his gaze.

She thought he was very handsome when he was shy like this, and she was enjoying making him nervous.

"Great conversations are what I do best," he said, mustering bravado. "Otherwise, what is the point of talking?" He extended his arm. "Shall we?"

She took his arm and they strutted along together, making a joke of it. At the vaulted entrance to an unmarked building, they stopped. A guard opened the door for them, and they walked up three flights of stairs, their footsteps echoing. They pushed open a metal door and arrived on a veranda-like deck enclosed in glass. A number of people, some their age but most of them older, sat at tables overlooking the street, eating and drinking and talking.

Frederick Cardew-Boston moved through the crowd with an ease that suggested deep familiarity, and the staff acknowledged him with a kind of reverence that suggested a deference not just to money but to power. Who was this fellow, and who were his family? And did she really want to know yet? Maybe it was better just to enjoy the dream, not to analyze it while she was in it. There would be plenty of time for that when she awoke.

A waiter led them to a corner table with an excellent view and a little privacy. "So have you taken other girls here to impress them?" Khoudi said when they were seated.

"No, this is the first time," he said. "I usually come here with my sister to meet my father for lunch." It struck Khoudiemata that he must have asked Mahawa for more information about her and he must have gone to the salon looking for her. After all, where else did Mahawa know to send him? That was why Kadiatou had been so cryptic!

The waiter rushed to unfurl their cloth napkins for them.

Frederick Cardew-Boston signaled that they wanted to be left alone for a moment.

"Does your family own this place or something?" Khoudi laughed, indicating the conspicuously attentive service and also trying to learn a little more about him but without asking direct questions.

"No," he said seriously. "They just know who my father is." He fidgeted in his chair and then unbuttoned his jacket and loosened his tie. Then he stood up and took the jacket off entirely, starting to hang it on the back of his chair until the waiter approached silently and whisked it away. Though he still seemed slightly nervous around Khoudi, there was a quiet ease to the way he wore a suit—or took it off. He turned back the cuffs of his sleeves and sat back down.

Khoudi felt something tighten in her belly. She forced a smile to hide it.

"Well, I am glad I don't have to dance for that smile this time," Frederick Cardew-Boston said softly.

"Don't take that for granted," she said. "I only give it when I want to." She looked around the room. Seeing how beautifully the other women held themselves made her straighten up.

"I noticed," he said. "But I like fooling myself that I have something to do with it." Khoudi could feel his eyes on her face, studying her, but when she turned back toward him, he averted his gaze, as though meeting hers would do something to him that he wasn't prepared for.

"So when do you think you will find the courage to look at me directly, Frederick Cardew-Boston?" Khoudi searched for his eyes, but he managed to evade her, signaling for the waiter he had shooed away. His phone rang again, and he picked it up and moved away from the table to speak. He was far enough away that Khoudi couldn't hear him, but she could tell by his gestures and his pacing that he wasn't having a pleasant conversation. The waiter hovered by the table with Khoudi.

"Apologies again. Something I had to handle," Frederick Cardew-Boston said when he returned to the table, holding up his phone to indicate its insistence. "Please." He gestured to the waiter to continue.

"Good to see you again, sir," said the waiter. "And what will you be having today?"

"We will have jollof rice with fish. And two bottles of Heineken." The waiter's face registered surprise at the order, which wasn't on the regular menu here either—nor, plainly, was it what Frederick Cardew-Boston usually ordered.

Khoudi was annoyed at his presumptuousness. "I do not want jollof rice. I would prefer groundnut soup, if you have that, and a Star beer. Thank you." The waiter looked even more astonished and turned to Frederick Cardew-Boston for confirmation.

"You heard her," he said. "She will have what she asked for." When the waiter left, he said, "I am sorry. I thought I was being a gentleman by ordering for you."

"There is a difference between being a gentleman and being controlling. I am perfectly capable of speaking for myself."

It was obvious that this young man wasn't used to being challenged, especially by women. But once again she was struck by the fact that her enjoyment of his company outweighed her annoyance. "Frederick Cardew-Boston," she said, slowly and deliberately, and he looked up with an expression of chagrin, bracing himself to be set straight about something else. "We are just getting to know each other. You don't know what I want yet. Okay? Now, let's have that great conversation you promised me." She tried to ease the tension between them.

"Khoudiemata," he said, seriously. "Can I be honest? I was under the impression that girls—women—like a man who is in charge. That is what I am used to." His phone rang, but this time he put it facedown on the table and silenced it. Then he picked it up, sent a text, and put it back, facedown. "So, what else can you teach me?" he asked. "I mean, about yourself."

"Don't be cheeky now," said Khoudi. To her relief, the waiter arrived with their beers. She hoisted hers and proposed a toast. "To the boy with the longest-living colonial name." She laughed.

"I am not to be blamed for my name, you know. My father gave it to me." But he paused there, and it seemed he was not going to be much more forthcoming about the details of his background than she was about hers. Why was he dancing around the subject? Khoudi wondered. Most people threw their family names and histories around freely, especially when that family had so much as a piece of land and a pile of sand and some bags of cement ready to make into bricks to build a house. And this young fellow's body language suggested that he had not tasted any of the bitterness of life with which she was familiar.

By the end of the meal plus several more beers, though, she had found out a few things about Frederick Cardew-Boston and his family. To begin with, their affinity for very long, very English names had started with his great-grandfather, who had changed the family name to Cummings. He did not mention what name he had changed it from, however.

"My father's name is Wilberforce Granville Cummings," he said, looking chagrined. "I used to send my résumé for job openings at banks

ISHMAEL BEAH

or international companies, and just for a prank, I would list all sorts of achievements. Invariably they called me right away and offered me the job over the phone, without even meeting me or verifying the information. The power of my name was sufficient." He laughed.

"I mean, with a name like that you cannot help but have an air of pomposity about you," Khoudi teased him.

"Yeah, sure! I got to live up to it, you know." He laughed. "We are businesspeople, though; we are a family of businesses." He drank some water.

"I am not aware of your family name, and I read the newspapers," said Khoudi, certain that she would have heard it from Elimane in his endless digesting and discussion of the news. Business in their country was, after all, ultimately controlled by a very few clans.

"Maybe we only use our colonial names for certain things, eh? Good morning, sir, I am Frederick Cardew-Boston Granville Cummings." He sighed.

"Really, you got the 'Granville' as well?"

He looked pained. "My grandfather—my father's father—wanted our family to be perceived as sophisticated. This is at least what my mother's mother thought. She used to say that he was 'a clever spineless fool.'" He laughed and shook his head. "My family on my grandmother's side was the opposite. They embraced their traditions, so we had this constant bickering about all matters relating to etiquette and identity."

"Are fools with spines better than the ones without?" Khoudi asked, trying to be funny.

"Yes, says my grandmother. Because fools with spines can from time to time remember the truth within them even if they do not act on it as often as they should." He sighed, and they were silent for a while, drinking more beer.

Despite herself, Khoudi was beginning to feel sorry for him. She had set out to mock him, and to keep the attention on his story so that he didn't ask too much about hers, but she could see he felt truly burdened by his legacy.

"Our library at home, in the city here, is filled with books about the Europeans we are named after," he said. "Stories of the heroism of these men were my bedtime stories as a child. I preferred the stories that my grandmother told me, from 'the countryside,' as my father would say. Many of them were fables, about cunning spiders or foxes or speaking birds. Or fish that walked on land, and houses flying into the night. Strange as they were, I could see myself in those stories. They showed me possibilities, taught me how to imagine. There were serious ones about learning from mistakes, and even with practical information in them, like how certain plants can cure you or kill you. The whole world was alive in those stories. My father didn't want me to hear them, because he believed they were the products of 'backward imaginations.' Somehow, I sensed that he was passing on a fabricated truth that he had made himself believe. How can imagination be backward? My grandmother didn't care what my father thought, and kept telling me the stories anyway. But as I got older, my father took my education more and more in hand. We made fewer trips to the village, and what was read to me now became more powerful than the stories my grandmother had told me." Frederick Cardew-Boston hailed the waiter and ordered another round of drinks, taking care to ask Khoudi if she wanted more of the same or something else.

"And who wrote those books, the ones that your father read to you?" Khoudi pushed on.

"The same people all the men in my family are named after. In our house, we read only books written about us by others. My father prided himself on his intelligence, and he is very intelligent, but you could drive a bulldozer into his blind spots. And he is very stubborn and very strict." He sighed again.

"Why do you sigh so much when you speak of a house filled with books?" Khoudiemata asked him. Such a life couldn't have been all that bad, she thought. And the fact that he was even questioning it meant that his rebellious childhood mind was alive.

"I told my father once that I noticed how quickly a newly arrived missionary whose book about our country I was reading had formed negative opinions about our way of life, just because it was different from what he knew. My father told me I was not educated enough to understand what had been written." He laughed.

"So somehow you knew there was another side to the story," Khoudi said.

"Yes, I did. I remember reading a description of blacks as 'savages in every aspect of their lives,' even the way they chased down live-stock with spears and cut the animals' throats with knives or clubbed them to death without any remorse, and then moved on to another activity. I laughed when I read this, and my teacher reported my be-havior to my father, who reprimanded me." He paused. "But I had been to Europe, and I suspected that their chickens, goats, and cows did not walk to the supermarket and ask to be packaged for con-sumption. I mean, after all, they do call their own places that per-form such tasks 'slaughterhouses,' and the people who perform them 'butchers.' If they have figured out a way to coax animals that they must die for our sustenance, I have not heard of it!"

By now, Khoudi was laughing loudly and uncontrollably, and he caught the contagion of it too. They laughed so long and hard that they cried, banging on the table. When Khoudi noticed others at nearby tables glancing at them, annoyed, she stopped and sat up straight again.

"Don't stop because of them," he said, loudly enough that they could hear. "Who cares what they think?"

Khoudiemata was again impressed at the character Frederick Cardew-Boston was beginning to reveal to her. Which was truer, though, this one or the one he displayed around the beautiful people? She wondered if she dared bring him to see Shadrach the Messiah, who could tell him a thing or two about his colonial namesake.

"Thank you, Khoudi," he said, looking at her with gratitude. "I have not been able to speak about such things in a while. No one my own age seems to think or care about such matters. And I can't remember the last time I laughed like that." His face was relaxed, and now he met her gaze easily.

"You are welcome, my young African friend with the heavy colonial burden," she said, and they both laughed.

"To be fair, you have encouraged my curiosities and answered my many questions," she said. "What are yours, Frederick of the British Empire?"

He hesitated, as if there was something important he wanted to tell her, but what came out was, "Are you going with someone?" As soon as he had said it, he looked aghast, whether because of the answer he anticipated or because of the question itself, she could not tell.

"That is not a classy thing to ask a young woman," she reprimanded him, "especially for someone who has read all those books. And you were doing so well!" But he looked so deflated by her mockery that she added, more gently, "No. I am not with anyone. I am by myself, and I like it just fine."

They sat in companionable silence for a while, and then Khoudi said, "I am tired of pronouncing your whole name. Can we pick something shorter?"

He took her hand from the table and placed it inside his. "What do you have in mind?" he said.

"How about FCB?" she said.

He laughed. "It sounds like a bank. Or a football club."

His phone rang. This time, as soon as it stopped, it began again. The mood was broken. He stood up and answered. "I will call you in a minute," he said into it, a hard edge returning to his voice. Then he put his jacket back on and straightened his tie.

For the first time since they had sat down, Khoudi wondered how much time had passed. Suddenly she missed her little family and longed to get back to them. She picked up her handbag and said, "Young boy, the conversation was as good as you promised."

"Young boy?" he said. "We have to come up with a better name than that!"

He put his hand lightly on her back as they exited the restaurant, but at the door she turned. "We are forgetting to pay."

"I took care of it," he said.

"When?" she said. "I didn't see it."

"It was a way to say thank you for a wonderful conversation and afternoon. For me, at any rate! If it wasn't truly wonderful for you, then I should pay for torturing you with my presence and my words."

On the street, several serious-looking men were standing in front of the restaurant, waiting. Security guards, obviously, though Khoudi was certain no one had been there when they'd arrived.

"Your people?" Khoudi joked.

"I am afraid so," he said ruefully. "It comes with being a member of a properly colonized family."

She laughed, and said lightly, "I don't think anyone wants to steal your colonial burden." But she was wondering why even a well-to-do young man from a business family needed this much protection. How much damage had they done to others to require it? Even children of politicians didn't have this much protection.

"Young master," said one of them, "we have to go. Orders from your father."

Frederick Cardew-Boston's phone rang again, and this time he answered it with a sharp and angry tone. "You wait for me there. Tell them to wait. Now." He hung up, and the guards who had been shadowing them walked toward a luxury sedan with its engine running. One of them opened the door for Frederick Cardew-Boston, and another hesitated on the other side of the vehicle, looking at Khoudiemata. But she stepped back, to indicate the parting of their worlds for now.

Frederick Cardew-Boston turned to her. "Take my number," he said. She hesitated, then pulled out her cheap phone and typed it in. If he thought anything of it, he didn't show it. He also didn't ask her if she needed a lift. Perhaps he assumed, correctly, that she would refuse. He went to the sedan and lowered himself into the backseat. The car flashed its lights as it sped away, led by a Land Rover that didn't stop for traffic. Or perhaps he hadn't offered her a lift because wherever he was going, he couldn't bring her.

She looked up to see a few women nearby eyeing her, with jealousy, she thought. Did they think she was a fool or a loser for not doing whatever it took to go along with someone so clearly wealthy and important? Khoudi understood what desperation could make you do, but something in her resisted going down this particular path blindly.

"A Njamete, eh?" one of the women muttered. "Pretty ambitious for a girl with a flip phone."

Khoudi started. Njamete! That was the name he had been keeping from her. Where had she heard it before? The women went on gossiping about the family, plainly aware that she could hear them, but Khoudi was no longer listening. The name had conjured a host of associations, drilled into her from long rainy afternoons hearing from Elimane about the doings of the rich and powerful. The telecommunication monopoly. A supermarket chain as well, she thought. And some sort of embezzlement charge? She was hazy about that—there had been so many such charges. She recalled the waiter's extreme deference, the magical settling of the bill, the muscular bodyguards, and so many of them. She was almost tempted to call Frederick Cardew-Boston that minute to tell him she had figured it out, but she needed to sit with this information a bit. Did she really want to be involved even in friendship with someone from a family like that?

She walked away as quickly as she could, trying to shake off what she imagined were the judgmental stares that followed her. She needed to speak with Mahawa about this, but she had to be careful not to betray too much of her own reaction. No one in Mahawa's circle would see anything disturbing in a background like his.

She was walking so fast that before long, she found herself in a more run-down neighborhood. She commanded an attention that eluded her when she was in her hoodie and beanie, but she noticed that her new assertiveness remained with her, and it seemed to keep some of the calls and whistles at bay. She was far from home, and thinking of the long walk ahead and the money in her bag, she contemplated calling Manga Sewa. When she saw an empty taxi, she hailed it. Even if other passengers got in along the route, she would be able to claim her space. She gave the driver the address and climbed in.

Approaching the first roundabout, the taxi slowed in traffic, and she spotted them, making their way along the road in formation. Elimane was on the right side, in the lead. He was taking his time, so his pace alarmed no one, but his eyes darted here and there, searching for what might need guarding against, what might be corrupted. Slightly behind him strolled Ndevui, his long hands swinging with an apparent nonchalance that was its own distraction. Near him was Namsa, her hands crossed behind her back as she kept close to a woman who held the hands of her two small children. Namsa kept enough distance so as not to waken the woman's suspicion but stayed near enough to make it credible to others that she was traveling with them. Kpindi brought up the rear, in the same sort of proximity to some schoolboys.

As the taxi passed them, Khoudiemata noticed how focused and intent their faces were. It occurred to her that she was the only one in the world who would recognize them as a group. It gave her a pang not to be able to simply pull over and ask them to climb in, but she was not ready to reveal this other self to them yet. So separate did her new identity seem that she did not bother to hide, either, certain that their eyes were incapable of noticing her from afar, in a taxi and in unfamiliar clothes.

The taxi was almost abreast of Elimane now, and just as it passed him, his head turned in her direction, and she thought she saw his eyes light up in recognition. She looked past him determinedly, the way other people always looked past them, hoping he would assume he had only seen someone who looked like her.

The traffic thinned, and the taxi sped up. Khoudi managed to get to 96 Degrees, change, hide her fancy clothes and bag, and get back to the plane before the others arrived. She went inside and lay on her bed. She wanted to return to the evening with Frederick Cardew-Boston, before she had found out who his family was, before she had seen Elimane and the others. But instead a sharp memory surfaced in her mind, like a shard working its way to the surface of her skin.

She is sitting at a table, on her mother's lap, curled beneath her mother's long neck. Her mother is teaching her how to write in cursive. "Try to imagine the shape of the word, to picture it and *feel* it before you write it. Then you will be able to form it with confidence." The voice is soothing, so soothing it is painful. Khoudi sat up with a start, to break the hold of this memory, even though the memories came so rarely. Why was it only the sweet ones that surfaced, when they did? Would she prefer the others?

She thought about her double lives and wondered how long she could keep them apart. Was there a way to bring them together? She looked down at her sweatshirt and baggy pants. She had left her other clothes at 96 Degrees, but maybe she could take a small step. She removed her beanie.

Her phone vibrated in the silence, making her jump because she wasn't used to having one. That was another thing she could do—not keep it hidden. She looked to see who had texted. It was Mahawa, of course—who else had her number? She wanted to meet Khoudi at a beach bar the following night to discuss "weekend plans." What weekend plans? Her excitement warred with her worry as she waited for the others to return.

Namsa announced their arrival with her high-pitched whistle, which stopped short when she noticed Khoudi in the entrance to the plane. Her jaw dropped.

"If your hair is so beautiful, why have you been hiding it?" she cried, her eyes sparkling in amazement. "Can you take me so that I can get my hair plaited like that too?" She took off her beanie and threw it into the trees, and both of them burst out laughing.

The boys emerged into the clearing, and their eyes widened at the sight of Khoudi. "Wow, I never knew our big sister was actually a girl. You know, a *girl*," said Kpindi. He seemed to be struggling to understand how this strikingly beautiful young woman had been in their midst all this time.

"Elimane, what do you think of our new Khoudi? I would really love to hear your take," teased Ndevui.

Only Elimane remained low-key. "Khoudi has always had her own elegance," he said in a low voice.

"Wait, we didn't really hear you!" Kpindi called after him, but he ignored them. Elimane seemed to be searching for an activity to distract himself, to change the subject. Then he remembered the money that needed to be shared. He laid it out on the table in five equal shares and took his.

"I have to get back to town for an errand," he said. "I will see all of you later on." He started back off across the clearing. The others watched until his frame disappeared. Then all eyes turned to Khoudi, searching her face for the state of her own feelings.

But all she said was, "Come, we have money! Let's go to the night market and be there before night arrives." They each took their share of the money and hid it in different parts of their pants and shirts. They always preferred to take their money with them rather than leave it at home, as who knew if something might prevent them from returning to the plane?

"Namsa, will you lead us?" Khoudi asked. The girl was already heading for the clearing, whistling a song none of them knew, but when she heard Khoudi's request, she stopped abruptly and assumed her role with gravity.

The market was already in full swing when they arrived, with a boisterousness unique to those for whom such pleasures were scarce. They made their way from cluster to cluster, eavesdropping on political debates, listening to radios and televisions rigged up in the most fantastical ways and blaring music of all kinds, football matches, and telenovelas at the same time. They bought themselves bread and sardines and beers, and a bissap juice for Namsa, and sat together, eating and drinking and watching. Here, they didn't need to pretend to be apart.

For the moment, Khoudi forgot about Frederick Cardew-Boston, the beautiful people, and weekend plans. Someone had corrupted a movie projector and was showing an old kung fu film against the wall of an unfinished and apparently abandoned house nearby. People in the crowd had seen it before, and they began to act out the parts in front of the makeshift screen. Others who were intent on watching the movie pushed them out of the way, and a skirmish broke out. It was as if two kung fu films were showing, one live and local and the other foreign—and the audience watched both, shouting and laughing.

Khoudi glanced to the side and noticed that Elimane had joined them. Whatever errand he had had must not have taken long. His good humor seemed to have returned as well, and he was following the movie with avid attention. She offered him something to eat and some of her beer.

He gestured at the movie. "I read somewhere," he said, and Ndevui groaned, but Elimane pushed on, "that with good aim, and a strong kick to the balls, you can push both testicles inside. Do you think I could do it?" He stood and assumed a kung fu pose. The boys burst into laughter, and Namsa joined in. Tenderly, Khoudi watched them all. They stayed at the market until sleepiness claimed their bodies. Then they made their way back to the plane, their feet knowing the path even in the darkness, and they all slept late into the following day.

8

Elimane's phone woke them, chiming repeatedly until Ndevui located it on the floor, under some discarded clothing. He accepted the call and, without saying anything, pressed the phone to Elimane's reluctant ear, standing over him in his boxers with a tattered piece of cloth that passed for a bedsheet draped over his shoulders.

It was William Handkerchief, of course, with another mission for them. Elimane regretted having charged the battery at the night market, as they had enough money now to last them for a while. But he did not think they could safely refuse William Handkerchief's request for help, especially as sooner or later they would need access to a new supply of cash.

Khoudiemata had her own reservations. She was anxious not to miss her date with Mahawa, and worried about getting back in time to make the necessary preparations. But she said nothing, only helped Namsa to get ready in the privacy of the plane while the boys took their clothes outside to dress, then joined the others in washing their faces and brushing their teeth with water from a jerry can.

Today's assignment would be in Point View, and William Hand-kerchief would pick them up at the roundabout. Their destination was explanation enough: William Handkerchief wouldn't want them showing up on foot or in a dilapidated taxi in the richest part of town, for fear of arousing suspicion. Wearing dark glasses, he picked them up in a Land Rover. He didn't even acknowledge them as they climbed into the back. Namsa, sitting on Khoudi's lap, was so excited that she kept her hands clasped to control the urge to touch every-thing inside this cool car with tinted glass. How could this machine contain an entirely different season as it pushed through the heat of the day? "So they can't see us, but we can see them?" she whispered to Khoudi, who nodded and gently placed a finger on the little one's lips to communicate *No more questions.*

William Handkerchief drove fast, his hands keeping up a nervous beat on the steering wheel as he made small talk with Elimane. In no time, they were driving through the tree-lined streets of Point View, passing mansion after mansion, some of them seemingly empty of life even when the lights were on. It wasn't until they pulled up to a high white fence, behind which stood one of the biggest homes they had ever seen, that he explained the day's work: The owners of the house had departed. Elimane and the others would be packing up whatever possessions remained and loading them into a phalanx of luxury vehicles—also the owners'—parked in the driveway.

Thanks once again to Elimane, they had some context for this mysterious assignment. Painted in red on the fence were the words PROPERTY UNDER FACC INVESTIGATION—TRESPASSERS WILL BE PUNISHED. From listening to Elimane review the news, they knew that the FACC was the Federal Anti-Corruption Commission, which had been expanding its investigations into alleged corruption on the part of government officials. They also knew that such investigations were usually an elaborate sham. Usually they targeted former officials who had gotten greedy and refused to share the money they had embezzled, bringing the wrath of their peers down on their heads. Once their houses had been so marked, the owners would take their valuables and leave the country. If the accused relocated elsewhere in the country, it meant they had merely taken a fall for a scandal so egregious that it could not be swept under the rug. Then the FACC would pretend to search for "evidence"—a process that could take years, until the public forgot about it and the red paint had faded, at which point the case would be closed, with no resulting prosecution or explanation. The house would be sold to a foreigner or rented to a foreign company, and everyone would move on.

They entered the house with trepidation. The ceilings were as high as a cathedral's, and there were so many rooms that the little family worried about getting lost. Everything was painted bright white, and the furniture and floor tiles were white as well, which cast into relief the gold-colored staircase with its matching gold railing. Given the blinding brightness all around, light wasn't really needed, and the shadows cast by the sun ran along the walls and floors, making the five of them feel that someone was following them at all times. The tile was so polished that it squeaked under their feet as they hurried about their tasks. But the job went smoothly. They worked quickly, not talking but whistling to keep one another within earshot. There was not a great deal left in the house but stools and nightstands and coat hangers, and a great many stacks of papers and files, and before they knew it, they were a hundred dollars richer and William Handkerchief had dropped them at a junction where they could catch a taxi back to the plane.

"Your boss man is everywhere," Kpindi said. "I like how he pays, though."

As soon as they were back at the plane, the others went to nap, exhausted from the previous night's antics and the day's labors, but Khoudi took her bag and left. At 96 Degrees, she changed into the black lace dress, slipping the black jeans underneath it. She wasn't quite ready to bare her legs.

Mahawa was sitting at a table on the veranda of the Sea Cliff Bar, not far from the bar where Khoudi had first joined her and her friends. It was early, the place not yet crowded, and Mahawa, her eyes on the waves shimmering in the near-dark, didn't notice her approach. Khoudi had gained confidence in entering such establishments, breezing through them with the air of entitlement she had learned from Mahawa and her friends, without waiting to be seated.

"Excuse me, young lady, may I interrupt your conversation with the ocean?" Khoudiemata pulled up a chair and sat down, as Mahawa turned to her, beaming, gave her a kiss on both cheeks, then held her face in her hands, looking into her eyes. Khoudiemata was struck by the subtlety of Mahawa's makeup, which avoided the masklike look she saw on so many other black faces. She would have to ask Mahawa how she did it. But she could not hold the intensity of her new friend's gaze for long, blushing and smiling and looking away.

"I have missed you, my friend," said Mahawa. "You always have such interesting things to say. I am getting bored with my other friends, who just talk about the same things over and over again. I tell them this all the time, but everyone remains who they are, I guess."

She raised her hand to summon the waiter and ordered a bottle of 2007 Cabernet. "Since you made that beautiful remark about drinking red wine, that is all I have wanted to drink! This will be a special bottle, just right to celebrate us girls hanging out." She took Khoudiemata's hand and they laughed together, inhaling the salty air.

The bottle must have been very special, because the manager himself came to present it to them, holding it before himself like a trophy, pouring a little for Mahawa to taste. She twirled it in the glass and smelled it, then took a sip as Khoudiemata had done when they were at Noire Point. Mahawa nodded her approval to the manager, who poured them a glass each, set the bottle on the table, and bowed away.

Mahawa took a sip of her wine. "So I have heard some rumors. Tell me they are true—otherwise, I will have to kill my sources. I mean, what is the point of having unreliable gossip?"

"What rumors?" Khoudiemata asked. She knew full well what, but it was fun teasing this way, especially with Mahawa.

"Are you going to make me beg?" Mahawa said, taking up the game.

"Oh, I think I know of one." Khoudi pretended to ponder for a moment. "No, it is gone. My memory is so fluid! Perhaps more wine will help." She took a sip from her glass. But she couldn't hold her silence against Mahawa's relentless seduction, and by the time they were halfway through a second bottle, Mahawa had heard all about her lunch with Frederick Cardew-Boston.

As it turned out, Mahawa had already heard Frederick Cardew-Boston's own account. "He said you were 'intriguing.'" She twirled her glass and offered a toast toward the moon.

"Intriguing, eh? Well, why didn't he tell me that?" Khoudiemata said curtly, but inwardly she was delighted. She knew she was intelligent and observant and street-smart and tough, but no one had ever called her intriguing.

"He kept me on the phone for quite a while, also unlike him," said

Mahawa. "Anyway, he is inviting us away for the weekend, out of town, at the beach. Me, you, my man Musa, and him—all expenses paid. You have to learn how to take a gift, my stubborn friend," she added with a mock-chiding expression, when she saw Khoudi's look of concern. "In fact," she said, "I am going to give you some practice right now." She reached into her handbag and pulled out a tissue-wrapped parcel, which she placed on the table between them and indicated that Khoudi should open it. It was a beautiful new blue two-piece bathing suit. Khoudi hesitated. Mahawa stood up, holding the top and bottom to her own body without a shred of self-consciousness. "I couldn't resist," she said. "I could just see it on that sexy body of yours."

Khoudi felt herself blush, and she looked around to see who else might have overheard.

"But it is true!" cried Mahawa, looking her up and down. "So why shouldn't we say it?" She put the suit in front of Khoudi and took her seat again. "Anyway, I got myself another just like it, in red. You can have that one if you prefer it. We'll match!"

Khoudi picked up her wineglass again. "So why hasn't he asked me directly? I might not be available, after all, as my schedule is packed." When she looked up, she saw that Mahawa was frowning, and she burst out laughing. Well, it was reasonable to assume—and actually true—that like most young people of school age, she was relatively free on the weekends these days.

"He is quite smitten by you, you know," said Mahawa. "This is the first time I have seen him excited about a girl, in fact. He is used to getting what he wants. You know," she added, growing sober, "he is a Njamete."

Khoudi's uneasiness returned. If he was getting that interested in her, it would be only a matter of time before he found out the truth about her.

"He didn't tell me himself," she said. "I had to find it out for myself."

"I know how people talk about his family, but he is a good person," said Mahawa. "We all come with the burden of our families, after all."

Her phone rang. She glanced at the number, then answered. "Hello?" she said uncertainly. Then her face relaxed. "Oh, hello, young man . . . You are at my house? . . . No, I am not at home. I am at Sea Cliff." She looked at Khoudiemata and mouthed, *It's him*. "No, I am not doing that for you, my dear friend. You can ask her for it yourself when you see her. Okay, bye." She hung up and gave Khoudiemata a look of triumph. "He's going to come by. He will be pleasantly surprised to find you here."

"Well, let him come, and perhaps he will have the strength to ask me whatever it is that he wants to ask."

Khoudi raised her glass, then froze with it pressed to her lips. She had just spotted Elimane among the growing crowd at the bar. It was a shock to see him, their other lives colliding here and now, of all nights and places. He was wearing a white suit jacket, black pants, and a tie. The bartender handed him a drink, and when he turned, she spotted William Handkerchief behind him, in his brown suit, holding a carved stick before him like he was some kind of tribal chief. Their eyes roved the place; they were waiting for someone. Khoudi waited for his glance to fall on her, and to see what he would do if it did. She was certain he wouldn't give her away, if for no other reason than that William Handkerchief wouldn't want any uninvited witnesses to whatever swindle they were hatching.

The alcohol had quieted Mahawa, her growing silence, punctuated by drunken giggles, and sighs, allowing Khoudiemata to keep her eyes on Elimane. She was struck by the easy way he wore his suit. It was the same way he read books, natural and unforced, like something he had done all his life.

Two white men carrying briefcases entered the restaurant. William Handkerchief went to greet them, and then a waiter promptly seated the four of them. They ordered drinks and food, which were brought to them promptly. Khoudi noticed that the two white men ate quickly, and pushed back their chairs and left before the bill came. She also noticed that they left without their briefcases. Then William Handkerchief departed, carrying both briefcases and leaving a wad of cash on the table, presumably for Elimane to settle the bill.

Frederick Cardew-Boston entered and made his way across the space. Khoudi's heart leaped as she watched him, forgetting all about Elimane. But if she had been watching him still, she would have seen a shadow cross his face as his gaze alighted on her at last and he registered her sudden happiness at the new arrival. She would have seen Elimane hoist his glass in her direction, and she might even have seen his mouth form the words he said aloud—"I am glad to see you embrace your elegance"—causing a passing waiter to smile, mistakenly thinking that the comment was for her. Noticing, Elimane smiled back at the waiter, as a prelude to the inquiries he wanted to make, about a certain elegant young man across the room.

"Good evening, ladies," Frederick Cardew-Boston said when he reached their table. "May I have the pleasure of your company?" He did not look surprised to see Khoudi there, but he did look pleased.

"I told you he would come," said Mahawa. "He is a bee now, and

you are his flower. Whoops, bad analogy, but you know what I mean."
She stood, swaying slightly. "I am going to get us one more bottle,"
she said, "and perhaps mister here can help us finish it." Giggling, she
made her way to the bar.

"Please, have a seat, Mr. Uninvited." Khoudiemata pushed out a
chair for him with her feet. He took it and pulled himself closer
to her.

"I have something to say to you before Mahawa gets back," he
said. "I am used to being the one who's in control, but somehow your
presence dismantles me completely and I like it. I don't like that I like
it, but I do. Do you know what I am trying to say to you?"

"No," said Khoudi, "but I have a question for you. How many
'likes' did you use?" She pretended to count them on her fingers, but
he didn't laugh as he usually did. She continued. "Suggestion. Try
and look into my eyes directly and say what you want succinctly. You
know the meaning of the word, right?" She sat up straight and faced
him. He closed his eyes tight for an instant, then opened them and
looked directly into Khoudiemata's.

"I wish I could just look at you like this all the time," he said, and
this moment was so intense that she was quiet too. "I am falling for
you, I think," he stammered.

Khoudi had to do something to break the intensity. "You think
you are falling for me, eh? So why are you sitting down?"

But he held her gaze fast. "No jokes. I just want to be with you all
the time."

"Please continue, Mr. Njamete," she said, propping her head
against one hand, her elbow on the table. "I am listening."

He gave her a wry look. "So you've found out about my family," he
said. "And now what?"

Mahawa returned to the table, brandishing another bottle of

wine. "I am back! I hope I gave you lovebirds enough time." She had brought two extra glasses with her, and she set one before Frederick Cardew-Boston and poured them each a healthy amount.

He held his aloft. "Before we drink—Khoudiemata, would you please come with me and Mahawa and her boyfriend for the weekend? I need a break from the city. I have booked some rooms for us at a beautiful spot along the peninsula. Two days and nights of pure relaxation and great conversation. Please come with us." His phone rang. He glanced at in, then silenced it.

"Make him beg, Khoudiemata," said Mahawa. Khoudi lifted her glass and drank, and the others followed suit.

"That's a yes," said Mahawa. "I know that even the smartest men don't always have the emotional intelligence to read a woman." She laughed, and Frederick Cardew-Boston's face lit up.

Sudden drumming drew their attention to the beach. A group of dancers had painted their bodies like skeletons, with neon paint. Khoudi, Mahawa, and Frederick Cardew-Boston watched and applauded as the dancers pirouetted and leaped through rings of fire, each one livelier and more daring than the last. When they had finished, they doused the flames in the surf and washed the paint off their bodies.

"Aren't they wonderful?" said a voice. "Though they always make me melancholic." Even without turning, Khoudi knew it was Elimane, but she didn't want to turn around to confirm it. Was he talking to her? She didn't think so. But why was he at their table?

"Ah, I thought you had made me bring the glass for nothing. Everyone, please meet Conrad Jean-Claude. I just met him at the bar. He is a sharp young man and has a beautiful command of language. And this is Khoudiemata and Frederick Cardew-Boston," Mahawa said, introducing them.

"It is a pleasure to meet you both. Your friend Mahawa here was telling me that if I wanted witty conversation, this is the table for that. Though I am not exactly known for my brevity." Elimane took a seat and helped himself to the wine and took a long swallow, looking at Khoudiemata through his glass.

"I told you he had a way with words," said Mahawa. "I am thinking Ophelia might be a match," she added, smiling slyly.

Khoudiemata was not happy with this intrusion into her world, though she tried not to show it.

"So what is your story?" Frederick Cardew-Boston asked. "What do you do, and where did you go to school?"

Elimane was ready for him. "I studied in Paris and London, but it's a while since I completed university—I started young. I now run my family business, and in my spare time I read history. A lot of history," he said, with significance. He stood up and unbuttoned his jacket, then sat down again.

"Paris and London? Are your parents from here?" Frederick Cardew-Boston sounded impressed.

"My father is from here, and my mother is from Côte d'Ivoire. Hence my name," said Elimane. "So I grew up with arguments about who was worse, the French or the British." He took another sip of wine.

Frederick Cardew-Boston leaned forward. "So you said something about your family business? What kind of business?"

"Ah, let's leave business talk for daylight. I joined you for that witty conversation, after all." Elimane set his wineglass down on the table and leaned back, but his phone must have vibrated, because he pulled it out of his pocket and looked at it, and stood abruptly. "I will have to look forward to that another time, however, because unfortunately I must go. I have some business to attend to in the morning, as it turns out, and I must have all my wits about me then. You know how that goes." He shook hands with Frederick Cardew-Boston, then turned to the women. He kissed Mahawa twice on both cheeks, and then it was Khoudi's turn. It was strange to take in his familiar scent while pretending they had only just met. He shook hands with Frederick Cardew-Boston once again, holding his gaze for a moment, then he disappeared into the night.

When he was gone, Khoudi tried hard to rekindle her former gaiety, though she could not stop wondering what he and Mahawa had discussed at the bar. Had they exchanged numbers? Then she remembered that Mahawa had left her phone on the table, so it seemed unlikely. Unless he had texted her? She resisted the temptation to glance at Mahawa's phone, and instead poured herself another glass of wine to calm her nerves.

Khoudiemata wondered what she should do for the remainder of the night. She didn't want to go home, because it entailed going first to 96 Degrees to change, which seemed too much for this late hour, when even the moon was looking for an excuse to sleep under the cover of clouds. Besides, she was angry enough with Elimane for invading her private world that she worried she would say something she would regret if she encountered him again tonight. But she did not feel like going home with Mahawa either, even though she knew an invitation would be eagerly offered. She didn't trust herself not to disclose more than she intended under her new friend's relentless attention. Frederick Cardew-Boston was out of the question. It was too soon.

It had begun to rain softly. The best thing to do would be to return to one of the unoccupied houses by the beach. As she sat there drinking, the sea breeze against her face, the music from the bar harmonizing with the sound of the waves and rain, she indulged a fantasy of spending the rainy season alone. What a relief it would be not to have to shift between worlds! How would she even manage all those stops at 96 Degrees, as the rains grew heavier? But what about Namsa? Khoudi had never seriously imagined leaving her behind for an extended period of time.

Khoudi swallowed the last of the wine in her glass and returned her attention to the table, only to discover that Mahawa had already paid for their drinks. It was just as well. She needed to start saving her money if she was seriously going to plan an escape for herself.

"I have to get going," she and Mahawa said at the same time. Mahawa laughed, though Frederick Cardew-Boston looked crestfallen. "You should spend the night with me on Thursday so that we can get ready together," Mahawa continued. "Then on Friday we can drive up in my car. In the meantime, I am going to the hairdresser tomorrow if you want to join me there. I will text you the time." Mahawa gave Khoudiemata a kiss on both cheeks while eyeing Frederick Cardew-Boston. He was not the only one smitten with Khoudi, her look said, and he'd better be on his toes.

"I am going to walk along the beach for a while. By myself. Then I will call my taxi man," Khoudi added. Frederick Cardew-Boston looked disappointed but resigned. With this young woman, he was not in charge.

When he was gone, Khoudiemata took off her shoes and hoisted herself over the railing and onto the beach. It was quieter now, and the rain had lightened to a mist. She passed entwined lovers here and there, giggling, kissing, moaning, or just enjoying looking at the ocean. And then there were no more bars, and no more lovers, only quiet houses, some of them lit from within. She walked until she reached the house where she had slept recently. The lights were on inside, but she knew that meant nothing. She found some pebbles and threw them onto the veranda and the rafters. There was no response. It seemed that once again she was in luck.

She woke to the sounds of fishermen singing to wake the fish for their catch, and she was back on the road in time to encounter an early-morning evangelist with a bullhorn, intoning, "Wake up and pray, or Judgment Day will be a nightmare for you. Don't be tempted by the warm bed you are laying in now, or the warm hands of the woman next to you. Pry yourself away and come pray. Her nakedness is temptation. Her round breasts are tempting you. Her lush nipples are tempting you. God is testing you." Khoudiemata laughed to herself, certain that she wasn't the only one noticing that his plea was a better advertisement for sex than for prayer. Anyway, who was to say that lying in the arms of a lover before the day began wasn't a prayer in itself?

She passed Ndevui on the path to the plane, setting out for his daily run, his earphones already in, so she simply gave him a fist bump, and off he went into his other life.

Next was Kpindi, on his way to the guard post. "Big sister, you look like you had a good night. If you ever need a bodyguard, let me know and I will come along."

At the clearing in front of the plane, there was no one else in sight. Then Elimane emerged from the plane with a book, his face plainly thirsty for the sleep he had not gotten. He glanced at her and sat down at the table, opening the book he was carrying and giving it his apparently rapt attention.

Khoudi felt her anger at him flare again, but she spoke with deliberate calmness. "So go ahead and read, and I will tell you what I want you to hear and understand," she began. "This is not a discussion. I go away to have my own world, to discover something very important about myself. I want to do that all on my own. You want to keep this family going with me as part of it? Then you respect my private world, as I respect yours."

Elimane did not look at her, but gave a small, forced smile that acknowledged he had heard her. "Okay. I only want you to be safe, and it was with that intention that I crossed the line."

As she listened to him, her anger dissipated. Of course he wanted to protect her. He wanted to protect them all.

"Okay, then," she said. "I am going to the market."

"I hope you find its canvas as fulfilling as always." He almost chanted it like a prayer. "I know you have a great capacity for finding beauty anywhere." He turned to look at her, giving her a genuine smile now, and she returned it, nodding in acknowledgment of what felt like an agreement. Then he turned his attention back to his book.

By the time she got to the market, she had missed the moment of sigh. She was exhausted from the previous night, and she thought about simply buying food, but then she reminded herself of her plan to save. Besides, why squander her money when she had her wits to get by?

She took stock of her surroundings. The vendor at a baked goods stall looked jumpy and distracted every time a car pulled up or his phone rang. That was a possibility, but bread alone didn't feel like quite enough this morning. What she really wanted was some of the smoked fish that was being sold nearby and had attracted quite a queue. She moved closer, studying people's body language and eavesdropping on their conversations. A man with two teenage girls was just finishing placing a large order. "One of my daughters will come back to pick it up," he told the cashier, pointing over his shoulder as he paid. Reacting quickly, Khoudiemata leaned closer to him and made eye contact with the cashier. Then she walked away with them, waited ten minutes, and returned to pick up the wrapped bundle.

Next, she stood off to the side of the bakery stall and called the number written on a board in front. She watched as the nervous fellow picked up. She didn't speak but just breathed heavily into the phone and hung up. The man stood up, looked around anxiously, then ran around behind the stall, glancing back nervously. Khoudi walked swiftly to the counter and took several small loaves of bread, wrapped them in a piece of newspaper from the stack lying there, and pretended to leave money. Then she turned and strode confidently away from the stall and out of the market, not quickening her pace until she had turned the corner. When the sounds of the market were only faint on the wind, she stopped to catch her breath. Then she began to laugh, because her eyes had fallen on a familiar sight. It was the census man, this time with another ridiculously dressed and equally lost-looking partner, sitting on the ground with a sheaf of papers before them.

She took off her beanie and called out to them. "Excuse me, sirs. Have you started your counting this morning?"

The men looked at each other and then back at her, baffled.

"We are census and tax officers," the familiar one said. "Give us your name and where you live, how many people live with you. You don't happen to have your tax receipt on you, do you?" He elbowed his companion to open his ledger and take notes.

Khoudiemata laughed. "Have you two ever thought about becoming comedians?"

His partner, who looked younger, piped up, clearly trying to impress his boss. "This is not a joke, young woman. Everyone must be accounted for."

"Well, I have been around for a while now, and I think I know why the government is all of a sudden interested in accounting for me. It's because there is an election coming, and they want to rig the vote." She had slipped her knife from her raffia bag, and now she twirled it in her hand, casually but ominously. The census men looked at her warily, taking stock of both the audacity of this young woman and the size of her knife. They got to their feet and backed away, stuffing their papers into their knapsacks.

Khoudi came closer. "Yes, I have them!" she shouted at unseen companions. "Get ready to cut them off at the corner."

At that, the men took to their heels, scattering papers in their wake as they fled. Khoudi pursued them until they were out of sight; then she returned to where they had dropped their papers to see what they had left behind. The census forms she ignored; they were useless. But there was a bundle of unissued tax receipts. With the poor they would be worthless. No one with little money would give even a fraction of what they had to the government, which was already taking what belonged to everyone and giving nothing in return.

They might not even be authentic tax receipts anyway. Sometimes the tax collectors, or their bosses to be precise, made fake ones, so that they could pocket the monies they collected. Either way, they allowed those who possessed them to ward off subsequent shakedowns. The traders in the market would certainly welcome them. She and the others could sell them together, for money or in exchange for food or other provisions, certainly for less than the census cowards would have charged.

She was confident that the men wouldn't report what had happened. They were not going to admit that they had been terrified of a young woman with a pocketknife. They would make up some fantastic story about getting violently robbed by a gang of men instead, and someone else would possibly be wrongfully arrested.

Elimane was reading when she arrived home. Kpindi and Ndevui were kicking around a green-looking orange in the clearing, and Namsa emerged from the plane, yawning, at the sound of her return.

Khoudi tapped Elimane on the shoulder, and he looked up, his face sad but calm. She set her raffia bag on the table and began to unwrap the food. They gathered and helped themselves to bread and fish. For once there was more than enough, and they feasted.

9

Khoudi knew that prolonged goodbyes only brought up difficult emotions for them all, so when the weekend finally arrived, she simply announced to the others that she would be gone for a few days. Then she left, before any of them could say or ask too much. And even though she had never been away from them for so long, they simply waved her off, if a little hesitantly, and whistled their farewells.

At 96 Degrees, the sun was strong enough that she didn't need to rush to change out of her boyish outfit. For the first time Khoudie-mata stood naked and unafraid, and enjoyed her shadow on the sand. She tried on the bathing suit Mahawa had gotten her, remembering how Mahawa had praised her physique, and imagined walking around on a beach with other people and not feeling awkward. Then she took off the suit and went into the water, lowering herself in until only her head remained above. The water was warm, and her hand felt warmer still as it caressed her cheeks, lips, and neck, then gently traveled along her dark beautiful body, past her belly and down, where a tingling pleasure made her bite her lips. Afterward, she lingered on the sand, treasuring this haven of hers, this transitional place, feeling an unfamiliar sense of calm. She hoped no one else happened upon it while she was away. Or if someone did, she hoped it would be another young woman like her, who was discovering herself and needed a private place to do it.

She dwelled on these thoughts as she retrieved her suitcase and began to get ready for her night at Mahawa's house, and the weekend beyond. She dressed with a new confidence about how to prepare for a life that was fast becoming normal for her. And yet she recognized that entering this new world also meant shedding the sense of invincibility that carried her through the life she had been leading as she sailed the streets, invisible to most, seeing opportunities that others missed, creating new ways to survive each day—like taking possession of those tax receipts and figuring out what could be done with them. Kpindi had laughed when she'd recounted her adventure. "So it was you!" he cried. Ndevui had let out a whistle—not a signal, just a low whistle of appreciation—and Namsa had looked at her with little-sisterly awe. Even Elimane had been impressed. "Nice work," he'd congratulated her. "I always wanted to corrupt something from the government." And then he'd added, "Take care. The number-one thieves do not take kindly to competition."

But the thrill of remembering the courage and ingenuity with which she'd acted lost its vibrancy as her mind replayed her encounters with Mahawa and her friends, the ease with which they sat and talked and ate and drank, fearlessly inviting the gaze of whoever passed by. She closed her eyes tightly and experienced again that profound calm within, almost like a deep, short sleep. Holding on to that feeling, she concentrated on the image of her little family, the way they looked when they returned home, as though from another dimension, their faces sharp and hard. Well, they could keep the receipts. Elimane would help them figure out how to sell them gradually, so as not to raise suspicion. And the money and necessities that selling the receipts would bring them would keep them going for a while, even if their work for William Handkerchief disappeared, as at some point it must.

At the entrance to her haven, Khoudi noticed beer bottles littering the ground. No, it would not be long before others discovered her secret spot. She removed her phone from the back pocket of her jeans and called Manga Sewa.

His voice sounded distant, but as always, he was there in a shorter time than seemed possible. She waited as he put her suitcase in the trunk and held the back door open for her.

"How come you are always nearby when I call you? Are you just waiting around here for me all the time?" Khoudiemata said playfully, as he got into the driver's seat.

"I have the power of anticipation," he said. "I am where I know my best customers need me even before they think about it." He looked at her in the mirror. "So where to this time? You are going on a trip?"

"Perhaps you can anticipate where I am going," Khoudi said, her eyes and her smile wide.

"I am afraid my powers are running low this evening." He laughed, and she gave him Mahawa's address.

"Nice part of town," he remarked.

"Some new friends I have made." She checked her phone to see if she had missed any texts.

"Do you want me to turn on the AC?" he asked.

Khoudi thought a minute. "No. Let's roll down the windows a bit so that we can invite the air in."

"I was hoping you would say that," he said.

The air outside was almost as hot as the air within, and dusty, but the breeze was welcome, and they rode along in companionable silence for a while as evening fell. She thought how, if you were not from this land, such air would make you cough and you would hate it. But if you had lived here until the land began to embrace you, and then you left, the very dust and heat might be among the things you would miss.

She met Manga Sewa's eyes in the mirror.

"Last time I saw you, you asked me whether I had ever found something I thought I had lost. Is that something that happened to you?" It was unlike her to ask such questions, as she did not want to be questioned in return. But she was no longer who she had been, she was beginning to realize.

"Yes, so to speak." Manga Sewa's face was painted with a curious mix of melancholy and pleasure. "Or at least, I found a way to hold on to what I had lost."

Something in his manner made her hesitate about pressing him further, and they returned to silence. Before she knew it, night had come, and they had arrived at the gate of a compound ablaze with lights brighter than those of the night market. A guard opened the gate promptly, and Manga Sewa drove in more slowly than the smoothness of the driveway warranted, as if reluctant to bring the ride to an end. The rest of their conversation would have to wait for another ride.

She got out of the car, and he went to retrieve her suitcase, which he set down on the impossibly smooth pavement next to her. She was glad now that she had been able to afford only a used one. Well-worn luggage made it look like she was used to taking such excursions. "I will call you if I need rescue," she said to Manga Sewa. "Otherwise, I will see you Monday sometime."

She followed his taillights down the driveway, then turned to face the massive house, the mango trees lining the entryway as painstakingly groomed as her hair. But before she had a chance to take it all in properly, Mahawa came rushing out in shorts and a T-shirt. She hugged Khoudiemata tightly, pressing her entire body against her, whispering, "I might just have to make love to you!" Her breath made Khoudi's ears tingle. Then she released her grip and laughed. Unsure how to respond—surely this was a joke?—Khoudi hesitated for a second. Then she laughed too, once again in awe of her friend's free spirit. But she was glad Manga Sewa had left before he had gotten a look at her. She had a feeling he wouldn't approve.

A young girl about Namsa's age materialized and vanished with Khoudi's bag before she could say she had just as soon carry it herself. Then Mahawa took her hand and pulled her into the house, which seemed to spread endlessly into the night, as ablaze inside as out.

"Do you want to go to your room first and freshen up, or shall we get straight to drinking before dinner? Your choice." Mahawa was walking backward, holding both of Khoudi's hands in hers, and she steered them into the dining room. Through its windows, Khoudi could look down the valley. In the distance, she could see the fainter, more familiar lights of kerosene lamps. Some of them, she knew, were still in motion, going back and forth with those who kept searching for something the day had not given them.

"May I have a drink first, and then go to my room to 'freshen up,' as you say?" She looked around discreetly, conscious of not letting her eyes give too much away. The room was perfectly cool, but there was no air conditioner visible. Instead, the coolness seemed to be coming from vents in the polished wooden floor. The bookcases lining the room made it feel both sophisticated and inviting. A phalanx of binoculars and a telescope sat on the wide windowsills, and giant potted plants stood in the corners, breathing their own coolness into the room. Khoudi attempted to mask her insatiable curiosity by holding up her phone and pretending to stare at the screen while her eyes stared beyond it, feasting on the elegance and scale of the house. Why would anyone who lived here ever want to leave?

"You needn't be so formal!" Mahawa chided her. "Do what you like, okay? I am drinking beer, as it is so hot this evening, but help yourself to whatever you like. If we don't have it, I can send someone to get it." She went behind the bar that occupied one end of the room and opened a cabinet. It was lined with bottles full of all kinds of clear and amber-colored liquor.

Khoudi thought of Ndevui and Kpindi, who got drunk on whatever they could find, then pushed that thought out of her head. "Beer, please," she said, though she intended to study and perhaps taste some of the liquors while she was here, in case she ever had to order them at a restaurant. Mahawa handed her a bottle of Star beer from a small refrigerator under the bar, and then led her down hallways and past what seemed like innumerable doors to the guest room, as Mahawa called it. It was the biggest room Khoudi had ever seen, with its own bathroom and veranda. The bed could sleep six people if they arranged themselves properly. She tried not to show how overwhelmed she felt. How many rooms were there in this house? Where were Mahawa's parents? Why did they leave her alone with so much to drink?

"My room is right down the hall, so come by when you are ready, and we can go have dinner then. Feel at home, my friend." Mahawa closed the door and left. Khoudiemata stood there drinking her beer, unable to think about what to do in the space. She looked around and sat on the bed, then headed to the bathroom, where she washed her face with warm water. She sat on the bed again for what seemed like a decent interval, then stepped into the hallway, taking her handbag with her. In the hallway, which seemed to stretch before her endlessly, she heard music. She followed it around a corner to a door with light spilling from underneath. That must be Mahawa's. She knocked.

"Come in," called Mahawa.

The room was even bigger than Khoudiemata's, impossible as that seemed. Instead of two large windows, there were six, and between them hung large, colorful paintings with shapes that looked vaguely like women. There were built-in shelves here too, filled with books and knickknacks that Khoudi guessed came from Mahawa's travels. It wasn't so much a room as a suite, with an enormous canopied bed in an alcove and a sofa and chairs, like her very own living room, and to the side, a table and two chairs, even a little refrigerator. The door to the closet was ajar, and it looked like a clothing store, lined with pairs and pairs of shoes and racks and shelves of colorful, neatly pressed and folded clothing.

"We can eat in my room if you don't want to deal with sitting at the table and all that formality my parents like. They tell me each time someone comes into our home for the first time, I should host them that way. I am making an exception for you because I know you won't be impressed, Ms. Enigmatic." When Khoudi didn't answer, Mahawa picked up the phone and pressed a button. "Can you bring dinner for us in my room?" She listened. "No, just a bit of supper. Yes, that's good."

She hung up and turned to Khoudi, then burst out laughing. "Silly, why did you bring your bag with you? You could have left it in your room. No one is going to steal it!"

Khoudi hesitated to set it down, though she knew how ridiculous she looked. The bag held all the money she had in the world. She set it on the far side of the bed, where her eyes wouldn't constantly strain to find it.

On the wall next to the bed were framed photos she took to be of Mahawa's family. Three different babies, two boys and a girl. A family of five. The father, tall and dark, had his arms wrapped around an elegantly dressed woman. There were two older boys—those boy babies, presumably—and a little girl who was clearly Mahawa, despite the missing front teeth. She sported the same mischievous smile. "Where are your parents?" Khoudi asked, as casually as she could, while Mahawa opened the fridge and took out more beers. She didn't want Mahawa to return to her comment about how enigmatic she was.

"They have gone to visit my older brothers, who are at university in the US and the UK." She added information that Khoudiemata hadn't asked, reigniting Khoudi's worry about what questions Mahawa might ask her in return. She reminded herself how much Mahawa liked to be heard and in charge, to be the center of attention.

"So you are all alone here?"

"No, the cooks and housekeepers and guards are here." There was a knock at the door—had Mahawa conjured it?—and a young woman stepped into the room, carrying a large bamboo basket. She set it down and took a few covered dishes from it, which she placed on the table. Then, one after the other, she took out porcelain plates, bowls, and cups, silver and napkins, and set the table.

"You have okra sauce and jollof rice with fish stew. If you leave it covered, it will stay warm." The woman stepped back from the table. "Let me know if you need anything else, miss." With a nod of acknowledgment from Mahawa, she left the room. Khoudiemata stared after her, aghast not at what she was saying but at the sickly pinkish hue to her skin. Only at the knuckles and elbows could you see that her natural tone was as dark as Khoudi's.

Mahawa caught the look on Khoudi's face. "My mother did

everything she could, even confiscated her whitening creams and threw them away, but somehow she managed to get her hands on more." She sighed. "Anyway, that is a vexing issue and will make drinking melancholic, so what do you say we drop it?" She raised her bottle. "To the weekend!"

Khoudi raised her bottle to meet Mahawa's, and they drank. Then the two of them went to the table and sat and uncovered the food, releasing its delicious aromas.

It was an unforgettable night, first for the sheer luxury of savoring the food, one mouthful at a time, and drinking, a sip at a time, until everything was amusing. Mahawa told stories about her travels and her life, and Khoudi asked question after question to keep her going. There was the time Mahawa's family had gone to Switzerland but had found it so unpleasantly cold that her father chartered a plane to take them home early. Another time, they went to London for what was supposed to be a long weekend. But turmoil broke out back home, so they ended up staying in London for six months, renting an entire floor in a hotel whose name Mahawa couldn't recall, though she remembered it had the word "Lord." Her parents hired tutors to give the children lessons, and when they got home they found they were ahead of their classmates in their studies. Khoudi nodded along with these stories as if such occurrences were normal, though inwardly she marveled yet again at how consistently good life could be to some people.

By two in the morning, they had migrated from the table to the wonderfully comfortable carpet. Khoudi was just beginning to doze off when Mahawa got to her feet and went into the bathroom, leaving the door open. Khoudiemata could see her in the mirror as she took off her clothes and changed into the bathing suit like the one she had given Khoudiemata. She came out of the bathroom like a model on a catwalk, stopping right in front of Khoudi and striking an exaggeratedly sexy pose.

"What do you think?" Abashed, Khoudi tried to avoid looking at her, but Mahawa lowered herself to the floor right next to her. "You are more shy about a woman's naked body than most boys I know," she teased. Then her face took on an air of seriousness.

"Khoudiemata. I know you try your utmost to avoid talking about yourself. I don't know why, but I believe that people have the right to decide what to share about their personal lives, so I don't pry. I like what I know and see of you. You are intelligent, you think for yourself, and it doesn't hurt that you are very beautiful." She winked at Khoudi flirtatiously; then her face went serious again. "But now that you and Frederick Cardew-Boston are starting something, whatever it may become, everyone—especially the girls who will envy you—is going to want to dig into your past. I am on your side, no matter what, but you should be aware of that."

Khoudiemata raised her eyes, and Mahawa met her gaze. She felt awake and alert and no longer drunk, and Mahawa seemed the same. They smiled, acknowledging that for the moment, no more needed to be said. Then Mahawa leaned in closer and kissed her. Khoudi hesitated for a moment, then kissed her back. They both sat back, easy with the energy that flowed between them.

Mahawa got to her feet and pulled Khoudi to hers. She put on some music, a song Khoudi recognized and thought was very sexy. *I dey mad over you girl, say you are my woman, eh eh, my super-woman*, they sang, dancing together until sleepiness began to overtake them.

"I think I need directions back to my room," said Khoudi. "Your house is like a small town."

"Stay here," said Mahawa. "My bed is big enough for both of us."

And without even answering, Khoudi fell across the enormous bed, and sleep possessed her.

She woke to brightness, disoriented until the delicious sequence of the night returned to her. Mahawa was not there, so Khoudi slipped out of the bed, put her clothes on, retrieved her handbag, and made her way down the hall with its seemingly endless rooms until she found her own.

She took off her clothes and went to the shower and turned on the water. When the temperature was right, she stepped in. She stood there for a while, luxuriating in the steady pulsing of warmth down her back, a seeming miracle after her ocean and river baths. She stayed in longer than she needed to but got out sooner than she wanted to, afraid of using up all the hot water. Most good things, she knew, come to an end.

She dressed in denim shorts and a white tank top and went into the hallway. At Mahawa's door she heard the sound of the shower running and music playing, something melancholy in a language she didn't recognize. She waited a bit, but when neither water nor music came to an end, she decided to follow her nose to breakfast.

It took her out onto the veranda, where daylight revealed a stunning view, and a table so elaborately set with cutlery and crystal and china that she nearly ran back inside. There were breads and meats and jams and fruits of all kinds, some of which she had never laid eyes on before. Just as she was debating whether to retrace her steps, she heard Mahawa behind her.

"Good morning, my party friend. Come, let's eat, and then hit the road. I am so excited!" She took Khoudiemata's hand and pulled her to the table.

Khoudi filled her plate and began to eat. "I am surprised to find you in such a good mood," she commented.

"Why?" Mahawa looked up from her tea with an expectant face.

"The music you were listening to in the shower was sort of depressing." Khoudi bit into a slice of buttered bread with jam.

"Ah, I see!" said Mahawa. "That was Cesária Évora. I don't find her depressing. I just love the longing in her voice." She paused, then continued with her usual mischief: "But next time I will play one of those cheesy R&B songs and maybe you'll come join me."

She met Khoudi's reproving look with a defiant one of her own. "I am not going to stop until I see you casting off your shell and letting yourself blossom into the fantastic woman you are."

"Fair enough." Khoudi didn't want to let the conversation continue any further in this direction, though part of her wanted to ask when this blossoming into a fantastic woman was likely to be completed. To her relief, Mahawa concentrated on her breakfast, and they ate in silence, enjoying the breeze and the birds that sang, celebrating the day.

After breakfast they went out to the driveway, where Mahawa's car, a shiny black Jeep with an open top, sat, its engine humming as servants stood to either side, holding open the doors for them. Khoudiemata climbed into the passenger seat, but not before she took a quick look in the back. Sure enough, her bags were there, packed by unseen hands. She relaxed, making a vow then and there to try to enjoy this adventure as much as possible. What did she have to lose? If it never happened again, so be it.

Before long, they were cruising along the ocean, music blaring from the car and Mahawa dancing in her seat as she sang along. Gradually

Khoudiemata joined in, and before long she too was shimmying in her seat, her face against the wind. She stopped only when Mahawa slowed down at the approach of a village. Young people rushed the car, hawking bread, cold water, cigarettes, anything they had managed to lay their hands on that someone else might want. Looking at their faces, Khoudi pictured those of her little family. They had done this sort of hustling before they got better at living at the edges of society. She tried to get a sense of which of them were connected to each other, the way she, Elimane, Kpindi, Ndevui, and Namsa were. But then they were past it, and Mahawa stepped on the gas, and Khoudi let the image go and joined in singing again, until the next town.

After about an hour and a half, they left the tar road for a red dirt one, the tires squealing their disagreement. "Here we come!" said Mahawa. Twisting and turning, the road led them down to where the ocean kissed a blanket of the whitest sand Khoudiemata had ever seen. Even Mahawa, who had been here before, stopped singing and turned off the music. They listened to the breeze that cascaded through the trees like a waterfall, and looked out at the glistening blue water.

At last Khoudi found her voice. "We could just sit here in the car for days, and I would be fulfilled." They sat there for some minutes more, until Mahawa broke the trance by grabbing her handbag and passing Khoudiemata hers. There was already a young fellow by the car waiting to carry their bags.

"The young masters are waiting for you at the restaurant," he announced. "They instructed me to take your bags to the rooms."

Mahawa laughed. "So they are calling themselves masters already." But instead of guiding her straight to the restaurant, Mahawa took Khoudiemata on a detour to the beach. She bent down to remove her shoes and indicated that Khoudiemata should do the same so that they could walk along barefoot, relishing the beauty of the place before they joined their companions.

They eventually found Musa and Frederick Cardew-Boston at a table facing the ocean, with several empty beer bottles before them. Frederick Cardew-Boston jumped up. "Well, well, I am pleased that you made it! I wasn't certain, because my supposed friend here hasn't answered her phone since last night." He indicated Mahawa with a chiding glance, but she was deep in a hello kiss with Musa.

Frederick Cardew-Boston pulled out a chair for Khoudi. "I have not presumed to order for you, but I have inquired about the red wine selection, in case you prefer that."

Mahawa emerged from Musa's embrace. "Well, look at what you have done, Khoudiemata. You've tamed his pomposity. Good for you, young woman!" She snapped her fingers for the waiter.

"I think that he secretly wanted to be a gentleman," Khoudi said. Frederick Cardew-Boston fidgeted self-consciously under her gaze.

"The young man is trying. I will give him some pointers." Musa boxed Frederick Cardew-Boston's arm lightly, until he joined in the laughter, sensing that it was all in good spirit. The sun had chased away every cloud in the sky, and the occasional breeze caressed the surface of the ocean, making it ripple. They ordered more beer, then lunch and another round of beer. They spoke as they drank and ate, slowly, savoring the leisurely pace of the day. Khoudi noticed that none of them, not even Frederick Cardew-Boston, had their phones out, and so there was nothing to interrupt their time together.

After lunch they decided to retire to their rooms, and to meet again for a swim in a couple of hours. Musa and Mahawa went down the hall hand in hand. Khoudi hesitated, uncertain where to go, until Frederick Cardew-Boston dug into his pocket and presented her with a key.

"This is for your room," he said. Seeing the look of uncertainty on her face, he added, "Your own room. I am so pleased that you came, and that you did not leave your teasing and sarcasm at home. I will see you shortly, Khoudiemata."

Her suite was on the second floor, supported by the sturdy concrete structure underneath. Upon entering, she looked straight out the windows onto the ocean. The tide was low, and the expanse of sand gleamed against the sky; to one side, a tributary flowed into the sea. There was a veranda right outside, with a hammock-like chair. She opened the windows to invite the sound of the waves inside.

Only then did she look around the suite itself. There was a sort of parlor, and a private bathroom with an abundance of fresh towels. There was a telephone, a television, and vases of cut flowers. Even though she had slept here and there in rich people's homes during the rainy season, she had never been in a situation to enjoy what they offered without fear of being caught.

She closed the door and locked it. You must never let your guard down, especially in unfamiliar places, she reminded herself—especially in places where life was so soft and gentle, because when things broke there, they tended to break with a shock. She walked toward the bed and fell onto it, overwhelmed. The suite was too spacious for her, and she wondered if she should have come. Then she sat up and looked around again, to take in everything. As she did, a decision formed in her head: She was going to start enjoying everything that was in the room, in the suite, in the resort.

She got up and went to each of the vases of flowers, smelling them and arranging them so that they maximized the elegance of the room. The one next to her bed had an envelope with a handwritten note leaning against it. She opened it.

I thought you might like these words that I have borrowed from Léopold Sédar Senghor. They are from a poem fittingly called "To a Dark Girl."

Tu as laissé glisser sur moi
L'amitié d'un rayon de lune.
Et tu m'as souri doucement.

That means:

You let the friendship of moonlight
Glide on me. And you smiled sweetly.

Khoudiemata read and reread the note. It thrilled her that she could make someone feel the way Frederick Cardew-Boston seemed to feel about her. But at the same time, she thought of the little family with melancholy. How she would have loved to ask Elimane about Léopold Sédar Senghor, whom she was aware of as a Senegalese statesman, not as a poet. She was certain Elimane had read him. She resolved to tell them all about her adventures when she returned, and that made her feel better.

She decided to have some time alone on the beach before the others joined her. Standing before the mirror in her new bathing suit, she summoned the courage to go outside. She put on her sunglasses and hoisted her bag on her shoulder, draping over it a panya that she could lie on but also wrap around her waist if she needed it. She helped herself to a bottle of cold water from the refrigerator in the parlor. Then she took a deep breath and opened the door.

The beach was long and beautiful, and it wasn't difficult to find a secluded spot. She spread her panya on the sand and anchored it at one end with her bag so that the wind couldn't make a kite of it. Then she lay down and looked up at the sky. She could feel how her skin greeted the sun with pleasure, the warmth bringing out its natural oils. She closed her eyes and, without looking, felt how her long legs, her hands, and her cheekbones glistened under the sun's caress. She rested her hands on her belly and imagined: If this were her real life all the time, what would she do with it?

An image—a memory?—floated up. A child was running after her mother and father on a beach very much like this one. Then the parents stopped and sat on the sand, admiring her as she turned cartwheels and twirled around, making herself so dizzy that she fell down. She got to her feet and started running circles around them, until the father stood up and began chasing after her, making her shriek with laughter. The scene was so vivid that Khoudiemata gasped and sat up abruptly, looking around to be sure that it wasn't something that was actually occurring. But there was only a handful of people nearby, all of them either asleep or relaxing on their panyas as she had been.

Her heart was racing, and she could feel herself breathing fast too. She opened the bottle of water and took a sip, but it was impossible for her to regain her previous state of relaxation. Lying down wasn't going to help. She stood, shook out the panya and wrapped it around her waist, and went for a walk, heading farther away from the resort. She pulled her pensive shadow along with her, and all her fantasies, dreams, and nightmares. All this time she suddenly had on her hands, freed from the need to survive, was uprooting things in her memory. She tried not to chase the images away but to let them float across her mind as she walked, her feet tasting the warm water at the ocean's edge. Now the man and woman were chasing the little girl along the beach; the girl giggled and ran ahead, and they followed, laughing too. It pleased her to imagine that she might have had such a life, a family that seemed happy in these glimpses.

Her meanderings had taken her to a nearby village, full of crumbling two-story wooden houses in the colonial style. Elderly people sat out on the verandas that wrapped every home, in rickety chairs and hammocks. Clusters of young people sat around a few kiosks that lined the red dirt road, listening to music that they cranked as loud on their phones as it could go. A child darted in and out of the ruins of an abandoned home, shouting, "You can't catch me!" with a couple of her playmates in pursuit.

Khoudiemata looked at her phone and realized that she had been walking for almost an hour. She turned around and retraced her steps, back to the resort, back to the present.

"As they say, great minds think alike. Or in this case, a great mind influences a curious one." At the sound of a familiar voice, she looked up. Frederick Cardew-Boston was standing in her path. He was wearing shorts and running shoes and was sweating, his muscular chest heaving. He mopped his face and neck with the shirt he held in his hand, then put it on.

"I read that somewhere recently," he said, "and it struck me so much that I memorized it. I thought now was the right time to use it." She tried to suppress a laugh at the idea of him rehearsing sentences to say to her.

"I couldn't stay in my room in such a beautiful place, on such a beautiful day, especially knowing the rains will come soon enough." Khoudi watched as he tried to avoid looking at her body. She wanted to readjust her panya, which was coming loose, but didn't want to risk drawing even more attention to herself. She reminded herself that this was surely not the first time he had seen a woman's body.

She remembered the flowers in her room, and the note, and she thanked him. "I did not know Senghor was a poet. I had only known of him as a politician." She was pensive for a moment. "Can you imagine how different the world might be if all our politicians were poets?"

Frederick Cardew-Boston looked relieved to have something to talk about. Since meeting her, he told her, he had started to search out books beyond the ones in his father's library, especially seeking out African writers.

There was something else he wanted to tell her. He had another name, a name his grandmother had chosen for him before his father had chosen Frederick Cardew-Boston. It had been included on his birth certificate as his middle name, but since then, his father had included only the initial, S, in his passports and other official documents. Speaking with Khoudi had stirred his curiosity about it.

"So what is it?" she asked.

"Suluku."

"Suluku," she repeated. "I like it."

He had learned that his namesake was a great nineteenth-century ruler from the northern part of their country who, through sheer political cunning, had managed to maintain his independence from the British. He was convinced, he told her, that his grandmother had given him the name in hopes that it would help him to resist accepting anything he did not have the opportunity to question.

Khoudi already knew about Suluku, and much more besides. "Your grandmother sounds like she was an incredible woman," she said. "She reminds me of Nyarroh—have you ever heard of her?" And she told him what she knew about the female chief who had helped mastermind resistance against the Europeans' attempt to impose their way of life. "Her name belongs with others who did the same: Bai Bureh, Suluku, Kailondo, Manga Sewa, Momoh Jah, and so on."

"That's not how I learned the history!" Frederick Cardew-Boston exclaimed. "I was under the impression that almost all of those men simply surrendered to the British. There was no mention of any resistance—let alone a resistance led by a woman." He shook his head. "It never made sense to me that such proud and independent people would just give in. But how do you know all this?" he asked.

She recalled Elimane's history lessons. "Well, there are bits and pieces in books, but it's hard to find a comprehensive account. I've learned much of it from a fellow who calls himself Shadrach the Messiah. He isn't your usual historian," she continued, "but he makes sense in his own maddening way."

"I would love to meet him. Where can I find him?" said Frederick Cardew-Boston. "This fellow should be speaking at the National Library—before Parliament, from the sound of it."

"Suluku"—she gently tried out the name—"forget about Parliament. They are not interested in history, especially the kind of history that makes them think about their own people. And have you ever been to the National Library? There is nothing national there. It is full of books by foreigners, all about us." She was struck by her own passion as she channeled what she knew from Elimane, and she felt a little guilty at the thought.

"One day I will take you to hear Shadrach for yourself," she told him.

"Well, maybe you can tell me some bedtime stories from him." He flirtatiously broke the serious mood, and she playfully swatted him away and he swatted back, accidentally brushing against her breast. They both stepped back in embarrassment.

"Aren't we supposed to meet Mahawa and Musa around now?" Khoudiemata half hoped he would say, "We'll go when we are ready." But instead he agreed that they were late to meet their friends, and they went in search of them.

They found Mahawa and Musa on the beach in front of the resort, sitting on a mat and drinking fruity drinks. The four of them sat there until the sun turned red on the horizon, talking, snacking, and laughing at stories that Mahawa, Musa, and Frederick Cardew-Boston told about their past adventures and mutual acquaintances, with Khoudi punctuating the narrative with witty comments.

Yet carefree as she seemed, she could not help reflecting that none of the people who walked by them would know the kind of life she was used to leading. What a complete nonentity she was, as far as there being any official record of her existence. She thought of the others who shared her fate. What were they doing now? She imagined them on their way home, after corrupting what they could from the day. Or maybe they had just relaxed at home for once, since they had enough money to last them for a while.

"I am getting a little cold." She stood up and wrapped herself in her panya. "I'm going to go change." The others waved her off, with plans to meet for dinner on the beach.

Strong as her imagination was, Khoudi could not know that, as she was making her way back to the suite, Namsa was leading Kpindi and Ndevui from town, triumphant with the provisions they had scored. But Elimane wasn't with them. He had gone to the docks to pick up a box for William Handkerchief, and he had gained entry without any hassle, but somehow the box wasn't there. Even more disconcerting, when he had called William Handkerchief to tell him about it, his usually volatile boss man had seemed unconcerned. William Handkerchief wasn't the type to let little things pass.

This time, Khoudi stood for a bit longer under the shower, enjoying it until the thought arose that she'd better not get used to something she wouldn't always be able to have. She turned the water off along with her thoughts and stepped out of the bathroom, wrapped in a towel, to contemplate what she would wear that night. She chose a colorful skirt of yellow and black, and a top of the same pattern, with a head wrap to boot. It pleased her to know that everything she wore was from the land she stood upon.

She bent toward the mirror to apply black lipstick and subtle dots of white stone powder to her cheeks. She peered closer, surprised to discover little beauty marks on each cheekbone that were darker than the rest of her skin. How had she never noticed them?

She sensed a hush when she entered the beach restaurant, many eyes on her as she scanned the crowd for her friends and made her way to them, at a table with a fire pit blazing nearby. They were all dashingly dressed for the evening.

Musa gave a low whistle, and Mahawa exclaimed, "It seems I don't have much to teach you, after all. You are stunning!" Only Frederick Cardew-Boston remained speechless, until Khoudi said, "Well, if you're not going to speak, you might as well go back to your room and eat by yourself."

"You know, Khoudi," said Musa, "sometimes it's enough simply to be quiet and let how you feel show on your face. I think my young friend here is learning that."

"This calls for a toast," said Mahawa. "The fact that we are together in this beautiful place and that we have begun to tame some of the psychological nonsense that has been planted in the minds of these boys. Perhaps they may at last become real men!"

"What qualifies us for manhood in the eyes of women like yourselves—women who are in possession of their own intelligence and strength?" asked Musa.

"Yes, do tell," said Frederick Cardew-Boston. "It seems to me that women want a man to be strong, almost emotionless, and at the same time they want us to be affectionate and vulnerable with them. It's a difficult balancing act, especially for those of us who were raised not to show our emotions." He looked up at his friend. "Musa, your thoughts?" But Musa's response was simply to put his beer to his mouth. I have survived my own awakening, he seemed to be saying, and I'm not about to undergo another.

"Well, we women are complicated people, and we mature faster than you boys do, so we will give you a pass this time," said Khoudi, and they put serious matters to rest, joking and listening to the band, who were playing reggae covers.

After the band had finished, a DJ played popular songs from around the continent, and the intoxicating beats drew them to the dance floor. Mahawa and Musa held each other close, and as one number merged into the next under the DJ's capable hands, the distance between Khoudi and Frederick Cardew-Boston closed. The party went on until the night itself sighed with exhaustion and began sending the moon, the stars, and finally the darkness itself to bed. By the time Khoudi and Frederick Cardew-Boston had disentangled themselves, the DJ had packed up his equipment, and Mahawa and Musa were nowhere to be found.

"I was afraid you had gone to sleep." Seeing the light on Khoudi's veranda, Frederick Cardew-Boston had come up to find her, folded inside the hammock-chair. "I brought us this, to make our silences pleasurable," he said, holding up a bottle and two glasses he had gotten from the bar. He poured the wine and handed her a glass. She sat up in the hammock and took a sip.

After a few minutes, she stood and went inside without a word.

He drank quietly for a while. Then he called after her, in a loud whisper. "*Khou-di.* Are you coming back to me?" There was no answer. He turned and saw that the door to the suite was opened slightly. He hesitated, then walked in. She was not in the parlor. "Hello. Hey!" he called into the empty room, so he would not startle her. Not getting any response, he entered the bedroom. And there she was on the bed, completely naked, one hand on her breast and the other between her legs. She was looking right at him, and her eyes told that she was expecting him.

Later, he would not remember how his legs carried him to the bed. But he would remember how she locked eyes with him. How she removed her hand from her breast and replaced it with his own. How she grasped him by the neck and pulled him close. How, when they were both naked, he touched her face longingly and cupped his hands under her head to look deep into her being, his eyes filled with pure longing. How nothing in the world existed except her warm breath, her legs wrapped around his buttocks, her chin up, exposing her beautiful neck. It was not the first time she had been penetrated, but it was the first time she had made love on her own terms, willingly, joyfully. And it was the first time he had allowed the sensuality of a woman to completely inhabit his body. The energy between them pulled them together again and again until the night was completely gone, and then they slept.

In the morning, he was gone. She showered and went down to breakfast at the café on the beach, expecting to find him there, but there was no one she recognized until Mahawa joined her.

"So, how was your night, you conqueror of young men?" Mahawa laughed loudly, and Khoudiemata, embarrassed, looked about, hoping no one had heard. Fortunately, everyone seemed to be in their own world, or hiding in newspapers or books or headphones.

"Well, you are in a good mood. How was your own night?" Khoudiemata countered quietly, her uneasy mood a poor match for her teasing words.

Mahawa seemed not to notice. "Oh, that young man isn't going to be able to wake up until noon," she said with a wink.

That must be where Frederick Cardew-Boston was, Khoudi told herself, sleeping off his exertions in his room. And she forced herself to sigh along with Mahawa, as if remembering her own conquest.

Yet the day did not improve from there. The restaurant began to fill up with weekenders who had arrived to enjoy the sunny days that were now numbered as the rainy season approached, and those who had come in search of other pleasures. A group of middle-aged white men, their eyes filled with self-satisfaction, ogled them until Mahawa gave them the finger. After them came a group of men who looked to be at least forty, some perhaps well into their sixties, with girls who could not have been out of their teens. The girls were dressed more skimpily than Khoudi had imagined it was possible to dress, as though with the sole purpose of sustaining the lust of these grandfathers, who could not keep from touching them in full view of the rest of the company. Khoudi reflected on the irony that there was a policeman stationed just outside the entrance to the resort while men like these entered with underage girls.

"Let's go for a walk on the beach," said Mahawa, attempting to break the mood.

They went back to their rooms to put on their bathing suits under their outfits, in case they decided to go for a swim. Khoudi got back downstairs first, and was fending off a stranger's come-on by the time Mahawa returned.

"Had trouble putting on your bathing suit? Those things can be tricky," Khoudi joked.

The man mistook their laughter for an invitation, and Mahawa had to interrupt him with a hard stare. "Let's go before I beat someone up." They headed out to the beach.

The day seemed to be polluted. They got a boat to take them on a tour past the village where Khoudi had wandered the day before, to another resort, which was even more overrun with older men and underage girls than their own. And while they were resting on the beach there, a guard raced by them, in pursuit of a boy no older than seven, who was selling coconuts and other fruits to the beachgoers. When he caught the boy, the guard began to beat him with his baton. "How many times have I told you not to sell to the visitors!" Under the thrashing, the coconuts and other fruits went flying into the sand. Khoudi stared at the boy, imagining Namsa in his place—or any of the little family when they were younger. She wondered how many of the "guests" were foreign and local human rights workers, getting paid to do the work of protection when they weren't off enjoying themselves at the beach, apparently oblivious of the scene playing out in front of their eyes. The guard stopped only when a young African woman with a small child intervened, chastising him for his behavior.

"Shall we leave?" Mahawa saw that Khoudiemata was troubled by what had transpired.

"Yes," said Khoudi, looking at the guard, who was laughing while the boy ran away in pain. He would return the next day, Khoudi was willing to bet on it. He'd simply hope to escape another beating, or at least to sell all his wares before it descended on him. What would happen to a boy with such a life if he should ever taste power? she wondered.

On the boat back, Mahawa asked Khoudi if she was okay.

"It bothers me especially to see how we dehumanize one another in front of foreigners," said Khoudi. "In effect we are telling them to do the same to us."

"You may be right," said Mahawa. "But he has already beaten the boy. Let's not give him the power to destroy our day as well."

When they returned to their resort, they found Musa pacing up and down the beach, with Frederick Cardew-Boston nowhere in sight. "He got called into town," Musa explained. "His father sent some men for him. He didn't say when he'd be back."

Khoudi had known it would be so, she told herself. Life always disappointed you.

"Khoudiemata, don't worry," said Mahawa. "I am sure it is nothing."

Khoudi excused herself to go shower, with promises to meet them at the bar. In her private bathroom, she stood under the torrent of water, allowing herself to enjoy it as long as she liked. She had always known that this strange new life would come to an end, and it seemed to be ending even faster than she had expected. Something was about to break. She could feel it in the air even though she didn't know what it was.

She came out of the shower and wrapped herself in two fresh towels, one for her body and one as a turban for her hair. She sat in the plush armchair and looked at herself in the mirror. She thought about how she had never chosen the expected ways in life. She had not become a prostitute, for example, or a consort to a man fit to be her grandfather. She knew that those were not actually easy paths to take, psychologically, but they required less resilience and ingenuity than what she had been through. She knew that most young women did it because they had no viable alternatives. She had been determined to find—no, to create—a viable alternative.

When she went to join Mahawa and Musa at the bar, she was surprised to see that Frederick Cardew-Boston was with them. She had convinced herself that he wasn't coming back. Perhaps she had been mistaken. If he had returned, maybe her new life wasn't over—or wasn't over just yet.

"So how was the summoning?" she joked. Frederick Cardew-Boston gave her a smile, but she could tell that he was forcing it. And she noticed that his hands were once again gripping his phone, as if expecting it to ring at any second.

It did. He answered it, walking away from the bar, shouting insults at someone as he went.

"Each time he gets on that phone, he becomes someone else." Khoudi sighed with exasperation.

"He is under a lot of pressure from his family," said Mahawa. "They expect each of their sons to take his place in the business as soon as they are out of school. But he will be fine."

Frederick Cardew-Boston returned to the table full of apologies. "I am sorry. That was just something I needed to deal with. Now I am really back with you all, full time. Please carry on." He took a swig from the fresh round of beers Mahawa had ordered for them. But he kept his phone holstered in his hand, and Khoudi could see that he was not fine. Not really.

It's over, said a voice in her head. And this time she did not try to ignore it.

The rest of the night was punctuated with phone calls and apologies. By the time the last call came, he no longer left the table to answer; he glanced sideways at Khoudiemata as he listened. "Good," he said. And again, "Good. Let me know when it's completed." This time, when he hung up, he put the phone away in his pocket.

"Is everything all right?" Musa asked.

"Yes," he said. "All is good." And he raised his bottle to join theirs.

And indeed, his mood seemed to have lifted. His phone stayed in his pocket, his face brightened, and he brought his chair closer to Khoudiemata and whispered little jokes in her ear. When the DJ started to play dance music, he pulled her onto the floor, and at the end of the first dance he clasped her to him and kissed her, long and hard.

And just as he did, she was seized with a sudden, urgent desire for morning to come. She could not wait to see her little family once again.

King's property, king's property, everything is correct, she heard in her mind's ear.

And then the answer came. *King's property, king's property, everything is correct.*

10

King's property, king's property, everything is correct. The refrain was in her head as she neared home. But she had no idea whether the others would be there. She had been gone long enough that she had fallen out of their rhythms.

It was both a disappointment and a relief to be back in her baggy clothes and beanie. She was invisible again, and nothing in the demeanor of the boys and men she passed indicated that they acknowledged her existence. She was already craving some of the attention that she had gotten used to, but most of all she longed to return to her own world, where she could be herself and didn't have to pretend at anything. Her feet rushed her toward the plane.

She entered the clearing. *King's property, king's property, everything is correct.*

But everything was not correct. Something was terribly wrong.

She smelled smoke. She looked up to see it rising toward the sky before her.

She ran through the shrubs as fast as she could, until the plane came into view. It was on fire, burning from the inside out, the door hanging open and the inside smoldering with black, sooty smoke. How long had it been burning? For hours? For days?

She circled the plane, consumed with guilt and fear. No sound came from within except the crackle of flames as they consumed the last of their belongings. Where were the others? Was anyone inside? Why had she left them here to fend for themselves? What had she been thinking, running away to a life she knew wasn't hers?

She stopped and forced herself to think. For all that the little family had endured in the time they had lived together in the plane, nothing of this magnitude had ever happened. What were they to do in such a circumstance? She remembered: If they were separated by chaos or violence, they were to meet at Encounter One. If their home was taken over by others, they were to meet at Encounter Two. What if their home was destroyed? They had not prepared for that eventuality. But this seemed closer to Encounter Two. That was where she must go next.

Khoudi began running through the bushes, taking a shortcut she knew. It was overgrown with shrubs, and branches slapped at her face and scratched her legs. They seemed to be asking, "Where have you been? Where are you going now?"

She slowed only when she neared the boundary that was indicated by an old stone wall, in which were embedded the skeletal remains of a cannon that faced the sea. Behind the cannon were the ruins of an old house that itself had burned down long before. Flowers grew where they had been planted, though, their blossoms tasting the sea air.

King's property, king's property, everything is correct.
King's property, king's property, everything is correct.
No answer.

Khoudi sat on the stone wall to think.

Then, from behind the cannon, Namsa emerged. She rushed into Khoudi's arms. She was trembling.

"Are you okay?" said Khoudi. "Where are the others?"

It was a while before Namsa responded.

She didn't know where the others were. She too was only just returning home. The day before, she had been arrested by the police near the market and loaded into one of several trucks filled with other children. They had been driven out of the city in a convoy and dropped the children a couple of hours away, beyond the city limits. It was something the authorities often did to children on the street, especially when they were preparing for visiting dignitaries or other formalities, and wanted to look their best. It had happened to Khoudi more than once in her younger days, but as far as she knew, Namsa had avoided it. Nevertheless, Namsa had found her way back, hitching rides and walking, traveling in a pack with some of the other children for safety.

She had arrived only some hours before and, like Khoudi, had found the plane in flames, with no sign of the others.

At least she had not been in the plane when the fire broke out, Khoudi thought.

"And what about you?" said Namsa. "Did you at least have a good time where you went? I hope so. In our lives we should always have a good time when we can, because the rest is a struggle."

Khoudi looked at her in surprise.

"You taught me that." Namsa looked at Khoudi for a moment, then nudged her gently. "Something besides the fire is on your mind, big sister. You are here, but your spirit is scattered everywhere."

Khoudi took a breath. "Yes. It was good. And then it wasn't. I don't want to make a habit of it." She put her arms around Namsa again and held her tightly. It felt good to give and receive this frank expression of love and care.

"Or maybe you are just thinking too much about it," said Namsa softly. "Life happens, for good or bad."

Khoudiemata released her. "How did you become so wise, little one? Perhaps you should get arrested more often."

They heard footsteps on the dried leaves in the bushes, followed by the introductory whistles they knew so well. Jumping to their feet, they responded in unison.

Ndevui and Kpindi emerged together, distraught-looking but unharmed. They had been out partying when the fire broke out, and had returned home early in the morning to find the plane at full blaze. Elimane, as far as they knew, had been on an errand for William Handkerchief. Nothing had been amiss when they left. They suspected the fire had been set deliberately. But by whom?

"Is it because of the tax papers?" Ndevui asked. "Whatever it is, we are with you. We are a family!" Ndevui looked earnestly at Khoudiemata.

"No. That isn't possible," said Khoudi. There was no way of tracing the papers to their home, and besides, who in their land of corruption would take such a theft so personally?

She was deeply relieved to have reason to believe that Elimane was all right. But why wasn't he here? It was he who had originally designated their emergency meeting points, and the circumstances in which to use them. Now where was he, and when would he arrive?

They waited in silence, each of them worrying about Elimane and wondering about the bigger questions that lay beyond. Where would they find their next home? Would they stay together? It was Elimane who had brought them all together, and it was hard to imagine the rest of them without him.

Khoudiemata's phone rang. She thought it might be Elimane, and her heart leapt, but then she remembered that he didn't have her number. She looked at her phone and saw that it was Frederick Cardew-Boston. She answered.

"Hey. I really need to talk to you." His voice was heavy with worry, quite unlike his usual self. "Can we meet tonight, or anytime? Please." He was almost begging.

"I am not sure. Is it something that can wait?" Khoudi looked at the others.

"Perhaps. But there is something I want you to hear from me."

"I will think about it and let you know later," Khoudiemata said. She hung up.

"Weekend people?" Ndevui asked, but Khoudi didn't answer. The weekend, the resort, all of it seemed not just another world, but another universe.

They waited until night began to announce itself. A breeze rose, making the trees sway goodbye to the day, then fell to a whisper. Normally they would enjoy such a quiet evening, but tonight it came on with a ghastly feeling.

And then twigs snapped, echoing in the silence. The little family stood up, readying themselves for fight or flight.

Slowly, Elimane came from the bushes. He was wearing his suit, but his face looked haggard. For the first time Khoudi could recall, he had forgotten to signal his approach.

"I don't know where to begin," he said, standing before them. "I am so sorry."

"What are you talking about?" said Ndevui. "What are you sorry for?"

"I let my guard down in a way I shouldn't have." Elimane broke into a wail. "Ah, even my books are gone!"

Ndevui came toward him, his fists clenched. "We lost our home, with the rainy season upon us, and all you can think about are your books?"

"I just wanted to make sure you were safe!" At last Elimane looked directly at Khoudi.

Kpindi was in Ndevui's path, but he wasn't fast enough to block Khoudi. She grabbed his collar with both hands, nearly choking him. "Tell us!" she hissed into his face. "What did you do?"

And so Elimane told them all.

After he had encountered Khoudi and her new friends in the bar, Elimane explained, he began following Frederick Cardew-Boston.

"I know how men like that think," he said defensively, rubbing his neck. "I know how their families think. Trust me."

But unbeknownst to him, Frederick Cardew-Boston's bodyguards had noticed, and had assigned one of their own to follow him.

"You idiot!" Khoudi broke in. "Did I ask you to check up on me?"

Elimane waved her off. That wasn't all. The bodyguards had reported Elimane's detective stunt to Frederick Cardew-Boston's father, who took the security of his family extremely seriously. ("As you should well have known!" Khoudi said.) Not content to leave the mission in the hands of his son's bodyguard, he had called in one of his enforcers—one of the minions he employed to carry out whatever tasks he needed, when he needed them to be off the books and out of sight. And who was that enforcer? Elimane gazed at them all, in helpless defeat. William Handkerchief.

It was a coincidence that they were already acquainted, and it proved to be the perfect foil. Once William Handkerchief had received his orders, he redoubled Elimane's assignments. The steady stream of work that Elimane was so proud of was partly a sham. Many of the tasks that had seemed so mysterious were simply unnecessary errands, invented to bring him out and have him followed, until William Handkerchief had discovered where he lived.

In retrospect, Elimane should have been suspicious. Just as he'd returned to the plane from the phantom box pickup, William Handkerchief had sent him a text to meet at a bar by the beach for a new assignment. It was one of their typical deals: an overexcited foreigner, a briefcase, a guarantee of safe passage through airport security. But this time the mark was solo, and Elimane had wondered fleetingly why his presence was needed at all.

"Well, that went smoothly," he'd remarked when the foreigner departed, preparing to leave as well.

"Stay and chat a bit, Sam," said William Handkerchief, much to Elimane's surprise. He never stayed a minute longer than necessary after such transactions. Elimane was wary, but he told himself that even in such a relationship, to which distrust was essential, something resembling intimacy eventually crept in.

"So, young fellow, have you ever heard of Bai Bureh, the fellow who fought against the British because he didn't want to pay taxes to them for his hut?" Again Elimane was caught by surprise. They'd never spoken of history, or any personal interest at all. He hesitated before responding, taking a long swig of his beer to buy time.

"About Bai Bureh, I know only what I have learned in school, like everyone else," he said.

"Ah, school," said William Handkerchief. "That is where they give intelligent minds the false idea of hope instead of cultivating the cunning and maliciousness that are needed to survive here." He laughed quietly and swallowed the rest of his gin in one gulp.

Elimane sensed that something was up, but he couldn't quite put his finger on it in the words that had been spoken. Something about how they had been spoken was making him uneasy. Casually, with the edge of sarcasm William Handkerchief seemed to enjoy in him, Elimane asked, "What made you ask about Bai Bureh? I didn't take you as a man who cared for history."

"Oh, I only care for history if it can make me some cash." William Handkerchief laughed. "Otherwise the past remains dead to me. You, on the other hand, take reading seriously. I always see you reading a book when we are waiting for business, and you seem lost in it, not like I pretend to be when in fact I am observing people." And with that, he stood up, paid for the drinks, shook Elimane's hand, and left, without a word of a next meeting or assignment.

Elimane had gone to join Ndevui, Kpindi, and Namsa at the night market, where they wanted to watch the people as much as the Spanish soap operas no one understood. He arrived during one of the many commercials about skin-bleaching products, which made him think of Khoudiemata and her fierce hatred of them. Where was she, and what was she doing? he wondered. By the time the family had returned to their home, he was drunk enough to forget the strange conversation with William Handkerchief, and fell asleep.

The next morning, Elimane had slept late, uncharacteristically. He had slept while Ndevui left for his run, and while he and Kpindi dribbled their latest soccer ball—an unripe pumpkin—around the clearing. He was still sleeping when the boys and Namsa left for the market, and when Namsa, without his watchful eye, was picked up by the police and carted out of town. It was only the sound of a flock of birds taking sudden flight nearby that finally woke him.

He left the plane to urinate, and that was when it happened. He heard movement in the bushes, and instinctively he moved deeper into the brush to hide. First to emerge were two of the bodyguards he recognized from Frederick Cardew-Boston's lot. But why were they here? Were they following Khoudiemata? That would make sense—like all wealthy men, the father was a suspicious sort. But Khoudi hadn't been there since Thursday morning. That was when it came to him: *He* was the one they had followed. It was he who had brought them to the invisible world of the little family that he had worked so hard to build and to protect.

Behind the men, William Handkerchief came into the clearing. "Burn it," he ordered them. "Burn it so that they can never live in it again." He lit a cigarette and stood smoking as his men went to work. The men left only when they saw that the fire had truly taken hold, gaining an appetite that would not be easy to contain.

Elimane waited in the bushes until he was certain that the men were gone. Covering his face with his shirt, he tried to make his way back inside the plane. But the thick toxic smoke and heat were too much for him. He took what water there was in the plastic buckets outside and came as close as he could to dumping it on the blaze, but it did nothing but encourage the flames to lick at the buckets too. He was forced to back off before the fire tried to devour him as well.

At the main road, he saw the tire marks left by the hasty departure of 4x4s. He knew he must find Khoudiemata to warn her, but he had no idea where she was. He went to all the bars along the beach and other places that he knew the beautiful people frequented. It was only when he had exhausted his search that he had come to Encounter Two.

"They must have been looking for you too, Khoudiemata," Elimane said bitterly. "I may have made a mistake by following Frederick Cardew-Boston, but you're the one who found yourself a Njamete."

The others turned to her for explanation, but she was silent.

"It's our freedom that makes us so dangerous," said Ndevui. "We don't owe anyone favors, we live by our wits, we can interpret our history and circumstances as they make sense to us, not the way anyone else wants us to." The others were surprised. Ordinarily, Ndevui could scarcely stand to listen to such theories, let alone give voice to them.

"I couldn't have put it better," said Elimane. "You have been listening to Shadrach the Messiah, and now you have tasted the strength of your own intelligence."

"Philosophy is not enough to get you off the hook," said Khoudi. "No matter what, the fact remains that your jealousy brought about the destruction of our home. You couldn't just let me be on my own."

Her phone rang. She looked at it, then shut it off without answering.

The others turned from one to the other, as if hoping for an apology. But once the truth had been stated, there was no taking it back. A line had been crossed. Something had come to an end.

Ndevui began to pace, the fear of abandonment upon him.

Kpindi turned to Khoudi. "Sister, you know all the places to look for us, once you have cooled off." He gave her a hug, and she hugged him back, marveling once again how much like a brother he felt to her, wondering if it was the last time.

Namsa tugged at her hand, tears in her eyes.

Khoudi looked down at her. "You are coming with me, little one."

Khoudi looked at Elimane, with pity and love. She and he, above all, could not afford to say goodbye. They knew that if they allowed the emotions dancing within them to play fully outside and among them, it would weaken them not only for the task of surviving but for the extra sharpness and effort to help others survive. Elimane looked back at her, and they acknowledged all that had been good between them, and all that had been painful. Then Khoudiemata took Namsa by the hand, and the two of them made their way toward the road.

Only Namsa turned to watch the boys as they went, until the three of them had disappeared into the bushes. She and Khoudi emerged onto the road, the skeleton of a new family.

How strange—or perhaps it wasn't strange at all—that they would all meet again at the entrance to the beach, where an old lookout tower remained intact, though its body was aged with the salty wind from the sea and the rains that came and went, and the sunlight that shone every day on this forgotten place where someone might once have stood and watched the arrival of what changed everything. This morning, however, it was a stage for Shadrach the Messiah, and a couple dozen people had paused in their day to be entertained by him.

"Good morning," he cried. "Good morning, my sons and daughters, my friends, my compatriots of this land heavy with lies and deceit." The air was cool, and it escaped his mouth, a mist, as he danced to his own words, his colorful patchwork robe swirling around him.

"You! All of you, and especially you who suffer every day as you carry our history, the history as it has been taught to you. But if you learn your true history, you will be able to carry it in a way that it emboldens you, and your life will not be such a burden to you."

As he spoke, he began to weave his way among the listeners. And as their eyes followed him, they found one another. Ndevui with his running shoes around his neck and his earphones, intent on the music in his own head. Kpindi with his eyes averted, pretending not to see Khoudi with Namsa, in matching traditional cotton robes and head wraps, toting Khoudi's suitcase. Elimane sitting on a rock nearby. He was writing vigorously in a new notebook, and it was not clear whether he had looked up long enough to see them, but he seemed absorbed and content.

"Once, there were three women and two men, warriors all, who wanted to hear from those who had come across the seas, supposedly to befriend us. Even though they didn't know we existed," Shadrach added with a laugh, and some of the crowd laughed with him.

"But every visit with their new friends was by appointment. What sort of friendship was that? So the three women and two men took white clay from the river, and charcoal, and they painted their bodies so that they looked like skeletons. They drank medicine from a plant that would bring complete stillness to their bodies, and then they climbed into an elaborately carved boat that was delivered to the new friends as a gift, a work of art from the natives, as they called us. The colonial boss proudly accepted the gift and put it on display in his living room, where he conducted the affairs of his so-called empire. The warriors sat still for five days, until they had learned everything they needed to know about the truth of our new friends. On the fifth night, during a feast, the skeletons came alive, stood up, and carried the boat on their shoulders out the door, disappearing into the night.

"The colonials were in shock. By the time they recovered, it was too late to catch those lively skeletons. For the rest of that season of the sun and later the rains, the soldiers from another land searched for the lively skeletons in vain."

Shadrach paused and regarded his audience. "May you all be the lively skeletons of whatever season you choose." And with that, he jumped into the air and took a bow, then continued on his way, mumbling gibberish.

Khoudi looked at her phone to check the time. Manga Sewa

would be here soon. What was it he had said? *Have you ever lost something, and after you have given up finding it, the most wonderful thing happens?*

As she waited for him and whatever would come next, Khoudie-mata whistled a new little tune to herself, set to Shadrach's words. *The lively skeletons, the lively skeletons, everything is correct.* She liked the sound of it.

acknowledgments

I am deeply indebted to my family, my tribe—my wife, Priscillia, and our children, Kema, Farah, and Kailondo. Your presence has expanded and deepened my imagination and added to my life in the most remarkable and beautiful ways I could ever imagine. You are the very definition of life, and I love you all so very much. I am blessed to see the world through your eyes every single day. And Priscillia, *merci* for always believing in every idea and vision of mine, and for diligently reading my earlier drafts.

I wrote this book while living in Nouakchott, Mauritania; Saint-Louis, Dakar, and Gorée Island in Senegal; Sierra Leone; Nigeria; and Los Angeles, USA. These settings and the people I met there helped me imagine the characters and landscape of this novel. I am thankful for having had the opportunity to live in all these places, and to have them become part of me.

Throughout the writing of this book, I have become reacquainted with old friends, and made new ones who have now become family, a part of my growing and evolving tribe. Thank you, Eyal Aronoff and family, for offering to my family the beach home where I incubated and wrote parts of this book. Ann Norman, I so appreciate your checking in and offering the necessary connections and support. Tremendous thanks to Pam and Bill Bruns, and to Patty and Kenneth Turan, for welcoming us to the west side of Los Angeles and becoming the foundation we needed to call this place home, and for your encouragement of Priscillia's artistic endeavors and mine. Most important, you introduced us to Devin Williams, who joined the tribe as my sister. I will be forever grateful that our paths crossed.

Thank you to every other member of our family, near and far. Laura Simms, Fran Silverberg, Ira Silverberg . . . you are all with me, no matter where I am in this journey of life and writing.

I am lucky and honored to join the brilliant Riverhead family. It was a love-at-first-sight sort of thing! Thank you to my amazing editor, Rebecca Saletan, for your insights, patience, and hard work and for always staying faithful to the characters, the world, and the integrity of this novel. Looking forward to working on the next book and books with you.

My gratitude to my literary agent, Philippa Brophy at Sterling Lord Literistic, for believing in the universe I want to create in my books. And thank you to Nell Pierce at Sterling Lord Literistic as well, for your responsiveness and patience.